Cha.

CHALK

Paul Cornell

A TOM DOHERTY ASSOCIATES BOOK

NEW YORK

CHALK

Cover photographs © Getty Images
Cover design by Peter Lutjen

Edited by Lee Harris

A Tor.com Book
Published by Tom Doherty Associates
175 Fifth Avenue
New York, NY 10010

www.tor.com

Tor® is a registered trademark of
Macmillan Publishing Company, LLC.

ISBN 978-0-7653-9094-3 (ebook)
ISBN 978-0-7653-9095-0 (trade paperback)

First Edition: March 2017

Chalk

One

We're talking about the West Country of Great Britain, the farming country, below Wales and above Cornwall. Find the county of Wiltshire, then the town of Calne. Move your cursor east for about two miles along the A4 road. There's Cherhill Downs. Find some images. On almost all of them will be the Cherhill White Horse. It's one of many hill figures cut from the chalk soil on the uplands in this part of Britain. Some of them are relatively modern, some are ancient. The Uffington horse, further north, is the ancient one everyone knows. That one was cut, so the archaeologists tell us, by the nations of Iron Age people that lived in Wiltshire: the Durotriges or the Atrebates, as the Romans referred to them. They were rich. Their currency took the form of polished axe heads, never sharpened. They had vast resources, a large population and the commitment to build and maintain great monuments. The Uffington design is an indication, we're told, that they caught and tamed wild horses. The archaeologists think it's a model of what the tribes wanted to happen: this animal looks like it's running past, but actually we've captured it on this hillside.

The Cherhill White Horse, on the other hand, although it's beside an Iron Age hill fort, was cut in modern times. It looks domesticated. It turns the downs behind it from a forbidding fortress and place of suffering into the background of a painting. If the sunlight catches it at the right time of day, it's got a twinkle in its eye.

It was cut out of the chalk in 1780 on the instructions of one Dr. Christopher Allsop, who lived in Calne. According to the history books, they called Allsop 'the Mad Doctor'. They say he bellowed instructions to the men cutting the chalk from where he stood below the downs in the town of Cherhill. That's why this horse, uniquely, is designed for perspective, for a modern audience who are used to the illusion of that. I think Allsop suspected something about those downs. Perhaps he decided to put something up there to overwrite it.

So the Cherhill White Horse isn't old. But it's said locally that if a woman sits on the eye, originally made of lemonade bottles, she'll get pregnant. Nobody ever said, when I played on those downs as a child, with what, or who's the father?

It's like modern people know there's something there. That whatever it is wants to make new life. That it wants to get out. They put the horse there to *be* that thing, rather than think about what's been buried.

———————

The hill fort on Cherhill Downs is now called Oldbury Castle. The archaeological records show that when they heard the Romans were coming, the Iron Age tribes built huge new fortifications. They thought they could resist. There must have come a point when, the alarm raised, the legions approaching, they left their villages and evacuated to their stronghold. They would at least go down fighting.

The Romans didn't give them the chance. They had their decisive battles elsewhere. Then they built the road that's now the A4 right past the downs. You can imagine the tribes sitting up there, besieged only by themselves, watching the Romans march past.

———————————

Up close, the walls of that old hill fort are like waves rolling through the ground. They're huge. You're hidden when you walk those ditches. The wind drops, you're insulated. If you try to run up the other side, the pebbles of chalk will slide from under your shoes, and you'll have to use your hands, your fingers jamming into the soil, for a long clamber, and you'll have to stop when you get to the top, breathing hard, only to see another ditch and another rise in front of you.

When I was a small child, there was a copse up there where the sheep sheltered. I would sit there, on a fallen tree, to catch my breath. I watched the shadows of clouds pass over the big valleys below, that were made by glaciers. Or I would go and sit on the first step of the Lansdowne Monument, built in 1845 by Henry Petty-Fitzmaurice, of the family who still own the stately home down the A4 past Calne. The monument is a big spike of white stone. Or I would go and lie in the bowl barrow. It's a depression in the ground outside the bounds of the hill fort, in the form of a perfect circle. Before the First World War, everyone said it was where a keep had been built. Then it became where a zeppelin had dropped a bomb. Then it became where a German bomber had dropped a bomb.

But archaeologists tell us it's actually a grave.

At the bottom of the bowl, under the soil, lies a person, curled up like they're about to be born, on a bed of flint and charcoal, with a knife, a bow, wrist guards and a beaker full of beer. They say it's a loving burial, proof of belief in an afterlife, but I have my doubts. Perhaps the archaeologists weren't looking for the Threefold Death: the beating around the head; the wound in the throat; the suffocation. Perhaps they considered the stomach contents only in terms of food.

You'd still be able to see my family home from there. My parents still live in that house, a bungalow built by my dad. They still have my elderly Aunt Dar as their neighbour. Nearby there are a few scattered houses, a couple of villages, Calstone and Blackland, formed out of buildings that happen to lie along the same road. We got a church magazine that covered seven parishes, and they went way out into nowhere. The possibilities of the distant Salisbury Plain were always there when I was a child. I would hear thunder on a sunny day, and Mum would say that was the guns firing at the military bases up there, and I would be frightened at how loud they must be close up. Mum would hurry me inside, frightened too, as if the shells were about to start landing all around us.

How rich Mum and Dad were varied hugely when I was small. I went from private school to village school to private school. First I was the kid with the stupid accent, then I was the kid with the posh accent, then back again. That back-and-forth process, in some ways, explains everything. It's like the British class system is a magnetic field, and moving a conductor through it produces current.

————————

Every weekday morning, eight of us, kids from Calne and its surrounding villages, would stand on the town hall steps and wait for the minibus that took us to school in the village of Fasley. We'd be in uniform. Dad would drive me in on his way to work in Lyneham. He owned an insurance business that served the RAF base. He once had a laundry in the same building, then a betting shop. The insurance was the only thing that held on. The betting shop seems to have been a failed attempt to turn a passionate hobby into a career, to turn something that lost money into something that might possibly make some. Dad was always saying he'd made some small amount of money on the horses, or on Miss World, but he never mentioned all the times he must have lost.

In my first year at Fasley, when I was eleven, columns of workers would file into the Harris pie factory opposite as we were waiting on those steps. By my second year, the factory had closed down, and that was how it stayed, empty, argued over, six floors of windows.

The kids from John Bentley, the local comprehensive school—the state school, no uniforms—walked past us every morning. We'd get gobbed at, grabbed and slammed against the doors of the town hall, called at, get bits of food thrown at us.

———————

Fasley itself wasn't much of a village, there was nothing there really except the school. The building was an Edwardian mansion, with large windows at the front and gravel drives and playing fields. Imagine the sound of lots of kids' feet walking on gravel, and then on polished wooden floors. Chemistry and Physics were in a wooden lab down a smelly corridor that must have once been the stables. Biology was out in what must have once been servants' quarters, towards the woods. Maths was in what would have once been a guest bedroom. French and History were in the polished depths at the centre of all the stairs, near the staff room, the heart of the building, where the corridor smelt of cigarettes and soup. For PE, we went down the stairs into the cellars, all dust and moss. Bits of the school kept falling off. We were standing outside in lines at the end of break once when a gargoyle cracked from the gutter and fell. It was falling towards Mr. Rove, the headmaster, who was standing in front of us. There was one hopeful breath in from all of us as it dropped.

Mr. Rove was sure of everything. 'This will be the year in which eighty-five per cent of you get an A grade at "O" Level.' It didn't sound like an order or a challenge, but like he already knew. But much of what he said turned out to be wide of the mark. 'The only way to deal with children,' he once told my dad at a parents' evening, 'is to be certain.'

Dad told me that the same evening. 'Certain the school fees are going to go up,' he said.

The gargoyle shattered a few feet away from Mr. Rove. He glanced at it, then turned back to us without mentioning it.

———————

There were the woods out the back.

They were surrounded by a long stone wall, which we ran alongside when we were sent on cross-country runs. The woods were a sprint back to the bell at the end of break. The soil there was what got put into boxes and sifted on biology field trips. It was one of the two places where you smoked. If you did that. I didn't.

In front of the school buildings there was an old oak, the big tree. It had large, low horizontal branches you could walk along, or sit along like girls did. The bark was polished smooth by bodies. There were initials and patterns carved so deep into the wood they must have been there for years, the tree growing around the gashes, kept there by finger after finger pressing in.

Every now and then, I'll ask people if they have impossible memories of their childhoods. Sometimes someone will recall seeing fairies, or an imaginary friend they were sure they saw and heard. Nothing I've been told matches what I remember.

My name is Andrew Waggoner. At school, like most of us boys, I was known only by my surname.

But there was also someone else. He was called Waggoner too. Waggoner was someone else, but he also had my name and my face and my place in the world. Jeans, smoking, writing stuff on your bag, wearing your shirt out, wearing your collar up, wearing your tie thin—I didn't do any of those things. Waggoner did. Waggoner also did some terrible things.

It's going to be difficult, but I'm going to try to tell you something that's true.

Two

I should give you the full names of the five boys in Drake's lot, in order:

Vincent Lang. He was the first one. Lang was this thin kid who was right down with kids like me in the pecking order. Lang was always sniggering. He made up mocking songs and sang them under his breath, all the time. He was always laughing, always trying desperately to get higher up.

Second was Stewart Selway. He had a big round cock that he always got out and sat around with in the changing rooms. He'd point at it and talk about it, and about porn films it sounded like he was making up.

Carl Blewly used to hang around with our lot in the first year, but then didn't. He borrowed things and never returned them. He had glasses and a tight, puckered-up face, like he was always sucking on something sour.

Steven Rove was Mr. Rove the headmaster's son, fat and with big hands. He shoved faces into the mud, and slapped people, and even scratched. He never used the fact that he was the headmaster's son. In fact, whenever anyone said, that he got angry.

Then there's Drake himself. The pivot about which everything turns.

Anthony Drake was his name, but only one person ever called him Anthony. I have met nobody like him since, and everyone I've met has been like him.

In our first year, he punched a boy in the windpipe. The boy nearly died, but didn't tell. Neither did anyone who'd been watching. There was awe and tension around Drake and the boy after that. But Drake just kept going. The boy moved away when his parents did. Drake doing that never caught up with him. He kept on being who he was.

Drake was a football kid, so he hung around with Franklin and Goff and Sadiq, who didn't have to fight much. But he also hung around with Lang, Selway, Blewly and Rove. Drake had sandy hair that flopped down in a kind of random bowl. He had freckles. He looked like Tom Fucking Sawyer. He carried a knife in the bottom of his satchel. No teacher ever saw it. It was something like a Swiss Army knife, but bigger, with lots of longer and more complicated options, including a serrated blade. It was a farm knife. He used it to chop the tobacco for his roll-ups.

There. I've mentioned the knife.

Drake talked about driving tractors and stunt bikes on his dad's farm. He talked about going into the army. It felt like he was already in the army.

———————

I talk very little about my memories of school, impossible or otherwise. People sometimes say that what they've heard about my past doesn't make sense, because I remember things in strange orders, or that I've made up funny or defensive stories that have embedded themselves in my head so deeply that I think maybe they *are* the memories now.

My life is full of continuity errors. I hear stories about people with 'reclaimed memories', usually of child abuse, and I should sympathise with them, should believe them, but I don't. I remember everything, I just tell lies about it. I feel perhaps they're doing the same. I am hard on people, though. Sometimes frighteningly hard.

Still, mine is not a story about child abuse.

———————

Calne didn't have much to it apart from the factory. Dad was chairman of the Conservative Club. Mum and Dad went down there to play snooker and skittles. They won a lot of trophies.

One Christmas when I was little, Dad got me a junior snooker set. It was a small green plastic table with two small wooden cues. I walked around it with my cue held down on top of my foot, so I had to walk stiff legged. I liked twirling the cue from hand to hand. Dad tried to get me to play properly.

One night he took me down to the Club and let me into the big room at the back where there was an enormous snooker table. He told me that he'd hired the room for the whole night, which had cost three pounds—six weeks' pocket money. So we were going to have as much fun as we could. He went to get me a Britvic and a packet of Salt and Shake. There were a couple of old men there. They offered me a sup of their beer. I smiled at them. I got the chalk and chalked my cue by spinning the cue into the chalk.

I was just tall enough to be able to lean over the table. I was worried about splitting the felt with my first shot. Dad came back in with the drinks, shared a joke with the old men, asking if they'd got me drunk yet. 'Oh, ah,' one of them said, 'he's drunk like a trooper. Drunk like a trooper!'

I grinned at Dad. He came over and told me, his voice low, that the two old boys were on the Committee. Now I had to play properly. He was going to teach me. How he looked in front of the old boys was up to me. He showed me how to set up the table, the right way to arrange the balls into the triangle. He broke, and sent the white ball straight into one of the pockets. He winked at the two old lads. 'Two shots to you!'

I took my two shots, trying to remember how I was supposed to rest the cue on the backs of my knuckles. I ended up with a strange grasp, the cue hooked under one of my fingers. I liked the way that looked. Dad took my hand and hooked it out, put my hand on the table and replaced it several times, until he realised that the old lads had started to look at nothing but that. 'Do he want any help?' one of them asked. Dad said no, I'd get it. I was doing well at school, Fasley Grange actually, it looked like I was going to win the bursary this year, I was a quick learner.

'Takes after his dad,' said the other.

I made my hand into the right shape. I took my two shots. I missed every ball with the first one. Dad insisted I nicked a red. Then I sent the ball off the table. He only took one shot in return.

The old lads never left. It took three hours, all the time we had, but Dad was finally able to let me win. On the way home, I asked him if we had to go back next week. He was silent for a bit. Then he said, 'I'll make it up to you lad. I'll make it up to you.' The next day he brought home a snooker trivia board game. It looked very expensive. We played it once.

But there was something about the cues, or sticks, as I called them, that I really liked. I took my two junior snooker cues with me when I went up onto the downs. I twirled them,

I could spin them around my fingers to get them to go in a circle, for two or three spins at least. Like a drum major. Majorette, Dad said. And so I said that too, until he stopped me and said major. They were my swords. I used them to whack down the nettles. Linus carried a security blanket in the *Charlie Brown* cartoons, and whenever she saw me reading one of those books, Mum would say that the sticks were my security blanket. She said it like it was a great shame, only half a joke.

The man with two sticks. That was the comic strip I would have created about myself back then. That was how I saw myself. I said it to Mum, sometimes. I never felt able to say 'boy'.

But then I realised that there was another man with two sticks. I found him in a book.

When I was small, I'd often get a shock when I turned the pages of a book. I read books I shouldn't have. I scared myself with what I saw. This time I was more shocked than ever. Because the picture was of me. The picture was of a chalk hill figure, the Long Man of Wilmington. He still stands on the side of Windover Hill in Sussex, surrounded by long barrows. He's a sign, a model of something. But only I know of what. Or I think I do. He's an outline of a human figure. He has no face or genitals, but the outline looks male. He has his arms outstretched. In both of them he holds a stick as tall as he is.

That's why I went to the annual Fasley Grange School fancy dress Halloween disco in 1982 in exactly what I normally wore, and I carried my two sticks. I went dressed as myself, but was able to say that it was a costume. I was the Long Man.

You can see why I was such a target. Fucking little shit of a boy, pointing at himself. Didn't have brains enough to hide. What kind of costume requires an explanation?

The Halloween disco was on a Sunday night that year, with the half-term break having started on the Saturday, so it was one of those awkward going-back-into-school things. It was held, as always, in a room under the school, in what looked like it was originally a wine cellar. It was supposed to be rented out for corporate parties that we never saw, and might have been a pipe dream of Mr. Rove's. It was accessed by a narrow flight of steps. A disco had been set up with Mr. Rushden as DJ. Mr. Rushden was quite young, and looked and spoke like the pop star B. A. Robertson. He had very hairy legs. We knew this because he was the PE teacher. He was also the Religious Education teacher. His RE lessons were full of stories about sport. 'Just because I told Goff off in class before the match,' he would say, on the subject of forgiveness, 'doesn't mean I wouldn't pass the ball to him on the pitch, yeah?'

The sport metaphors meant I never had any idea what he was trying to say.

That night, he had big black and silver decks and two boxes of discs, mostly seven-inch singles. There was a dance floor of polished wood. There was a nonalcoholic bar, with a red cloth hung over the optics of the bottles of spirits and the beer barrel taps covered in little black smocks of felt. They looked ragged, like they'd been cut out at the last moment. A few of the teachers stood awkwardly around the room, dressed as monsters. Mr. Coxwell was there, looking round as if swearing under his breath, not dressed as anything other than himself. Mr. Coxwell was the deputy head. He taught French, and he was always angry. Whenever he entered a room, you felt the tension. He once told a joke in French, and then bellowed when somebody laughed. Because, he said, they couldn't possibly be laughing at the joke itself. 'This isn't a good enough school for that,' he'd said.

So here's the big memory I can hang everything else on, the break in the horror that lets me think about what happened that Halloween: Angie Boden in her witch outfit, a green ra-ra dress with black tights and a tiny witch hat, dancing to Culture Club. She had big black eye shadow on.

Back then, Angie Boden and I had never talked. There would have been laughter at me even approaching her.

Angie and her only friends, Netty, Jenn and Louise, wrote lyrics in Biro under their shirt collars. They had a different kind of shoes, they put badges on their lapels, but they were still good girls who did well in class. They were not popular with other girls. Even boys knew that. I once saw a girl slap Angie so hard she drew blood. It had been for saying the music the girl liked was old-fashioned; that's what the boys said afterwards. The boys had all laughed at that fight, trying to be above what girls did, scared by how big it felt.

Angie had a ferociously deep Wiltshire accent. I can hear it now, saying the lyrics to 'Cruel Summer', slowly and carefully. She had a face like she should be posh. Not as much as some of the girls, the ones who had braided hair right down their backs. Just posh enough so the accent was a shock. Angie had a short, flicked-over haircut, very Human League. It suited the frown she usually wore. That night, she was dancing like she always did, her hands balled into fists, leaping inappropriately up and down to 'Do You Really Want to Hurt Me', which was Number One at the time, her three friends beside her. The other girls who were dancing did it away from them, and were swaying tastefully. I'd only see makeup on these girls at the Halloween and Christmas discos, and then it'd look like part of their costumes, with big pink blusher and huge darkness around their eyes.

The only one of my lot to come along was Mark Ford, known as Fiesta. He was dressed as some sort of devil. He had his face painted red, but he was wearing a white jacket with the sleeves pushed up and a white vest underneath. Fiesta had that harmless nickname: Ford Fiesta. Teachers started to use it, because it was harmless, and then his parents became Mr. and Mrs. Fiesta, even to their faces. I saw once—at an assembly, from a wince when Mr. Rove made exactly that mistake, and of course didn't correct himself—that Fiesta hated that nickname. But he never asked us not to use it, because that would mean we'd use it more.

Fiesta asked what I'd come as, and I explained. ''Cos you look just like you would at home.'

'You don't know what I look like at home.'

'Yes I do. You look like that.'

Mrs. Parkin came over and said she didn't think I should keep the sticks, and that I'd look ridiculous dancing with them and might have somebody's eye out. She put them in the cloakroom. So now I was a man without a costume at a costume party. That's when dangerous things from two universes took an interest in me.

Three

Mum had said she didn't think it was much of a costume. 'They'll all laugh at you. I don't know how you'll ever get any friends. You'll come home a laughing stock, mark my words.' But in the end, she went along with it.

When we were in town, and Dad was trying to park somewhere, Mum would cry out, 'There's a policeman!' Once, when some medicine had tasted of aniseed, Mum had put the spoon in my mouth, and I'd thrown up. Mum had grabbed my lips and held them together, desperately trying to get me to keep it down. Then she'd burst into tears and run out of the room. I think that's my earliest memory.

This time, maybe I should have listened to her.

———————

Drake had come as a werewolf. He had big sideburns glued to his face, in a deliberately half-hearted way, and was wearing a leather jacket and jeans. He hadn't any fangs. He was hanging around with Lang and Rove and Selway and Blewly at the bar. He'd got pissed before he came here, and they were pretending they were too.

Drake had been looking at me since I'd had my sticks taken away, pointing at me and then laughing to his mates. Angie looked in Drake's direction and then looked away. I looked at her, and then looked away myself. Drake saw that. He came straight for me. The others followed him. Drake could see teachers, so he stopped just before he got to me. 'Cunt,' he said quietly. 'Little cunt. We're going to hang around with you. We want to come to your house and fuck your mum. Shouldn't mind that. You do it all the time. Has she got a big, furry muff, then? Have you seen it? Do you like the taste of it?' I was saying no, over and over. 'We've got something to show you,' he said. 'After. Fucknor Waggoner. Fucknor Waggoner. You'll be getting home to fuck your mum. That's what you like. You love her. You are her.' Then they went back to the bar.

I tried to hang around with Fiesta, but he wasn't interested. He danced by himself, at the side of where all the girls were dancing with each other, doing his Michael Jackson bit. He didn't seem to mind the boys laughing at him. I think the Fiesta family were so rich that when Fiesta went home, he got told that in three years he'd be driving a sports car, and he thought, okay, I'll just try and get through school without getting hit too much.

Laurie Coxwell was there. She was Mr. Coxwell's daughter. She was short, and had curly hair, like her mum, who taught us Maths. She'd played the flute at an assembly once. I'd clapped without being told to, and everyone had laughed at me. But afterwards, when we were passing in a corridor and there was nobody else in sight, she'd stopped and said thank you. She'd come tonight as a cat girl, with whiskers and a tail. 'Hi,' she said. Terrifyingly.

'Hi.'

'Are you going to be dancing later?'

'I'm waiting for the music to be good.'

'Don't you like Culture Club?'

I didn't know what to say. I knew what the answer would have been for Drake, but for a girl? I spent too long trying to guess the answer. Finally, she took her drink and smiled awkwardly at me and walked off back to her mum.

Angie's friend Louise Callidge put her arms up over her head to dance to Modern Romance's 'Best Years of Our Lives'. Louise, unlike Angie, had the accent to match her looks. She had hair that hung right down her back. It feels strange to be talking about her so offhandedly here. Right now, she's just a normal kid. Well, as normal as any of Angie's lot were. She'd brought a tray of cakes she'd made to the disco, like that was a thing you did, but girls were always doing things that boys didn't think you could do, and Angie's lot did that even more. The cakes sat there for the whole time I was there with nobody eating them until Angie's lot ate them all. Louise would look around as she danced, her gaze sweeping over the other girls, then she'd stop, examine something, judge it, away again. She danced to show off, bouncing her hips off Angie and Netty and Jenn. They looked like they should be really enjoying dancing, but did it with a seriousness that suggested this was hard work, that they were trying to achieve something.

I danced, the first time I'd done that with people watching. I leapt in and started jerking around, trying not to dance too much or too little, held within my tiny box of what was allowed. But dancing. Lots of laughter, but I felt like I was sticking it to them. I was a weird and normal kid then. I saw Drake watching. No expression. I think he'd already decided what was going to happen to me.

———

Around ten o'clock, kids started to leave to get to the driveway and find their parents getting out of their cars. I knew my dad was going to park his rusty white Renault Fourteen right up against the front of the school, and march in early in his cigar-smelling suit with chalk on the cuffs to have a quick word with a teacher.

We only had so much money. Just enough. That's why, for my parents, my school life was about me winning the bursary for my final year. The bursary was for the cleverest kids, the top boy and girl of each year. I'd been second last year. Mum and Dad kept mentioning the bursary to me, one and then the other, like they'd told each other they weren't going to say anything, but neither could keep to that agreement. The bursary was based on end-of-year exams. So I heard the words 'school fees' all the time at home. Once, on a caravan holiday, Mum and Dad yelled at each other for two days about school fees. The John Bentley comprehensive was a terrible vision for all of us, the pit they were working hard to keep me from falling into, where those kids that spat at us on the town hall steps came from. Sometimes I asked, and Mum and Dad would laugh and say no, no, I shouldn't worry; they'd do *anything* to keep me out of John Bentley. If Mr. Rove had had any kind of selection procedure based on class, Mum and Dad wouldn't have got past the interview. All the really posh kids at Fasley always looked like they'd been tricked. Upper-middle-class kids like Fiesta seemed marooned in the wrong place. Some of the houses these kids came from would have made better private schools than Fasley did.

I went to get my coat and sticks from Mrs. Parkin at the door. I was sweaty and worked up and thinking I'd done something really big, that I'd taken the test, and had sort of half failed and half passed it, but that tonight I was doing stuff for the girls watching, and not the boys, and that was weird, but great. That moment: my hand closing on the hood of my blue coat that could zip up to a tiny hole way in front of my face, and that had an orange lining.

That's our last sight of the normal and weird kid.

Drake's hands closed on me as I took the coat. 'Come on, mate! You're such an ace dancer!' Drake put one arm round my shoulder and dug his fingers in. The other four were by his side, around me, cutting me off from Mrs. Parkin, who was looking for the next coat anyway. I didn't get my sticks. I could see them in the corner of the cloakroom, but I couldn't ask for them with Drake there. That was the last time I saw them.

So, suddenly we hit the cold night, and I was looking round for my dad, hoping and not hoping he'd be there. There was no sign of him. Parents and kids thronged around us for a moment. That parent smell. Big coats and jewellery. Mothers slipping coats around their daughters' shoulders on the way to big cars. Where were Lang's parents? Why didn't Mr. Rove see his son going out and call him back?

'I have to wait for my dad!' I was saying, trying to get out of their grasp.

'What's that? You're waiting to fuck your mum?' They were guiding me quickly around the back of the building. I could have yelled, but it would have been a scream. That would have made me a victim again, so soon after I'd started to get free. We went straight off the gravel into the bushes and from there into the woods.

They kept me moving with shoves. They couldn't have long. They'd have to be back there in minutes. That wouldn't stop Drake, no rules for him. He was walking along quickly, knowing exactly where he was going, knowing his way through the trees. We entered a clearing. They pushed me up against a tree, so hard that the knots of wood punched my back. 'Right,' said Drake, and the others began to wrestle with me for the belt to my trousers.

Four

I started to yell. To scream. I was attempting to hold onto my belt as Lang grabbed my hands and Rove tried to undo the buckle, while the other two pulled my feet off the ground, and took off my shoes, throwing them aside. It felt terrible to have them take off my shoes. Rove was fumbling, his fingers slipping. I wrenched myself aside. Selway hit me hard across the jaw. I'd been hit a lot, but never so hard. The back of my skull bounced off the tree. My head rang. The world reeled. Several different pictures of the wood and the trees split off in my vision and collided again. I started to sob. They knew what they were after; they were going beyond anything they'd done to me before. All five cooperated in the task. There were just trees in all directions, darkness with lights beyond, help far off, all of us lit by the moon that was a night off full.

'I'll tell!' I shouted. 'You can't stop me telling! You can't stop me telling!'

'You tell and we'll fucking kill you,' muttered Selway.

Drake took a step back, took his knife out, flicked the switch and pulled out the very long blade with the serrated edge. 'Get his cock out,' he said.

'I don't want to touch it,' said Rove. 'Wait a sec.' He fumbled in his coat pockets and pulled out big, fur-lined driving gloves, which he struggled to put on.

My jaw had started to ache so hard I was having trouble

speaking. 'Please,' I said. 'Please don't.'

Lang held me hard against the tree, his breath wet in my face. 'Shut up. This is so you can't fuck your mum any more. It's *disguuuuuuuusting*.'

I thrashed and struggled, but then Selway slammed his body into my lower half, and I was pinned against the tree. Blewly got my belt loose, tried it round his own waist, then threw it away. He pulled the top of my trousers down. He sniggered at my blue Y-Fronts. He looked at the others, not knowing what to do now. He couldn't see any way he could touch me any further.

'Give it here.' Drake stepped forward.

He took the front of my underwear in his hand and pulled it down. He jerked the material about until my tiny dick and balls fell out. I could smell myself. They laughed. There was a fearful smile on Rove's face, a kind of awe at what Drake was doing.

Drake took me in his fist. 'Right, let's get rid of these.'

I screamed at the top of my voice. It carried as far as it could.

He tugged suddenly on my dick, pulling the skin forward.

Selway and Blewly had to hold my arms behind my back. I was thrashing and flailing. Drake raised the knife high over his head.

This is when he lets go, and they all run away laughing, I thought. That in itself was going to be so bad.

He chopped the knife down. There was a moment of intense pain. Like an injection.

I looked down. A tiny cord, a vein you might find in an egg, spitting blood. A flapping of meat that looked like nothing that could ever be part of me. A deep red gouge and strange colours inside it. I had been opened up. Drake held up a thin taper of flesh in his hand. 'You're a Jewboy now,' he said. He flicked it away with his finger. It landed amongst the mulch on the ground. He closed the knife and turned and started to walk away.

Selway and Blewly let go of me. They were looking at me carefully now. I was a thing of wonder. Lang reached down to try and pull up my underpants, but Rove stopped him.

'You're going to be all right,' said Selway. 'Aren't you?'

I actually nodded.

They walked off, looking back over their shoulders, following Drake. After a moment, all of them ran. They were running scared, but also they were running like they'd just scored a goal. I was that goal.

For a while, I stood there. I couldn't touch myself. Blood was running down my legs. Dribbling from the end of my dick. The shape of me was different. They'd made me different. I could feel a bunch of things flapping against my thigh, where there had been one thing.

That's still what it's like. It looks painful even now, and sometimes it is, when I piss or when I come. I'm suddenly panting, injured, freezing, and a long way away.

I've told everyone with whom I've been intimate, had to tell them way before we got to that, that I had an accident involving farm machinery.

I made myself step out from the tree. I nearly fell. I wanted to vomit, but I held it in. I fell to the ground and felt around until I found my belt and used the tree to get to my feet again. Everything felt slow and thumping. Everything was open. I was afraid of the mud getting into the blood, of becoming infected.

Over the years, I've found several mentions of infection

in my reading on this subject. Thank God I was inoculated against tetanus. My urethra was almost certainly narrowed. Which means I was lucky. If that process had gone slightly further, I would have begun to retain urine, which would have resulted in what is possibly the single most painful form of death. Perhaps I would have been made to see a doctor before it got that far. I doubt it. I think I would have fooled my parents, not told to the point where I fell into a coma. I've never shown it to a doctor. I've never had to. The average lad's doses of the clap are far less likely when you're someone whose cock requires an explanation.

In the days when circumcision was a medical matter, before it was decided that nonretractibility of the prepuce was something that would sort itself out, a Plastibell under the foreskin with a piece of string on the outside, or something called a Gomco clamp, was used to gently separate the skin over a few days. "A neat cosmetic result," I've read. Rabbis skilled in such matters, with sutures at hand, also leave something that looks tidy. My cock, however, does not look like anything cosmetic or traditional has happened to it. Unerect, it looks like a ragged lump, the foreskin parted down one side like a tear, red around the edges like lips, proceeding to the base as a glimpse into layers that were not meant to be glimpsed. Erect, it looks frighteningly exposed, painful, infected. It can't get to the angle it's supposed to. It's awkwardly skewed to one side.

Growing up, I saw penises in porn, clutched admiringly in the gentle hand of Shanine Linton. They looked comfortingly simple. That's not me.

In my life, whenever I've become close to a woman, there he is. There he is at every urinal. There he is. Drake. The closeness of a doctor or a mother. The intimacy. He made me.

I pulled up my Y-Fronts, feeling the material press against the wound. I got into my trousers, and, after fumbling with it for a while, I managed to fasten my belt.

The pain was getting worse. Walking was difficult. I did it slowly, with my legs as open as they could go. I hadn't pissed myself. It would have splashed over his hands. I was glad I hadn't done that. He would look at me and laugh next time I saw him, after half-term. All five of them would. They would make Jew jokes. They might tell other kids what they meant.

I moved in a circle. I couldn't find it. It was lost amongst the humus somewhere. Insects were already crawling in the blood. It was mine. It was mine. A doctor might need it to sew it back on. . . . Nobody was ever going to sew it back on. I got my hands and knees covered in mud. I couldn't find it.

Finally, I started heading back to the school. It took me a long time. Dad's car was the last one waiting in the drive. He was standing beside it, talking to Mr. Rove. I would not let it out. I would not let Dad know how his money was being spent. I would not make his attempt to push me up above him on his shoulders stupid. I had a story. To protect Dad. To protect the five of them. No, to protect Dad. No, to save me from John Bentley.

Between my legs was sticky with blood. So I had carefully smudged it on the pullover and the rest of the trousers, clenching my teeth at every downwards stretch. My muscles felt cold, the clench reaching up to my mouth, making my jaw hurt even more. The white lights along the drive would show it all. No getting straight into the car.

Dad and Mr. Rove turned and stared at me as I came round the corner of the house. I started to tell them how none of this was real.

Five

It's wrong to expect, to require, victims to be innocents. Victims often are the most difficult, the most aggressive, the nastiest, most compromised people. Of course they are. It's so tempting for me, when someone in the pub says, 'They should all be locked up', about anyone, to agree. Because they all *should* be locked up. We *all* should. But, because it *is* tempting, I tend to violently disagree.

I fight myself all the time.

Popular music; fashion; sport; the whole business of sex, from romance to family life—these are the things denied to bullied kids. It doesn't surprise me, these days, to see how geeks and hipsters have built whole subcultures on the absence, denial or modification of those things. The love of one of them, of pop music, was gifted to me. That break in the battle was Angie's part. Apart from that, if 'everyone' likes it, I can't. I associate mainstream culture with having my cock cut off. There are kids who went through school experiences like mine who will never watch football, and there are those who end up playing for Arsenal. Okay, who will end up with season tickets. Stockholm syndrome will only take you so far.

Enough about what I am now. That comes later.

When I was a kid, the view outside my bedroom window was always a problem. It was of the Cherhill White Horse, up there on the downs above our house. When I was eight, Dad planted a row of trees along the fence. By the time I'd started at Fasley, they'd formed a dark corridor, with the downs visible above them.

The corridor seemed to invite visitors. I'd look up from reading on my bed with the certainty that something had just passed the window.

———————

Halloween night, 1982, coming back from the disco after Drake had done that to me. Dad put a rug on the seat, and kept questioning me as he drove. That was my best pullover. How had I gotten fake blood all over it? Who were these other kids I'd been playing with? I said Rove, the headmaster's son. Dad was quiet for a bit. He asked me where my snooker cues were. I said I'd forgotten them, and he nodded. The pain between my legs was building now. How could it be getting worse? I wanted to curl up around it, but I didn't.

When we got home, I made the pullover the problem, taking it off and putting it straight into the washing machine. I was sly in a way that kids only think they are, like in stories, sly in the way that gets real kids caught. Mum cried out in anger and fright when she saw it, and I was gone into my bedroom and leaning on the door.

I listened to Dad telling Mum what had happened, at the tops of their voices. They were both going increasingly deaf. I still find myself yelling on the phone to them, to get through to Dad past what Mum's yelling in the background.

I sat on the bed, and, with a chair propped against the door, I started to undress. I nearly passed out getting my Y-Fronts off. That was something I'd never felt before. I had to hold myself up, breathing deeply, thinking about them finding me on the ground in the morning. The blood had stopped flowing. There was a caked wound at the end of my dick, and down it that streak I'm now familiar with. It looked like rust, gobbets of it in my pubic hair, all down my legs, and inside my trousers. I needed to wash it. I couldn't bring myself to.

There was a week off now, the half-term break. I wouldn't see the five of them for a week.

I put the dirty clothes in the wash basket. I'd wash them myself after everyone was asleep. I'd say I felt bad about the mess. Mum and Dad would ask, wouldn't they? I didn't want to be sly and get away with it. Parents in a TV show, the mum and dad from *Happy Days*, they'd know something was wrong and wouldn't rest until they got to the bottom of it.

I called to them that I was going to bed. They called back good night.

I sat on my bed. What did what had been done to me mean? I wasn't going to die. Probably. It only meant something if I let it mean something.

If I showed Mum and Dad and told them what had happened, Dad would march into the school and start yelling hopelessly about the headmaster's son, and that'd be the end of his ambitions for me, the end of his hopes that one of us would . . . escape. I'm not sure my young self could have put that feeling into words.

I waited until I was absolutely sure the bleeding had stopped, then got into my pyjamas. I could feel the dried blood against the fabric. It was like I'd grown spikes. I wasn't comfortable lying down or standing, so I sat on the edge of the bed. I hadn't closed the curtains. I'd been locked into a little box on the edge of the bed, hurting and afraid to move. So I was looking straight at the frame of the window, with the avenue of trees there and the downs above. I wanted to close the curtains, but I had it in my head, as I often did back then, that if I got up to do that, something else would get up from the other side of the window, and I would be facing it when I got there.

I usually closed my eyes and leapt at the window, and then made sure with my hands that there were no gaps in the curtains before I looked.

So I sat there, looking and looking. I found that for once I wasn't trying to stop the fear from coming in. I was wanting it, inviting it to join me. Above the downs that night was the moon, just off full. So close to full, in fact, that it looked like the light might slip round the edge at any moment, and the globe would be complete. The white light made the downs stand out. I could see the ridges and the troughs. I could see the horse sparkling like water. I waited until the sounds from the lounge and kitchen had stopped, and for the clunk of Mum's and Dad's bedroom door closing, and then I waited some more. I looked at the watch on my bedside table, and it had been an hour. I put my messed-up clothes in the washing machine.

In the kitchen, Dad had left the blinds open as well. The nearly full moon stood above me there too. Normally, Dad remembered to close the blinds for Mum's sake. She liked to have every window completely covered. There were two locks, four bolts and a security chain on the big wooden door. I went and undid them, as quietly as I had to. I went outside.

I stood under the moon. My breath bloomed, reflecting the light. There was the smell of the cold. There was just me, and the garden, and the curve of the road, and Aunt Dar next door, long in her bed, and the fields obscured by the tree hedge and the downs over all.

I walked around the back of the house. I walked anticlockwise around the house.

I walked down the dark corridor of trees. I walked past the window of the darkened bedroom of my parents.

I looked into my own bedroom window, and saw myself lying in my bed, asleep.

Because I had also started the washing machine, and gone back to my room, and got into my bed and gone to sleep.

It's all my fault. I had reached out for what had always fluttered around my window. This is where Waggoner began. He wasn't exactly what he had to be yet. He still bore my wound then. He was conceived at the moment of the cut. He was born outside my window, looking at me. That night on the downs, he was baptised into his own self.

Six

Waggoner left the window, and headed down the gravel track that led to the overgrown lane, that led to the downs. Waggoner walked quickly. The hedgerows hid him. Soon he was out of sight of the house. I always used my sticks to push the briars and blackberry bushes out of the way. Waggoner did it with his pyjama sleeves wrapped over his hands, catching thorns and leaves in the paisley material. Badgers lived up in the lane, in burrows with sprays of flint and dried chalk mud in front of them. Waggoner stepped between them as they snuffled. He fell sideways into a bush, and Mrs. Pheasant, as Mum called the bird, burst out into the night, screaming. Bats flickered around his head.

It's about a mile, at a sharp incline, up onto the back of the downs. His feet slipped in the mud, and gradually it coated up the sides of his pyjama trousers. Mum would say he got clarted. He kept walking, determined. He hauled himself up onto the stile at the end of the path. Beyond it were the uplands of the downs, marked with the National Trust sign. Waggoner sat getting his breath, and looked back to where he had come. Over there, RAF Lyneham, bright lines of white and yellow. In the distance, Waggoner saw the glow of Swindon, and there was Calne. The lights were cut off by the dark square of the Red Barn at the top of Mr. Maundrell's farm. The Maundrell and Angell farms both rented land off the big estates.

Waggoner looked up the hill. He was fearless. Suddenly there were lights.

There were often lights on the downs. Mum used to say they were torches. Hikers. Everyone seemed to say that, whenever I asked, without thinking any more about it.

These lights weren't the points of torches that flashed as someone moved through the ditches. These were big blue and red lights that swam into the sky and stayed there, floating like suspended fireworks, silently. The blue ones whipped off into the side of Waggoner's eyes and stayed there, no matter which way he turned his head. Waggoner put his freezing hands to his freezing face. The lights shrank back into the downs again. He shouted. He fell off the stile, into the mud.

I've heard such things called earthlights. It's said they're made when one huge thing rumbles against another, and both compete for the same space.

Waggoner scrambled to his feet and ran up the hill towards what he'd seen, the wind buffeting his ears, his shoes slipping. His body was cold like a stone. He used his hands to pull himself along, the wound in his groin opening, bleeding again. He pushed himself up the first hillside, to where the copse stood above the landscape of the valleys. There were no sheep now. They were taken in on winter nights. He leaned on one of the fallen trees. The elms were being cut down then, because of Dutch elm disease. He turned to look at the hill fort, across the dip that lay between this copse and the main body of the downs.

He couldn't see the fort. The whole of the downs was in shadow.

Not a shadow. It moved in the wind. It joined up in one moment, as if Waggoner had just realised it should be there, or it had moved suddenly out of the corners of his eyes and into full view. It swallowed the copse around him. He shouted. He was in darkness now. The darkness stayed put around him, and was in the way now, when he looked back to where he'd come from.

The darkness whispered. It was a natural darkness. It rustled. Creaked. Leafless branches, all around him now. Shadows that stood irregularly all around.

Suddenly, the downs had become home to a forest.

He made his way through it. He came to the banks and troughs of the hill fort. He stumbled down into the biggest of the troughs, the one that leads around to the 'gate' of the hill fort, where there's a gap in the banks that leads into the inner area. It really had been a gate once, archaeologists think, the place where large wooden doors had swung inwards. There was a light somewhere around the curve of the trough, from the other direction to the gate, anticlockwise around the hill fort. He headed towards it. It was a flickering white. It was like no real fire. Its origin came into view around the curve. The fire was like an animation of bright paper, sparkling in stop-motion. It was coming from between two sticks, held by a figure standing in the trough. He had one long stick in each hand, holding them wide apart, controlling the fire between them, buffeting and fluttering. The figure was like a sticker made to fit into a bigger picture in a sticker album. His edges and the background he stood in front of didn't quite match up. His features were concealed by the light. Waggoner could feel heat on his brow from the fire, prickling, like he was being sunburned.

The man with two sticks had placed himself at exactly the right point. He'd made things that usually ground together like two continents open up, creating a gap. Because of that, everything near him was under pressure. There was such stiff pain in him. He was a bottomless pit where a person had been. Carefully carrying the sticks and the fire, he inclined his head to Waggoner, then turned and began to walk away. Waggoner knew he should follow.

The man with two sticks led Waggoner round the outer wall. He turned off the main ditch, climbed the next bank and headed in a straight line away from the hill fort. Ahead of them, the trees thinned out a little. They reached the place where the monument stands. That night, however, Waggoner came to the edge of the trees and found he was looking down into a giant pit in the ground, its chalk wall round and white, with tree roots growing in from every side. In the centre of it stood a huge bright spur of chalk, imbedded flints shining. On top of it stood a big tree, the only oak of the forest, its branches covering and overhanging the pit, making the white walls ripple with the moon through the leaves. The bottom of the pit was full of water. The roots of the tree spread out down into the water like veins through the flesh of the rock. Between them were bones and skulls sticking out. The thing was at least as much bone as it was chalk.

My reading tells me that what Waggoner saw is called an omphalos. The tribes of Britain might have led huge processions around them. Perhaps when Henry Petty-Fitzmaurice looked at the Cherhill Downs, he realised something was missing, or wanted to keep something locked down, and so he built the monument.

The man with two sticks went to the edge of the pit. He shoved his sticks into the ground, squatted down, and took a cup from somewhere inside himself. It was golden, and it shone with reflected light. It was simple, smooth and perfect.

Waggoner looked at the cup and thought it was beautiful. He had an ache for it, a nostalgia for something he'd never experienced. It was like an often-told story in the shape of an object. The man with two sticks dipped the cup into the water, then brought it back to him. He showed Waggoner the cup in his nothing hands. Waggoner understood. He pulled his pyjama trousers down around his ankles. The man with two sticks looked at him. He poured the water from the cup onto the wound. Waggoner winced at the pressure of it. The dried blood was caked there, it felt like it was holding things together, but as the water found every concealed place upon him—

Waggoner became clean and whole again. His wound vanished. The pain was just an ache now, exciting, a new fire inside him.

The man stepped back, his task accomplished, expectant. He waited until Waggoner had pulled his trousers back on, pulled his sticks from the ground, then led him away once again.

———————

They were on guard at the hill fort that night, like they were every night. The empire would come for them. If it didn't happen tonight it would tomorrow. They held their iron shields to reflect the moon, and watched through a chink beside their eyes. They could see right to the horizon. They were never unaware of anything that approached. They were never dull to any possibility of future harm.

They valued revenge, above all, because of what had been done to them. Their law was absolute, to protect those who had had such wrong done to them. They were the only ones who remembered the importance of their culture, the epic nature of their plight, so they would remember it hard and carefully, in important songs and serious verse. They had been here forever, since the point they had escaped from the real world, and time meant nothing to them now, except on this one night, when the wise ones among them could escape their trap and see the world they kept themselves from. They had no children of their own now, and wanted them desperately, but there were terrible penalties for admitting desires like that, as for so many things.

Waggoner was shown the shape of the downs that night. He walked the bounds of the hill fort itself. He saw where those who stood guard on that special night were hiding, ready to emerge when the time was right. He exchanged a few words with one of them. She told him she was the one chosen to go ahead, that she was ready to do her duty in the next life. He was shown what I called the quarry, where some workings had once been cut into the hill fort, and a little water comes to the surface and winds down through the gravel, and the grass around is soggy, apart from at the height of summer. Here it was a rough pool of wet grass, desperately lapped from when those who were trapped there couldn't venture beyond the hill fort. Outside the bounds of the fort, he saw an ancient chalk horse, just a cluster of wild lines, a horse undreamt of by archaeologists, where there was now the newer, more polite one. Its eye shone with potency. He was taken to the bowl barrow, far from the hill fort, and found it was now a round barrow, with something inside waiting to be born. He saw a small, shiny rock in its own crater, the edges of which were worn down by ritual, the rock itself polished by the same care. It was what we'd call a meteorite, missing completely from the modern downs, perhaps taken by some collector. Dried blood covered the ground all around, but the rock itself was kept pure, a prized possession of the people. At a lesser distance from the hill fort itself, he was shown the round house of sacrifice, a hut with the door locked, with desperate cries coming from inside.

Waggoner was given several things to take back with him. He solemnly put them in his pockets.

When Mum came in in the morning, she found that the curtains were open. She closed them quickly, then opened them again. I was already awake. I told her I'd washed the clothes overnight. She told me off for a bit, talking around and around it, frightened . . . but she didn't ask any questions. When she'd gone, I looked under the blankets, and pulled my pyjama trousers down. I hoped it would all be gone, that I'd be whole again.

I wasn't. There was the wound that I would live with all my life.

Then I realised. Someone was in bed with me. Waggoner was lying there. He was real. I wasn't inside his head any more, like I'd been when I was asleep. He pulled down his pyjama trousers and showed me he was whole.

'Why wasn't I healed?' I asked.

'You can only be healed when your revenge is complete.'

I didn't know if I believed him. I was afraid of what he was planning to do when we went back to school, because he was free to do what he liked.

On the Friday of half-term, November fifth, Dad brought a box of fireworks home from work, and set them off in the garden using the long blue taper provided in the box. They had been very expensive. Mum and I watched. Some of them were duds. Mum grabbed Dad by the arm and told him not to go back to them, *please* Frank! There were two rockets, which went up high over the lane, as if they were heading for the darkness of the downs. I closed my eyes so as not to see them against the hillside.

Waggoner was with me all the time that week. Finally, in bed the night before we went back, lying awake, I found something I could say to him. 'I'll tell,' I said. 'If you promise not to do it, I'll tell on them instead.'

'Okay,' he said. 'Try.'

Seven

On the first day back after half-term, it took an effort for me to get on the bus. For the first time, I was going to experience a school day with Waggoner.

How can I even begin to describe Waggoner? He looked and sounded exactly like me. He was also a fourteen-year-old schoolboy. When Mum had laid out my uniform on the bed that he and I had started sharing a week before, he was suddenly wearing one too. He was also going to Fasley Grange school.

Mum hadn't had to feed and clothe him throughout the holiday. He would just suddenly have what I had. He would find space to sit beside me even if there was no space. It was like the world kept bending out of shape just enough to let him in. Dad took us both in the car to the steps of the town hall. We both sat in one seat in the front.

We sat next to each other on the school minibus. I kept looking at Waggoner's face. I was wondering if I was good and he was evil, or maybe it was the other way round. His arrival hadn't made what Drake had done to me better, it had made it more frightening. There had to be rules against him existing, laws. So I was going to tell everything about what had been done to me to the first responsible adult I could find. That would make Waggoner vanish. That was the sort of story this was.

On the way into my class's form room, I saw Drake's lot from behind. I sucked in a breath. I had to grab Waggoner to stop him from bellowing something at them. He was baring his teeth, his eyes were fixed on them, looking like my eyes never could: certain and fearless and rough.

Something made Drake's lot stop and look around. They saw me there, but not Waggoner. They pointed and laughed to each other, all five of them, curled up around it, a laughter so big they couldn't let it all out there. They waggled their hands in front of their bodies and made mock anguished expressions. They used my name like a football chant. I had imagined they might be worried or scared about what they'd done, that they would keep away from me.

They hadn't noticed the big change.

It was good when they didn't notice the changes. It paralysed you when they did. It made you hate getting a haircut. You never wanted them to see you in your normal clothes. Your normal clothes weren't like their normal clothes.

I just about managed to hold Waggoner back. I staggered with him into the form room. Waggoner thumped down between me and Fiesta, somehow creating a third chair at a double desk. I looked to Fiesta, and he looked puzzled back at me: *What?* He was ignoring Waggoner. So couldn't anyone see him? Why was I afraid of what he could do if they couldn't see him?

I was still afraid.

Mrs. Mills, our form teacher, started calling out the register. She looked tired in the first moment of the first day of this half-term. Could I tell her my incredible story? Could I just shout it out now, like I wanted to?

I couldn't.

She called out the one name that stood for both of us, and we both said, 'Yes'.

———————

The first lesson of the week was double Woodwork. I'd completed just three woodwork projects in my time at school. I'd start whatever Mr. Sedge, who was some sort of handyman for Mr. Rove, told us to start, and then I'd spend two hours every week shaving it. Waggoner, to my surprise, turned out to be good at it, turning the lump over quickly in his hands, chiseling and planing. It was because he didn't care about anyone's reactions to a mistake, so he could have a go, see what worked. I kept looking between him and the others. So could they see what he was working on hovering in mid-air, like something out of *Rentaghost*? No. The alteration had been stranger than that. I couldn't keep on limiting what Waggoner was by describing him using the language of children's television.

Drake and the others kept their secret chant going, looking over and laughing. If any one of them had stopped, maybe the others might have got scared of what they'd done. Except Drake. They'd have been on the phone to each other, talking about me.

I think Mr. Sedge liked it when the boys in his class picked on each other. It was what boys were supposed to do. While we did woodwork, the girls did cookery. In the fifth year, boys could choose to do that too. That was when you could announce your plan to be a poof. Mr. Sedge wore an off-white apron; his hair was just a few curls at the back of his head. He looked at everything every boy was making, and he nodded with his mouth open, so you could see his little teeth.

Could I tell Mr. Sedge? No. Boys will be boys. He would look puzzled: why was I bringing something to him he wasn't qualified to consider?

Drake and the other four got Waggoner and me into a corner, because it turned out I didn't want them to touch me. They were asking whispered questions that didn't seek answers, or maybe this time they did, nudging at me, making the chisel I was trying to work with miss the wood. I was half hoping they'd do that to Waggoner, but no. Mr. Sedge walked past, his grin fixed in place. Waggoner was saying, I will kill you, you bastards, I will kill you. They weren't paying attention.

The chisel missed again. It ripped my hand, up the right thumb. They all stepped back and sniggered. They'd done it to me again.

It was all I could do to stop Waggoner from lashing out with the chisel. I fought and I fought. I stared at the rip in the skin. He finally relented. That was the extent of his promise: that he would relent, only for today, while I tried to find a way to tell.

Mr. Sedge turned back to us and with a big theatrical sigh told me I'd have to go and get that seen to.

———————

I went to the school nurse's office. Angie Boden was sitting on the bench outside.

I hesitated, but then, when she didn't acknowledge my presence, I sat down. Waggoner sat beside me, making space for himself, and she moved up an inch or two. For a moment, I thought she'd seen Waggoner. But no, of course not. I was wondering about telling my story to the nurse, of letting my problem move from the thumb to the more serious matter.

Angie kept glancing across at me, frowning as always. It wasn't a surprise to find her here. She was always missing lessons with notes from home, not doing PE, not running, sitting there with a book, not bowed down by her difference. She seemed more grown up because she didn't have to do all the school things. She started humming something under her breath. Then she stopped. 'What's wrong with you?' she asked, then corrected herself. 'I mean, what's the matter?'

Someone had asked. I was so thankful. That hurt. I almost told her, but I couldn't get it out. I showed her my thumb.

'That doesn't look so bad,' she said.

'Right,' I said. It felt really strange to talk to a girl now, when I hadn't done it much before. The door opened, and the nurse came out. She told Angie to come on in, and Angie did, without looking at me again.

———————

At three o'clock that day, the bell rang for the end of French, and Mr. Coxwell muttered angrily to us to walk, not run, and we hauled our bags out into the corridor, Waggoner and me and all the other kids. I hadn't been able to tell Mr. Coxwell. I had not succeeded in telling any teacher. I couldn't think of any teacher on any day who would be any different.

To get to the minibus, Waggoner and I walked from muddy tiles to rubber mud rug, to gravel and sunlight, out at the back past the science lab. I was walking with physical pain in the winter sunshine. There would even be pain in summer. I would never be able to tell. I'd have to hold Waggoner back all the time. Drake's lot were going to keep doing things to me. I was going to work hard to allow them to continue.

Or instead I was going to go home and kill myself.

How to do that? I was examining it, a project to distract me. I think I would have kept on considering that forever too. I mean, come on, how many things had I succeeded in making in Woodwork?

But instead, there was Angie.

She was standing on her own, across from the biology classroom, looking away into the distance, concerned as always. 'Back on the Chain Gang' by The Pretenders. The guitar riff from the start of that is what's on the soundtrack when I think of her in that moment. She had her enormous bag slung over one shoulder, with the Virgin Records slogan *I'm a Virgin* stenciled on it in red.

I stopped. I decided. I was going to rush up to her and blurt out that since she'd asked earlier–

But she was off, having decided something, marching, off behind the biology classroom, heading out towards the woods.

Everyone else from my bus was getting on board. It would be minutes before it left. This was my last chance. I had to take it. I rushed after Angie. Waggoner followed.

Angie didn't look back as she walked down the dirt track that led into the woods. I didn't call to her. Maybe I felt like I'd scare her. I gave up walking properly and for the first time that day let myself limp, thump thump along the path, a monster's gait.

The low sunshine had made a big, hard line between the playing fields and the shadow of the edge of the woods. Above us was the school, emptying, becoming a home again for the night. Mr. Rove and his son Rove would be doing whatever they did, making use of lounges and kitchens that we didn't get to see. I wonder if Mr. Rove was standing at one of his windows that afternoon, looking down at us, three small uniforms, the black and white of two boys, the blue-and-white stripe of a girl, moving from light to dark at the edge of the trees. Could he see all three uniforms? Maybe he might have for a moment, as we crossed the terminator, like a trick of the light.

It's hard to imagine him being uncertain.

Trying to catch my breath to say something, to make her look, I watched Angie walk. The march. The swing of the bag on her back. Waggoner was looking too. He looked hungry like I could never be. Angie would understand my problem, being an outsider herself, but the teachers trusted her.

It hadn't occurred to me to wonder why, at the end of a school day, she was walking into the woods. Then I realised. This path was horribly familiar. She wasn't just going into the woods.

She was going to the clearing.

I slowed down. She didn't know anything about this, did she?

I stopped. She vanished around the curve of the path.

Waggoner looked at me. Shouldn't we just go back? I could hear her, rustling leaves as she walked, heading into the clearing. I crept forward. Waggoner followed.

I heard a voice up ahead. I stopped again. I recognised the voice, and got sick.

Drake.

Through the foliage, I could see his shape in the clearing. I sat down at the side of the path, slowly and carefully as I had to, so I wouldn't cry out, so I could hear, but they wouldn't be able to see me.

'You always want to come here.' That was Angie's voice. 'Is this your special place?'

''Spose.'

The two shapes moved together. They embraced.

I had to hold in a noise. I tried to stand. I realised I couldn't move without them hearing me. Waggoner was looking at me questioningly.

'I told you,' I said, whispering through my teeth. 'I will find someone to tell.'

'You wanted to tell her,' he said, not whispering. 'How about I do that right in front of him?' Before I could reply, he'd leapt up, and burst through the bushes into the clearing. With a cry of pain, I hauled myself up and ran after him. Angie and Drake turned, startled, as we entered.

Waggoner skidded to a halt, pointed at Drake and theatrically took a deep breath to speak. He knew I was going to stop him. I grabbed him. I wrestled with him in front of them. I got my hand over his mouth. He was yelling through it, muffled, unintelligible. I had no idea which one of us they could see or if it was both.

Drake started to laugh.

Waggoner contorted in my grip, trying to get my hand out of his mouth. His teeth were in my hand, and it was hurting like everything else about me hurt. I was going to injure myself. I twisted in my own grip.

Drake was laughing and laughing. 'Got summat to say? Sorry, we don't understand you. You all right, then?' He reached out for me.

I jerked back, so fast his fingers missed. I found myself looking into Angie's eyes. I was surprised at what I saw there: fear. She was as afraid of me as I was of Drake. I had no idea how that could be possible.

I saw her lips form words under her breath.

I was running along the path back to the school. The bus was still there. I hauled myself up and stumbled into it. There was Waggoner, already sitting in the bus, looking around, startled, as if he'd just appeared there.

I sat down beside him. My mouth and lips and neck were hurting as much as anywhere else on my body. I could taste blood where I'd bitten the inside of my mouth.

Everyone was talking normally; they were late getting off, waiting for Elaine, who'd now appeared at the door, having had to pick up something from the biology lab. Marie was in the front with Grayson, and Bradley was hitting his sister over the head with the tray from her cookery.

I laughed. I stopped it. I started to cry. I stopped it. I tried to just be. I couldn't. I wanted to shout. I wanted to tell them all. I'd been given one last chance to tell today.

What about the driver? But she was already yelling at Bradley, in her powerless, not-a-teacher way, and saying in the end that it was none of her business what we did.

Waggoner was looking at me again. He looked serious, worried for the first time, needing a little desperately now for me to let him do what he was here to do.

I hadn't been able to tell. I wouldn't even let *him* tell. What exactly had happened back there? Angie had yelled at me, and I had run; of course that had been it. I still didn't understand how she could be afraid of me. I didn't understand how Waggoner could be worried about her. I didn't yet understand what she could do.

Someone locked the back doors of the bus. It drove off, and I looked behind as it went up the long drive, and turned onto the road outside the gates, leaving school behind.

When I got home, I told Mum the dressing on my thumb was for something small that had happened in Woodwork. I sat there through half an hour of her fear. I couldn't deal with it, so I didn't. I asked to go for a walk before dinner.

I headed straight up the lane that led to the downs. I went up onto them, painful and slow as that walk was. I wanted to encounter for myself what Waggoner had met. I was too afraid to be afraid. I wanted to say I didn't agree. I wanted to work out some sort of different deal. But what had been there for Waggoner wasn't for me. Waggoner came with me, telling me that all the way. Then I couldn't walk any more. I crumpled into the bowl barrow and lay curled there, with the winter sun low on the horizon. It was nearly dark. I was freezing, but I didn't care.

Waggoner lay beneath me, beside me, around me. I saw him with me, and he asked me again to let him do what he had been born to do.

I closed my eyes. 'What are you?' I asked.

'I want what happened to *mean* something. I want *everything* to mean something. I'm *free* to *make* that meaning.'

'What are you going to do?'

'It'll take a long time. You won't understand why I'm doing certain things. You'll need to keep faith with me. But in the end, I swear, I'm going to hurt them more than they hurt you. Then, when your revenge is complete, you'll get healed.'

I thought of Drake with Angie, like I could never be. 'Yes,' I said.

Eight

The head of a boy from John Bentley was butting into the door of the town hall. Bam, bam, bam, like his skull on the door was a call for something big to happen. Waggoner had grabbed by the collar one of the boys who always gobbed at us and flung him against that door. He'd landed flat on his palms, surprised, and Waggoner had grabbed him again, knocked his hands away and slammed his head on the wood three times. Then he let go, and the kid fell.

The John Bentley kids stepped back. None of them wanted to fight all eight of us about this kid. He got to his feet, too shocked to be angry. Waggoner reached to grab him again, and he fell back into the gutter, and crawled up the wall until he was on his feet again, staggering.

I remember everyone staring, an island of strangeness. Elaine said we were being very immature. The kid with the curly hair started shouting things at us as his mates helped him away, as our minibus pulled up. I was looking at how straight Waggoner was standing now, taller than me, at the way he smiled, like a hero, his breath billowing hot from his mouth. He had been testing himself on that boy. Now he could do whatever he wanted. I dreaded that, and I dreaded what was coming at the end of the day.

At school, I looked at the kids getting out of the buses from different village runs. I was walking with Waggoner, slowly, towards the back door of the school, wondering where and when he'd begin his plan. I suddenly realised that Angie's group of friends were walking past us. There was Angie. There was Louise, looking around quickly, her expression worried and intense as always. Everyone else had gone inside. Then Angie was right beside me.

Waggoner started to laugh. He was looking Angie up and down.

She put her head next to mine and whispered so quietly that I was sure even her friends couldn't hear. 'Don't you dare tell about what you saw in the clearing. Okay?' I was so angry I couldn't speak. I looked to Waggoner, and now he was glaring at her. She seemed frustrated at my lack of response. 'What happened to you? What's wrong with you?' I couldn't answer. Drake hadn't directly referred to what he'd done to me when she was there. Had he not told her? Would it make any difference to how she felt about him? It was impossible for me to even begin to tell her. She held my gaze for a long moment. Then she was off back to her friends, and they were off at high speed into the school.

I turned back to Waggoner and saw that he was calm, quiet, prepared.

I did my work that day, kept my head down. I heard, at a distance, about Eddy Grant going to Number One with 'I Don't Want to Dance'. That didn't mean much to me at the time, though of course I needed to know what was Number One like any kid did, to be able to answer if anyone asked that as a mocking question. You were supposed to know, like you were supposed to know which music was okay to like and which wasn't. Since then, I've become very aware of what was Number One at every point during the events I'm describing. I keep wondering how much those records influenced everything that happened. The pop charts lie alongside my impossible memories as an index. Angie yelled suddenly at the news, a shout of annoyance that, at the time, I took to be a hatred of Eddy Grant, which surprised me, but I always struggled with which music was okay to like. Meanwhile, Angie and Drake stayed in their separate groups. Outside the clearing, I'd never seen them together at all.

I made sure nobody was watching me, and found my way back to the clearing in the woods. There was my dried blood. It was still real. I looked around for what had been cut from me. I still couldn't find it. Maybe it had been eaten by a bird or something. I could imagine it in its beak, pulled at by other birds. I gave up, hating giving up, and went back.

A cramp was in my stomach. It tensed every time I thought of what was coming at the end of the day. Although Waggoner had told me his revenge would take a long time, part of me had hoped that somehow the end of the day would never happen.

At the end of the day was PE, and after that we'd have showers, and everyone would see what had happened to me. I couldn't make myself tell, but my body would. Waggoner must know that.

Maybe that was going to be his cue to begin his long plan.

———————

'Franklin's sister is *broad*,' I heard Lang sniggering through the noise of training shoes being stamped on the floor of the changing rooms to get the mud off them. 'Wouldn't it, wouldn't it, wouldn't it be funny, if Franklin's sister had a wooden tit, wouldn't it be funny?'

We could already feel the cold from outside. My lot, Surtees and Fiesta and Cath (who was a boy, not a girl called Catherine), were slowly and carefully taking our clothes off. I kept looking across at Drake, but he wasn't looking up. Maybe by now he knew Angie had warned me off talking about seeing them in the clearing. Maybe she and he spoke about things like that, but I could hardly believe it. He would never acknowledge I held any power over him, so I never would.

In my lot, Surtees was tall and awkward. His spine curved, so that he looked like he was always ducking down. If he'd stood tall, he'd have been looking out over all of us, and would have been alone. Surtees would say sniffy, insulting things about the football kids, under his breath, usually, with a little high-voiced Wiltshire ferret glance at the rest of us, biting his bottom lip in glee. 'He's got an anus as tight as a nun's chuff,' he once said to Cath about Lang. I think it was because he hated being with us. He wanted to be a football kid. He never really understood why he couldn't be. He was talking to me about his English Cricketers Top Trumps pack. He had four of the special cards now, one of which came free in every pack, and if you got five, you could send off for a Sports Cars pack.

I wasn't listening. I was looking over to where Lang was with Drake and the others. Drake saw me looking. He must have read the expression on my face. He faltered, looked awkward. He'd just realised about the showers too.

I wonder now if Rove or Lang or Selway or Blewly were surprised that I came back to school after half-term at all, that they weren't amazed I wasn't in hospital. Maybe they'd spent half-term in fear themselves, when they'd woken up the next morning, after the clearing, and realised what they'd been part of.

No. None of us *thought*. You read books about kids at school, and they're fucking *detectives*, like teenagers on telly, all plans and decisions and life choices. But no. None of us *thought*. Not like adults do.

They had been too busy laughing to think of being vulnerable. They weren't sure they were even now. They couldn't imagine my weakness harming them. But they were about to see the results of their actions. 'Broad' was one of those words of Lang's that might or might not mean something. 'Isn't Cath *ace*?' he asked me once. I said yes. Lang had run about, his hands balled into little fists, saying, 'Waggoner says Cath's ace!' Cath, from my lot, had a mane of frizzy hair. That on its own would have been enough to make him one of my lot. Or maybe not, because if you looked at Goff, with his spotty face and greasy hair, you'd think he'd be picked on, but he just wasn't. The hair made Cath look surprised all the time. I assumed, in those days, that that was how all Catholics looked. I didn't know what a Catholic was. Lang had said the 'ace' thing to Cath too, pointing at me like he was telling him about something bad. So Cath had hit me as best he could on the arm a couple of times.

Wincing now, I sat on the bench, and slowly tied the laces on my training shoes. I was aware of Drake's lot considering me. That I looked wounded now must have felt like a threat.

Mr. Rushden came in, in his red track suit with white piping, and clapped his hands together. 'Right! It's raining, so we're going to get going with a cross-country warm-up, yeah?'

There was a groan, which he joined in with.

———————

The rain fell on us as we ran along the pavement beside the wall that ran round the school. The football lads, with Drake, had run off into the distance after the first sprint up the drive, leaving my lot to fall to the back and all the kids in the middle to string out in-between. Runs were the pecking order. Fiesta gave up as soon as possible and started walking, unconcerned. He'd get there in time with a couple of jogs halfway. Cath and Surtees went off to end up somewhere in the middle. I jogged along for a while, but then, as always, I started wheezing, and now the wound between my legs was aching, and I found myself having to stop and put my legs together, feeling something terrible and muscular, like something inside was going to snap.

I should have realised. It was only going to get worse.

Fiesta walked past me, looking over his shoulder, puzzled for a moment, then walking on. I was alone, leaning on the wall, sucking in air, trying not to throw up. Waggoner stood beside me, calm. He didn't encourage me. That didn't seem to be his job.

Mr. Rushden came running back. The rain was getting harder and harder. 'What's up?' he said. 'Come on, you can do it. Forget your body; it's all in your head.' He tapped a finger against his temple.

I couldn't reply. I managed to stumble into a run.

'That's it, keep going.' He ran beside me, a comedy slow run. 'The more you do it, the better you'll be, yeah?' He rotated his fists in a little mock boxing cycle. Waggoner ran beside me and Mr. Rushden, like in *The Professionals*, his cheeks puffed out, his hands made into blades. But he stayed alongside me. 'You'll be all right, okay?' Mr. Rushden got fed up with staying back here and moved off up ahead again, looking back over his shoulder.

As soon he turned the corner, I fell against the wall again. I wanted to cry. Waggoner looked at me again. Then he leapt up onto the wall. He scrabbled for a moment, then hauled himself up to the top and sat there. He reached a hand down for me.

I looked back along the road. This was not allowed. But the alternative was Mr. Rushden coming back again, me throwing up, crying, to have everyone looking at me as I staggered back hours too late. I took Waggoner's hand. He hauled me up onto the wall as a car went by, tooting its horn happily at the cheating. Boys will be boys. The horn covered up the yell I'd come out with as the pain had stretched from my hand to my groin. I hauled my leg over, and sat on top of the wall for a moment before, as quickly as possible, dropping onto the forest floor on the other side. Waggoner dropped down beside me.

We stood in the woods, hearing the rain thumping onto the trees. Waggoner set off in the direction of the playing fields. I followed, trying to be like him, forcing myself not to go hiding from tree to tree. I felt very out of bounds. Was this something Waggoner was going to do now, lead me into doing bad stuff? We got to the edge of the trees and the expanse of the playing fields. Rain was sweeping across them. In one corner, the girls were playing volleyball, small figures in their blue-and-white sports kit. God, why didn't they let us do stuff like that? My eyes found Angie, in her normal uniform, sitting at a distance from the game, reading. She didn't seem bothered by the rain. I saw, even from this distance, her head turn in my direction.

I didn't want to think about her at that moment. Closer to

us was the football pitch, the lines newly white after half-term. At one corner of it, the football boys were already arriving, racing each other through the door in the wall, sprinting to be the first to get to the line that marked the edge of the pitch. If I joined them now, that'd give them something to think about. Do they tell on me, or do they like what I've done?

They tell on me.

Waggoner just walked out of the woods and headed for them. I swallowed back throwing up and followed him.

———————

Mr. Rushden came through the door in the wall at the moment I arrived at the group of boys. They were staring at me, laughing, amazed. I'd made a move to change my status with them. All possibilities were still in play. They looked expectant, like they were wondering if I'd break down in tears and claim that I'd got lost.

Amongst them, Drake was looking calmly at the ground, Selway was looking left and right, smirking. Rove, Blewly and Lang wouldn't arrive for a while yet.

'Hoi!' Mr. Rushden stepped forward, pointing at me. 'Did you climb over the wall?'

'Yes, sir,' I said.

'You can't run that distance, but you can climb over a wall.'

I nodded.

'Right!' He grabbed the back of my shirt and hauled me into standing upright, then pushed my shoulders, launching me forward. 'Do it again.'

Nine

The boys laughed. I caught a glimpse of ecstasy on Lang's face as he came through the door in the wall and was quickly informed what had happened. I could have said something then, told on them. No, I couldn't. There was no longer any possibility of me doing that.

I set off. It was a long run to the gravel walk at the side of the house, with them able to watch all the way, so I ran. My lungs felt like two fists. I could feel my face blazing warm in the rain, and the pain between my legs had become a sickening lurch every step. It was like two limps, one leg then the other.

'Go on!' shouted Mr. Rushden as I stumbled towards the house. 'Don't slow down, I'm timing you.'

I went round the corner. I fell over. I rolled onto the gravel and through a puddle. I threw up in a corner below one of the library windows. I kept on heaving for a couple of minutes, nothing coming. I didn't care if I was seen now. I'd have been an accusation just in myself. I managed to roll into the corner and curl up. It felt like I'd ripped something open again. The pain stabbed when I moved either leg. I kept moving both, kept kicking against the wall, like a dog having a dream, trying to find a point where there was no pain.

Waggoner stood there in the rain, looking down at me. He seemed to decide he had to do something. He reached down and helped me to my feet.

I shouted.

He put my arm around his shoulder, and his arm around my waist, and got us moving. We followed the gravel path past the ornamental urns with their lids falling off and cracks down their sides, soil spilling out of them, towards where the vast driveway led up to the doorway at the front of the school. With the help of Waggoner, I started down the drive a second time. We weren't so much running as staggering, him trying to push us on as fast as possible, me about to fall. Was anyone watching from the house? We reached the gates. I grabbed the huge bolts, had to haul a spike out of a hole in the gravel, swung them open.

Back on the road. On the pavement. The rain broken by trees. Cars went past. Splashes up the pavement. The pain came and went. I got glimpses of figures through the rain. Breathe in. There they were. Standing there. Watching. So many of them. In the rain from the sky. The water shining. Breathe out. Car breaks the image.

They were seething, waiting to be loose, to have their revenge.

We passed the point where I'd misbehaved. A splash of brick dust on the pavement, washing away. Could I keep going? Could I keep my story going? If I fell, then Dad would know. Find the wound in hospital. Or worse, the school nurse. My body would tell.

Breathe in. There they are. Breathe out. Gone.

Another stretch of nothing.

And there's the door ahead. The rain in my eyes. The non-warmth of Waggoner beside me. There's the door. It's been closed again. Is it locked? If it's locked, then I'll wander off, I'll just walk and see what car picks me up and tell everything to whoever's driving it and let them take me home.

I couldn't. Mum and Dad. This is for them.

We fell against it. Staggered through it. A few steps down the path. There was the white line at the edge of the pitch. They'd all got their football boots on now and were playing a match. Mr. Rushden, with the whistle round his neck, looked around, came trotting over.

I'd staggered to a halt. I was looking at the white line.

He stopped, blew the whistle, waved his arm in the air for everyone to come over. They came running. He looked proud. 'Go on,' he said. 'Over the line.'

I continued to look at the line. They'd gathered now, staring.

'Give him some encouragement!' roared Mr. Rushden.

They didn't know what to do. 'Yay,' said Fiesta, and then shut up again.

'I said clap! Go on!' roared Mr. Rushden.

They started applauding in a sarcastic way.

'Andy,' said Lang. 'You're so ace.' And he should know.

I am still considering that line. Story of my life, that line.

Mr. Rushden was looking at me, wondering what was going on. He came forward, slapped me on the back, and so 'accidentally' pushed me over the line, my feet nearly tripping over it. 'There you go. Well done, Andy. You took your punishment and now we're quits, yeah? You can play football now.'

I did not deliberately cross that line. After that, I never did.

I'm the person who, when the shop assistant goes, 'That's two for the price of one; you might as well get another', shakes my head and says, no, you told me to do that, so no, I will decide not to, even against my own benefit.

I went and sat on the bench where all the Adidas bags were propped, with bottles of Panda Pop lined up. The others had gone back to the game. I got my boots on. My feet were far away. I waited as long as I could. That had been the first half of Double Games. An hour to go. I stood up again.

Waggoner was watching the match. He ran onto the field, and I followed.

I tried to stand in one place. In an eleven-a-side match, that wasn't so hard. Waggoner leapt around. Mr. Rushden, as always, was playing as well as refereeing, running up and down the pitch, twisting and turning around the others, passing at the last minute with a look of you take over, oh you missed. Waggoner was man-marking him. I realised that now they could see Waggoner instead of me. That was something he could decide to allow. Mr. Rushden, and everyone watching, must have thought I'd suddenly started playing football with enthusiasm, molded by his discipline, hard but fair. Every time Mr. Rushden got the ball, Waggoner was on him. 'Man on!' shouted Mr. Rushden, turning this way and that, dummying, waving for kids to get into place for him to pass to them.

But Waggoner hangs on, hems him in, turns it into a dance. He stops Rushden getting past the centre line, weaves around and around, always back towards the penalty spot in front of Mr. Rushden's side's goal. In that goal, Fiesta is watching like he's a bystander at the scene of the crime. 'That's it,' Mr. Rushden is shouting. 'Don't give me a chance!'

They're twisting around each other on the penalty spot now. The rest of the players have gathered around close, both sides waiting for the pass. Rushden hops the ball up into the air. He's intending to head it to Fiesta for a safe catch.

Waggoner windmills his legs up into the air. A muddy stud misses the ball.

Mr. Rushden screams.

Something white is flying through the air. A trail of blood. The mass lands on the penalty spot.

Mr. Rushden fell to the ground, still roaring, his hands clutching the left side of his face. Everyone ran over to see. We looked down at him curled, his hairy legs pushed up to his chest. From over the other side of the playing fields, Mrs. Parkin was running over, yelling questions.

I went to see. I bent down, my own wound aching, to look at it more closely. The eye was broken, the blue amongst the white, a trail of dangling nerves impossibly tiny against the grass. A splash of dark blood and a mess of other colours. Water was falling on it, drops running across the eyeball, washing the stuff into the ground.

Mrs. Parkin made us all stand back. She helped Mr. Rushden to his feet.

We were all looking at the eye. Waggoner stood beside me. There were expressions of amazement, whispers. The others were looking awkwardly at me. They didn't know what to make of me now, what was going to happen to me. Lang laughed, turned it into a cough in his hand. Waggoner raised his foot and showed me the gore on his studs.

Mrs. Parkin took out her handkerchief and bent down, gathering up the eye. 'I'm going to get Mr. Rushden medical attention,' she said. 'Get your training shoes back on, go and change, and then go back to your form room. Quietly!' We went back to the bench as she led Mr. Rushden away, yelling to one of the girls to go and call an ambulance.

Everyone started talking as soon as they were out of earshot. Some of them ran straight to the penalty spot and stared at it. Did you see that? His whole eye! Sharpened studs!

Waggoner did it. (They meant me.) Do they know? Who's going to tell?

'Did you mean to do it?' asked Goff. 'Were you out to get him? Was it a professional foul?'

I didn't answer. Waggoner was silent too. He went to join the crowd at the penalty spot, came back. I felt like I was going to fall onto my face and sleep. Only my empty stomach stopped me throwing up again. Some of the girls had started to come over to see what was going on. I could feel Angie's eyes taking everything in. She knew there was something wrong. It disturbed her in a different way than it should. She was considering, not shocked. Her friends stood with her, frowning. I looked over to them and saw Louise looking past me, to one of the other boys, then away again. She nervously licked her lips. She and Angie and the others looked weirdly like detectives observing the scene of the crime.

The football kids went to look again at the penalty spot as everyone headed back to the changing rooms. They exclaimed at something. I went to see. Into the penalty spot had been shoved a Panda Pop lemonade bottle, top first. In that moment, the sun broke through the clouds and the bottom of the bottle shone, a flame on the ground, like something alive had been planted.

Someone said that maybe they should pull it out, but nobody wanted to touch it. I heard the voices of Angie's friends, asking questions, growing fainter behind me as they walked away. Louise's voice, asking what did it mean?

I stayed for a moment. Waggoner grinned at me and put his thumbs up. I wouldn't have to have a shower now.

Mr. Rove met us on the way to the changing rooms, and said he'd called my dad, who would come to collect me. Everything would soon be back to normal. I didn't know if I was in trouble or not. I was put in the car, with Waggoner. Mr. Rove closed the door, and I watched Dad carefully nod at everything the teacher had to say. He finally got back in, raised a hand to Mr. Rove and drove away.

'Hard tackle, was it?' He said it like he and Mum said a lot of things, like it was a slightly absurd line in a movie and they knew it. Mum and Dad always seemed to be waiting for bitter laughter to undercut them. This got more pronounced when they were angry. It was a bit like what I got a lot of at school, people mimicking your voice, saying something that was important to you in a funny way. Only Mum and Dad did it to themselves.

I said it was an accident. He nodded. He drove badly. He yelled at someone who overtook him on a narrow lane. In the end, he didn't say anything else to me about it.

———

Mr. Rove called me into his office first thing the next day. There'd been a phone call at home that night. Dad had been loud as always, but it was just him agreeing, and then thanking Mr. Rove, a couple of times. He called Mr. Rove 'Mr. Rove' throughout.

Mr. Rove even seemed to blink carefully and precisely. He smelt like something pressed in an old book. I couldn't imagine him being Rove's dad, of him coming home to find Rove watching *The Magic Roundabout* or sitting across the table from him at tea.

He asked me if I had deliberately attacked Mr. Rushden. Before I could start saying anything complicated, Waggoner said no, he'd been worrying about it all night, sir, it had been an accident. He wasn't that good at football, and he'd gone for the ball–

Mr. Rove said he could see I was upset, and that I shouldn't worry. Because I was in the clear. Now everything was back to normal.

————————

We were told at that morning's assembly that Mr. Rushden was in Chippenham hospital. Lots of people looked at me. Apart from Mr. Rove, onstage, who was looking straight ahead.

Selway said it had been an accident, that I wasn't tough enough to do that. He said that to me, like I'd argue. Drake was silent. But he looked right at me once, like he was puzzled. Something in his world didn't fit now. I was the wrong person to have done that, especially after what he'd done to me.

————————

The last lesson that day was Physics. Mr. Brandswick lit up a cigarette and blew it into a tank to show smoke particles being battered by all that was invisible around them. I had to keep my lips together and take tiny breaths through my nose. The smell of it got into all the interesting pieces of equipment that were never used. I was grateful to be sent, with Waggoner, to get an extra pipette from the Portakabin. I saw Mr. Rove and Mr. Coxwell ahead of me in the corridor. I could hear the whispers. Was it punk? There was that album cover. That band are local, aren't they? Someone who's good at art? He'd left it intact for the police. Was it to do with what happened to Scott? They saw me, and stopped. Mr. Rove asked me if I knew anything about the vandalism on the football pitch. I said I didn't.

Once we were outside, Waggoner set off before I could stop him, towards the football pitch. He waved for me to follow. I could see there was something different as I got closer. There were lines everywhere.

I stopped. The white line marker trolley stood beside the pitch. It had been used to do this. In the penalty spot, the bottle was still there, afternoon frost on the glass. Around it had been drawn a four-sided shape, with a couple more lines sticking out the front. It went right across the box, ignoring the older, duller lines underneath it. The white paint was shining almost as much as the penalty spot. From there, a long curve. There were branches and isolated lines out towards the other side of the pitch. It was white on the white of the frost. It took me a second to get it. Not until I took a step back.

Around the place where Mr. Rushden had lost his eye, there was now painted the shape Waggoner had seen on the downs, the shape of an ancient chalk horse.

Ten

When I was a kid, Mum and Dad would talk about how things would go missing from our garden, or from the garage, or from Mum's jewellery box. They used to call the people that supposedly did this 'the intruders'.

Dad was in Burma in World War Two. In the loft at home he keeps a samurai sword, with the jewels torn from its hilt. He got it off an officer, he used to say. Sometimes he shot that officer, sometimes he bayoneted him, sometimes he throttled him with his bare hands. Sometimes he said he never saw any action. Americans stole the gems. He could have made a fortune. He still occasionally suffers symptoms that are like malaria, and also vivid nightmares that he can't be woken from. The two for him are tied together, and no malaria treatment stops them happening. These days Dad would have a complaint, a name for his problem, a course of therapy. I think that could be good. He would think it bad.

The last time I went down there, they still had everything from my childhood in my old room. Even my old posters were still on the wall. I'm sure they're not waiting hopelessly for me to return, it's just that what's put stays put. Old is good, as long as it's dusted.

Whenever I used to go home, I'd sleep not in my old bedroom, but on the sofa in the lounge, with a chair shoved up against the door. Mum would knock on the door in the morning, and I'd move the chair aside so she could bring me a cup of tea.

———————————

On the night after the horse was painted on the football pitch, lying in bed with Waggoner, I asked him if he'd done it, and why. I hoped terrible things weren't going to happen to everyone I was angry at. That wouldn't be justice.

'I didn't do it by painting the lines,' he said. 'You can change the world by sacrifice. An eye for an eye. It had to be done to someone. It's the first big step towards your revenge on the kids that hurt you.'

———————————

The bell for the end of Friday didn't feel as great as it usually did. I saw Angie and her three friends going to their buses, glancing at me and then not. Louise was carrying a plate of what looked like homemade biscuits, which they were sharing, each taking one before they separated, nodding to each other like this was the most serious thing in the world.

I sat on the bus and listened to the fighting. Always fights on Fridays on the way home, something being let out.

When I got home, I sat on the edge of my bed and put a hand to my mouth. Mum and Dad hadn't heard yet about the horse painted on the pitch. They didn't know the parents of the other kids.

In the end, I did what I did most Friday nights. I stayed up late with a Pot Noodle, watching *The Old Grey Whistle Test*, and then flicking between what had just become four channels during *Newsnight*. I stayed up for two things: *The Outer Limits* and masturbation. I hadn't tried to come since I'd been mutilated. But it had been *twelve days*. Normally, I'd wank two or three times a day. It seems amazing now, the teenage boy's sheer monkey capacity for sex. Now I had an almost permanent, painful, erection, of the new and terrible shape. The association of Friday night and release from the tension of school was dragging me towards doing what I had to do, whether or not I was going to injure myself in the process.

The Outer Limits was a weird American black-and-white show that began with a voice saying, 'We control the horizontal, we control the vertical'. Aptly. There was always a monster. Since that night on the downs, there'd been no *Outer Limits* on, because of the snooker. Now I really wanted to see another monster.

I could hear Mum and Dad arguing through their bedroom door and through the lounge door and the chair. They always seemed to yell at each other on a Friday night, usually about money. After an hour or so, they were quiet.

Waggoner and I watched weird Eastern European animation during a prog rock track on *The Old Grey Whistle Test*. I still didn't feel able to touch myself. I'd been trying to avoid it when going to the toilet, holding myself between my knuckles. I'd already managed to make a ragged spray of urine into a steady stream by hitching one part of my skin at an angle and standing in a certain way. Now I couldn't let myself do what I wanted to do. Something might burst. Perhaps not everything was connected up any more. Maybe there would be sudden, guilt-fulfilling pain.

Every time I felt like touching myself, I smelt again the tobacco on Drake's breath, felt his hands. Now he was part of what coming was for me. Maybe I was a poof now? But Drake wasn't a poof.

We waited through *Newsnight*, which was mostly about Yuri Andropov now being in charge in the USSR, and how that made nuclear war, the three minute warning, sudden light bursting in to reduce us all to dust and shadows, a little more likely.

That night's episode of *The Outer Limits* was 'A Feasibility Study', which was about a small town where people kept seeing monsters. The edge of the town was a barrier of mist, and out of the mist came more and more of the monsters, masses of bulbous flesh, closing in on the humans. I found that my hand had closed around my cock, and it was okay; there was no new pain. The monsters invaded the town, and it turned out that the town had been secretly relocated onto their alien world. There was a model shot of it sitting there amongst craters and weird mountains. The townspeople were brought before the head monster, who looked like he was grown out of the rock. The townspeople held hands and decided to make a heroic sacrifice. The monsters closed in with their bulbous hands and their eyes at odd angles.

I looked at the monsters and I came and came and came.

Eleven

When I was a kid, going for a glass of water in the night in my family home, running, eyes half closed, I'd scare myself by glimpsing myself in a mirror in the hallway. I still have trouble with mirrors. My tie can never form a correct sort of knot. My shoes cannot be made shiny.

———————

On Monday, Mr. Rove announced in assembly that the football pitch would be out of action for the rest of term.

The walls of the main hall displayed coats of arms of the three houses of Fasley Grange School: Igdale, Lawston and Trevor. We were never told who those names originally belonged to. I was in Trevor, so I suppose Waggoner was too. There were boards of winners' names beneath the coats of arms, but the lists stopped in the 1970s. The three houses used to compete, it looked like, for the Trilateral Cup. The Cup was now kept in a case in the office of Mr. Clare, the bursar. Mr. Rove brought it onstage once at a special assembly, and said that the Cup wasn't the most valuable object in his charge (although it had been valued at over three hundred pounds); that was the collective brains and bodies of his pupils.

'And I hope that pleases the louts who did this,' said Mr. Rove from the stage now, 'that they have spoilt it for all the rest of you.'

They came for me at first break, as we headed out into the playground. Again they led me away. I had to stop myself from yelling and fighting them just at the touch. Waggoner grabbed my shoulder, reassured me. Wait. Where were they leading me? Not to the woods. Just around the corner of the building. They stopped and stood in a circle around me. 'You're so tough, mate,' said Blewly, 'you fouled Rushden, so we're going to see if you can be part of our gang.'

He said it like it was possible he meant it. Blewly was always coming over to see our lot, to talk to Surtees. He'd ask what our favourite football teams were.

'Bristol City!' Fiesta had blurted out once, making us all cringe. Blewly had laughed about that in a matey way, while something in his expression said that he was licking his lips and saving that one up to mention later.

I had a book, *The Making of Alien*, which Dad had found in a charity shop and put in my stocking one Christmas. Blewly had asked to borrow it. After a couple of weeks, I started asking him about it. He said he'd bring it back. Then he asked me, because I'd been talking about them, if I had any *Avengers* comics. I brought them in for him. After a couple of weeks, I asked him about those too.

'They're only comics,' he'd said, getting a snort out of Surtees.

He kept asking to borrow stuff. We'd lend him things. He'd keep them. Then he'd stop hanging around with us for a while, then come back again. It never felt like I had a choice about lending anything to him. He never made any threats. That's another impossible thing I remember from my time at Fasley. I have no idea why a thinking person who could draw conclusions would keep on giving items they owned to Blewly.

After he'd helped mutilate me, I'd waited for Blewly to ask to borrow something else, so Waggoner could say no, but he never did. Every time Blewly had come over to our lot, I thought about the things of mine he had, things Mum and Dad had bought me. I could always have told them. They would have gone to Mr. Blewly. 'It's *The Mighty Avengers*,' I could hear Mum saying. 'The one with Ant Man on the cover.' Thinking about them having to get into the detail of that, that was the worst part.

'No,' said Selway now, 'we really are.' Lang sniggered.

I managed not to say that I didn't want to, thanks. Or ta, I'd have said ta. Or maybe cheers. I'd have dropped my accent a couple of notches. They'd have laughed at that. I stayed silent.

'We're going to test you,' said Rove.

''Cos you're not gonna tell, we know that,' said Drake. 'You're not going to tell about *nothing*. You wouldn't fucking dare. You didn't tell your mum when you were in bed with her last night, licking her fanny.'

This time I stayed silent. I didn't say no and no and no. They didn't seem to notice that difference. I was waiting for Waggoner to do something. The others were laughing until they had to hold each other up. They were laughing deliberately, laughing hard.

Drake kept trying. He was taking care to look me in the eye. 'Didn't she like the shape of your new cock? Did she think you were a girl? Or does she like you licking her fanny better now you're a girl?'

He was actually *referring* to it.

But Selway was looking serious, like worry was lurking

nearby. 'Come on, let's test him.'

'Little fucker, he won't pass. I'll shake your fucking hand, and I'll have to wash it afterwards, mind, if you get in the gang, like, but you fucking won't.' He kept them laughing. Me being here was making it all right for them. Me still going along with it.

Drake got out his tin of tobacco and started rolling a cigarette. 'This is the test,' he said. 'You're so tough now.'

Two years before, I'd been in the woods one break time, and had walked into Drake and Blewly smoking together. I'd walked away, but Drake had caught up with me. 'Want one?' he said.

'No. Thanks. No, ta. Cheers.'

He'd pulled one from the packet and stuffed it in my mouth, had stopped me from taking it out again, then lit it up. I'd started coughing, tried to spit it out, but Drake had grabbed the end of it and shoved it back into my mouth, while Blewly held me there. 'Are you Superman?' Drake had laughed his head off. 'Are you fighting the evil Nick O'Teen? You're going to be so cool. Fucking go on. Long drag.' He'd finally pulled it out of my mouth. 'You've fucking ruined it. A good fag!' He'd rolled it up into a little ball, then popped it into my mouth, stuffed it in with his fingers, and told me to chew.

I couldn't. I'd swallowed, and missed, and swallowed and swallowed and started throwing up. They'd let me go and ran off as I vomited into the bushes.

Was Drake going to do that again? No. Looking over his shoulder, to make sure nobody was coming, Drake lit the cigarette. He blew on it, and the end glowed red. "Roll up his sleeve," he said.

Rove and Selway grabbed me.

I almost laughed. They expected me to be scared of *this*? After what they'd done before?

"It's going to be okay," said Waggoner.

I stayed still. I did not fight them.

Selway nodded approvingly. He didn't know what he was nodding at. He was looking more and more worried.

Rove's big fingers were fumbling with my cuff. Blewly grabbed it and pulled the sleeve right up. Lang laughed. 'Look at his arm.'

'Lang,' said Waggoner in my ear. 'Lang will be the first.'

I considered that.

'Question one,' said Selway. 'Who's the captain of Liverpool?'

Should I even answer? 'Kenny Dalgleish,' I said.

'No!' said Selway. 'Graeme Souness. Dur!'

Drake pressed the cigarette against my upper arm and held it there. I felt the sharp heat, and then it suddenly got worse. I could feel the burn blistering. I didn't cry out. I locked my legs still and remembered the other pain that still held me up and down my body. Drake took the cigarette away again and spat on the ground. 'Graeme Souness. Fucker.'

'Question two,' said Selway. 'Who's Mary Millington?'

The pain wasn't going to be any worse than last time. I saw the look Waggoner had on his face and mimicked it, letting my jaw go slack. 'Dunno. Is she in the second year?'

'She's in fucking porn. She gives blow jobs.' Selway sounded like I'd let him down.

Drake applied the cigarette again. He kept it there longer. I opened my teeth and let my gaze dance up and down all over them. They looked back, uneasy now. But Drake wasn't.

'Question three,' said Selway. He waited a second for Drake

to take the cigarette away, but he didn't. 'Question three–'

Drake took it away. I let my jaw work some of the pain away on the air.

'What is *Flogging a Dead Horse*?'

I knew from what I'd heard from other kids that that was an album by the Sex Pistols. But I saw it again in my head: that line on the football pitch. I pushed my teeth together.

'It's an album by the Sex Pistols,' said Waggoner.

I looked at him, horrified.

Selway's face lit up. 'Correct!'

He smiled at the rest of them. They smiled at him. They didn't quite know what this meant, but they liked it, they found it was freeing something in them, letting them off from their guilt.

Drake looked between them, furious. 'Fuck it.' He stuck the cigarette back into the burn and shoved it in all the way, poked the pieces with his finger and then let the mess fall down my arm onto the ground. He turned and walked away.

The others looked in his direction, then back to me. As one mass, they ran off after Drake, but they kept looking back, uneasy now.

I blew the remains of the cigarette off my arm, and started covering up so the traces wouldn't tell. I rolled my sleeve down carefully. That might need another trip to the washing machine. I was shaking, but not for the normal reasons. 'Why did you tell him?' I asked Waggoner.

'Because I could,' he said.

Mr. Land, the history teacher, walked round the corner as I was buttoning my cuff. 'Waggoner,' he said, 'what is going on here?'

I slipped the button into place. 'Nothing, sir.'

'Don't think I didn't see,' he said.

'Sorry, sir?' A sudden hope, from a direction I thought had been denied to me.

'The thing about bullies is that they're cowards at heart. You give them a good old thump on the nose and they'll never bother you again.'

I managed to keep my expression neutral.

'But there's a sort of boy,' he continued, stepping closer to me, 'who's always going to get picked on, no matter what. In those cases it's often more the fault of the bullied than the bullying. You take my advice. You don't want to become one of them.'

I couldn't be silent. 'What did you see, sir?' Maybe it sounded a little accusatory.

He blinked at me. The light in his eye went out. I would never learn. 'Horseplay,' he emphasised, straightening up. He headed off round the corner, and glanced back only once.

Waggoner watched him go. 'Well,' he said, 'at least he got that right.'

Twelve

Across that week, I heard what had really happened to the football pitch, from a lot of different kids. A gang of skinheads had broken in. It was Melmbury who'd done it, who were at the top of the Wiltshire schools football league. The police came. We didn't see them. A tarpaulin was put over the field. For the next couple of weeks, Double Games was volleyball. Mr. Rove took it, and didn't make us run or shower.

———————

Next Sunday, Mum and Dad took me and Waggoner to tend the graves of the dead aunts at St. Swithin's Church in Compton Bassett. It's on the spur of a slope. You get there through a maze of lanes. The dead aunts were bunched in a corner under some trees. The grass was long there, and Mum and Dad brought heavy gloves to pull it out in clumps. There was a side of the church that, because of the trees, was in permanent shadow. I wandered off around the corner. I didn't know what to do with my hands without my sticks. Waggoner followed. I didn't know how to deal with him when we weren't at school. The shadowed side of the church didn't have so many graves. You could only hear the calling of the rooks. It was colder than in the winter sunlight. The ground was covered in moss, and there were ferns. I put my hand to the top of my arm, and felt the weirdness of the scabs and blisters there.

I sat down on an abandoned wooden wheelbarrow with grass growing through it. I touched a blister and felt the small pain, lost amongst the bigger one. I looked at Waggoner, and saw him only as a sort of mirror. I raised my arm, but he didn't move his. I couldn't see another person in those eyes. He seemed to realise I wanted something from him. He reached into his pocket, and took out a 50p piece. He turned it on its side to show me. I'd seen him, over the last few days, scratching it now and then against any available hard surface. Now one side of it was sharp.

One Tuesday towards the end of November, Double Games was swimming instead of volleyball. Fasley's swimming pool was a square pavilion that formed part of one wing of the building, open to the air at the sides, but closed in above by the weight of the house. We hadn't often been swimming before. Mr. Rove probably didn't have the money to keep the pool chlorinated, or perhaps he used it himself and didn't like the idea of it being filled with children. It must have once been quite spectacular, with its hundreds of tiny ceramic tiles, black and white, arranged in chessboard fashion apart from where they alternated black or white strips to show where the lanes were. There were measurements in green, formerly golden, lettering, that showed distances in feet and inches. It was an Art Deco ruin.

I'd thought I'd gotten away with it, but swimming meant being naked in front of the others, and there were always showers afterwards.

There was no way to get to the swimming pool from the changing room corridors, so we had to change, then run, and it always was run, usually with Mr. Rushden exhorting us to go on, go on, right out of the changing rooms and around the corner of the building. Previously, this had only ever been done in the summer term. The night before, I looked down at myself in my underpants. The shape was different. It would look strange in trunks. I could have asked Mum for a note, but that would have meant an explanation.

In the changing rooms that afternoon, the boys were singing 'Beat Surrender' by The Jam. They sang it in a piss-take way, because none of them, not even the football kids, could risk trying to sing anything properly. Then that turned into, to the tune of 'Farmer Bill's Cowman': 'Kermit the Frog, sat on the bog, having it off with Miss Piggy.' Even under that I heard Drake's lot laughing, their specific laugh, sent to me. I'd taken off my shirt quite calmly, and Drake had said things that made them laugh about the spectacular scar on my upper arm. The football kids were looking in my direction, surprised, noting it. I pulled off my underpants and struggled to get my trunks on quickly. Waggoner did the same thing in one quick movement.

I felt Drake's lot moving to try and see. Someone wolf-whistled. It was Lang. He was looking around at the rest of Drake's lot, merry on their attention.

'Do you fancy me, Lang? You a fucking queer?' It was Waggoner. His voice sounded a bit like my voice, but it was my voice on tape, someone who seemed to have a character. Everyone shut up, looking at Waggoner. It hadn't burst out of him. It had been deliberate.

Drake was cool as always, Rove pouting, Blewly looking incredulous and up for it, a touch worried, but amazed at what this allowed to happen next, and how suddenly, and how good this was going to be. Selway was anxiously weighing things up. Lang spluttered with laughter. Where had this sudden impossibility come from? 'Takes one to know one.'

Waggoner dropped the towel from round his shoulders and walked towards Lang. 'Queer boy. Queer-o. Do you want to see what I've got down here?' He grabbed his trunks and waggled what was underneath, which in his case was smooth and strong. 'You love it, don't you? Like you love having Drake's cock up your anus.'

Lang went red with rage. 'You fucker!' He jumped at him with a trill in his voice, like the first line of some sort of spastic musical, like this was still comedy. But that was automatic. He failed in his kung fu kick to the balls and battered Waggoner with his fists.

Everybody started shouting as Waggoner went under. Fight! Go on, get him! Get into him boy! Kermit the Frog! Waggoner had said Lang would be first.

Waggoner slapped aside the pummeling. Suddenly he hit Lang very hard on the side of his head. Lang staggered. Waggoner did it again, in exactly the same place, sending him rolling again. Then once more.

Lang's smile vanished, and he fell sideways.

Cheat! Fucking foul! Goh! Fucking ace! Kermit the Frog! They rushed in to look down. Lang was twitching. There was an actual lump on the side of his head. Kids were looking at each other, right on the 'go for a teacher, macho bit of sensible, gone too far, get in trouble for this', axis. Then Lang's eyes focused, and he spat blood, and he swung to be helped up by Selway and Rove.

Go on! Kick his head in!

But he still wasn't right. He had trouble standing. 'Cunt. We'll fucking have this fight later,' he said, loudly, but sounding like his teeth were falling out.

In walked Mr. Rove and blew his whistle. A few of the football kids looked at him like they should say something, but nobody did.

The boys made exaggerated yells and cries as we ran out into the grounds. Our breath was one great cloud. There was frost on the grass. My skin stung with the shock of the air. I was exulting, full of it. Yes! It was like I had a bodyguard now! But was what he'd done to Lang really worse than what had happened to me? If that was all he was going to do, that was both annoyingly slight and a relief. I did and didn't want him to do more.

Waggoner ran with me, grinning like I was. His teeth shone in the low winter light. I suppose now that he was more attractive than me. He was free in the way he stood, not curled up. He took advantage of the fact that he was free in his choices about his hair and clothes.

Ahead of us was Drake. He had a big red mark between his shoulder blades. Kids said it was where he'd been kicked by a horse. He never made any effort to conceal it.

We ran fast round the corner of the house, Mr. Rove yelling at us to go on, go on, don't slow down, and now straight into the pool! It didn't seem for a moment like he'd never done this before. We ran up the steps and into the pavilion area, which at least cut us off from the wind. Led by Goff, the football kids leapt, bombed or even dove straight in, their cold splashes going over the rest of us who were in assorted levels of awkwardness trying to climb slowly down the ladders or over the sides. I stepped in carefully but relieved, proud to see Waggoner leap in beside me. Goff's head broke the surface. He laughed and started splashing for the far side. Mr. Rove started calling again, made another whistle. The noise of boys shouting. Fiesta had his mouth wide open, his arms held above the surface of the water like a puppet, in shock. Waggoner ducked his head straight under the water, astonishing me, who couldn't do that. He was underwater and in charge! David Wilkie!

A series of whistles, and everything died down. I couldn't see where Drake's lot were. I joined Fiesta and Surtees and Cath at the edge of the bigger group. Waggoner swam leisurely beside me. There was something odd about the shape under his trunks. I'd got used to looking because I was always comparing myself to him. It looked like he was hiding something in there.

There was a noise from outside the pool. The girls were on their way. They ran with their towels wrapped around them. Mrs. Parkin was with them. They were talking, shrieking. Amongst them, I was stunned to see Angie. She was wrapped in a huge red towel. She had her three friends around her, one on each side, as always: Louise and Jenn Jennings and Netty Lauter. Angie had a determined expression on her face. She wore a blue regulation swimming costume. It looked odd on her, newly bought. The girls were herded to the other end of the pool from the boys, the shallow end, carefully making their way down into the water. Angie dipped straight under, and appeared beside her friends to look at us. I looked straight back at her by accident. Then I realised and turned away. I'd been glancing at the very white legs and glimpses of bottoms that they tried to hide as they got in. The zits on backs and shoulders. I was hard in my ugly, misdirected way.

We were sent to swim a few lengths, then organised into a number of races: breast stroke; backstroke; freestyle. I couldn't turn properly, because I didn't like to get my head under. Waggoner smoothly glided and spun. He was a shadow under the surface, when I could see him amongst the splashing and the limbs.

Then everybody had to tread water. I could do that. Beside me, Surtees took hold of the rail to do it. I was just about okay with being in the middle. Someone started shouting. There was a sudden heave of bodies. I went under.

I saw under the water. There was Lang, pounded under by the thrashing legs above. There was a missing look on his face. He was surprised. He floated in the middle, at half pool height, jerking.

Then Waggoner was beside him, pulling something out of his trunks. The coin caught a shaft of sunlight. A tiny puff of red bloomed in the water.

I got my head above water and shouted. I saw Angie, with her girls, right at the side of the pool, not screaming, but looking.

Mr. Rove, fully clothed, broke the surface, with Lang in his arms.

Then we all fell sideways.

Thirteen

It snowed heavily that winter. Snow thinned out the population of Fasley Grange School. It closed down bus routes. I watched the footsteps that Waggoner was making in the snow beside me as we walked from the bus one Friday. There had been no Games since the incident in the swimming pool. Today, with only four days until the end of term, was the day Lang was coming back to school. In assembly, we'd heard about what had happened. A terrible accident, a brilliant group of doctors and nurses who deserved a round of applause, and, yes, step up Mr. Rove, the swift action of the Head. He'd applied artificial respiration, even held closed the shallow wound in Lang's throat that nobody could understand.

Nothing had been mentioned about the bruises and other small injuries of the kids who'd been smashed against one side of the pool, falling impossibly sideways as the water fled up and out.

I thought now that that had been the moment of the big change being made. The big change that was still in place.

I had been worried that Lang had seen who'd attacked him. But if he had, a policeman would have arrived at our door before now. I was more worried by how Lang was going to react to the change. I wasn't sure how I felt about it. I saw Mr. Rove getting out of his car. Maybe for him the low turnout caused by the snow was a vision of what his school would be like if parents starting taking kids away. He'd held that wound shut until his own hands were white. But he looked steady and certain as always.

There was Lang, getting out of his dad's car. I'd never seen his dad before. He was like a big Lang, thin and with a mop of reddish hair. It was strange seeing Lang being dealt with like he was a child. It was strange seeing nobody laugh at this care. Lang was white. He looked lost in the snow. He had a Spurs scarf wrapped tightly around his throat, and now there was only a faint scar on his head. He wandered up to Drake's lot, fell in beside them.

'All right,' Blewly said to Lang.

Waggoner and I joined them.

Lang looked startled.

'All right,' Selway said to Waggoner.

Drake nodded to us and grunted.

Lang looked slowly between us and the rest of them. Back and forth. Was this a joke? He looked back to his dad at the car, couldn't quite do the sniggering he wanted to. What was going on?

Waggoner took a kung fu magazine from his pocket, and started showing Drake pictures of the nunchaku he wanted to buy.

Lang burst forwards between them. He couldn't quite grab the magazine from Drake. He opened his mouth in an exclamation that couldn't come out. He looked around the group. Come on! This wasn't possible! What were me and Waggoner doing in Drake's lot? How had that suddenly changed?

'What?' said Drake.

Even after a couple of weeks, I hadn't got used to it. I still went to school every morning expecting to be beaten. I'd felt the change the moment Mr. Rove had broken the surface of the water, Lang in his arms. The world had shuddered, different images colliding in my eyes. Silence had crashed in, cutting off the shouts. Then we'd been falling, towards the other side of the pool! I'd grabbed the rail. The water had fallen away from me. I was left hanging there. Kids were falling, silently screaming, hitting the side of the pool, the water bursting up around them and over the other side. Then the water had slammed back against us. The silence became kids shouting again, as they floundered in the fizzing water that bashed from one side of the pool to the other.

Mr. Rove had concentrated only on Lang. He'd kept him alive.

I'd looked over my shoulder and I'd seen Angie, on the edge of the pool, having only just clambered out, forcing her friends into a wet, square huddle, urgent. Louise was taking big, shuddering breaths, scared when the rest of them were calm, professional.

Waggoner had grabbed me. 'Come on,' he'd said, urgent himself.

Mr. Rove was yelling for someone to call 999, and the rest of us to go back to the changing rooms. As we went, Drake's lot fell in, running, beside me and Waggoner. I was afraid they were going to do something. But then Waggoner had said fuck and Drake had said fuck back, and then suddenly Drake's lot were talking to me and Waggoner like we'd been in the same gang forever. Waggoner had started to laugh and run and leap up and down, water flying off his wet skin into the winter air. He was steaming like it was smoke pouring out of him.

Life as one of Drake's lot wasn't easy for me. It was easy for Waggoner. He'd flicked up his collar and messed his hair like Elvis Costello. He folded his tie thin. It didn't look like it'd look on me.

Drake would spend most of his time with his lot being silent. When he talked, it was about his dad, who sounded like a god and was always getting him stuff, or about how his mum was a fucking bitch. Every now and then he'd grab one of the others, almost always Rove, and push him over and laugh, or slap him around the face, just lightly. Rove would say stuff about how rich his dad was. 'Cath is a poofter,' he'd say. 'He likes it up the arse.' Which would set Selway off about how he'd seen these two girls together in this porn mag. Blewly would nod every time any of them mentioned some cool thing they had, and say he had it too.

In those two weeks, they got hold of Surtees a couple of times. My own lot hadn't tried to talk to me about how I wasn't going over to join them any more. I saw them looking in our direction a few times. Drake used his knife to slice right down the back of Surtees's blazer, leaving a flapping gap which they all laughed at. They grabbed Cath too, and walked him right round the playing fields, surrounding him, asking details about how he was a poof and what he wanted to do to Fiesta.

Waggoner started bringing things into school, magazines and sticker books and different sorts of fags. He always said he'd let Blewly borrow the magazines and never did. I didn't join in. They didn't notice me amongst them. I didn't know why Waggoner was doing this. It was better, maybe. It didn't feel as good as it should have.

———————

I looked over at Lang during Biology. He was sitting beside Rove, but was looking over at Drake all the time. Drake now sat beside Waggoner. That is, beside me. Fiesta had suddenly started sitting elsewhere, and nobody had said anything about it; it was just part of the change. I would look to one side, and see Waggoner at our twin desk, and then to the other side and see Drake there.

Lang looked translucently white. He still had an astonished expression on his face. I could see the wound round his throat, brown-red and twisted like old tree bark. Everyone was looking at it.

Mrs. Pepper wasn't going to say anything to stop them. She was older than most of the teachers. She had her hair pulled right back, and wore huge baggy dresses with deep pockets. Like a lot of the people Mr. Rove employed, she seems in retrospect to have been more like someone who worked on the estate. She nodded and tutted as if she was wise. 'Nothing you children say or do surprises me,' she once told Surtees, when she'd overheard him saying something pornographic about Blewly. 'Once children were brought up to go into professions or into service; now it's computers or the dole queue, and it's always obvious who's going to be who.' She was currently teaching us about how genes reproduced through a series of diagrams. She got us to draw the diagrams of the different stages. When one of the girls asked what happened in between, how you got from one shape to the other, Mrs. Pepper cheerfully said she didn't know. The diagrams would appear in the exam, same as every year, and after that none of us would have to worry about this stuff ever again. That got a laugh, as she'd known it would. She always said that, she said. Once things get fixed in a particular way, they stay fixed. Wasn't that a comforting thought? Lang put his hand up and asked to leave the room, and was gone until the end of the lesson.

———————

Lang got his courage together at first break. He came right up to Waggoner and me and said, 'Right, I owe you that fight.'

'Go on, then,' said Waggoner.

'I would, only you'd get in trouble for picking on me. Because you're a spasmodic spasmo!' He half sang the words like they were from a song he'd made up, accompanied by his usual high kick to thin air.

Drake was silent.

Lang kept on at Waggoner. 'How's your cock? Did you find it? Have you got it in a bottle? Does your mum take it out every night for her douchey dildo? Bet you kiss her muff under the mistletoe.' He pulled a sprig of mistletoe out of his pocket and wobbled it around at crotch level.

Waggoner flicked his 50p piece in the air. It caught the low winter sunlight.

Drake was still silent.

Lang looked between them. He burst into tears. He ran for the loos. Rove started laughing, but Drake thumped him on the arm, and he shut up.

———————

When we came in after break, I didn't see what happened. Lang and Waggoner weren't in sight. We were all crowding at the top of the little stairs, going back to the form rooms. Suddenly Lang broke away from a tussle in the group. 'All right now, now if you want it, you fucking fucker!' He did his awkward little dance again, showing gaps of white flesh between his trousers and his short socks. He'd backed to the top of the big stairs. He cried out as he tripped. He fell like a tree, his feet caught together as they slipped on a muddied, snowy footstep. His head hit the marble balustrade. Blood splashed onto the white.

The crowd rushed forward. The ones at the front nearly followed him, like a penny falls at an amusement arcade.

He was rolling down the stairs, arms together, a bundle.

At the bottom of the stairs, coming out of his office, was Mr. Rove. A shaft of sunlight through one of the big windows caught the body. Lang looked like a ghost. Mr. Rove looked down at Lang as he rolled against his shoes.

The neck wound had reopened, and Lang had swallowed his own tongue. He'd been asphyxiating when the ambulance men got there. Mr. Rove had once more been called upon to do first aid. They took Lang straight to Emergency.

Drake shook his head. 'Fuck,' he said.

Lang was taken to Chippenham hospital. Once again, he was going to be okay.

On December twenty-first, Lang woke in hospital at around 7:20 a.m. The time and date seem in retrospect like they might be important. Maybe the importance of something being about to happen was what had woken him. I, however, was still sleeping. Which is, I suppose, how I know all this.

The ward was in darkness. All the other patients were asleep. The nurse who should have been at her desk was elsewhere. Lang had been kept in for observation longer than expected, because his blood didn't seem to be clotting properly, and the throat wound was thus proving difficult. Depending on the test results, he was going to be home for Christmas. He reached for the glass of water beside his bed. There was someone standing there.

The blow to the head silenced him. It hit the old spot, the beauty of a bruise already there. It switched him off. The pillow shoved down over his face pushed him into a coma. The dressing around his throat was taken off, the stitches cut like entering a turkey. The blood was allowed to flow free this time, out of his throat and over the bedclothes in a perfect circle.

Time of Lang's third and final death: 7:26 a.m., at the moment of dawn on the solstice, just as the first rays of direct sunlight came into the room through the big window above his bed.

We were later told that it had taken awhile for anyone to notice anything was wrong. Perhaps Lang had been so pale he was almost invisible.

The coroner found mistletoe in his stomach.

Fourteen

Lang was dead.

The things in me that thudded and shifted against each other had made me feel sick, when I heard confirmed what I'd dreamt about Lang, from a shout Mum had made when hearing the news over the phone. Those feelings made me have to sit down or lean against the wall, sweating and tired. I'd felt immediately like telling. But telling what? Something impossible. Waggoner remained calm. He still had his 50p piece. The edge was bloody. I told him to clean it, but he shook his head.

On the Wednesday before Christmas, me and Aunt Dar decorated the lounge like we always did. Aunt Dar smelled of something sweet, and had the roughest hands. She wore pinnies. She said I was quiet. I was. I kept making myself remember Waggoner's promise that when all this was over, I'd be healed. If only I could keep going, I'd be whole again.

Just before the end of term, Renée and Renato had gone to Number One with 'Save Your Love'. Everyone hated it. Now I had it going round and round in my head, but I didn't want to get rid of it, because if I did, I'd start thinking about things.

There was going to be a parents and teachers meeting in the new year. By then, the police or the coroner might have something to say about what had happened.

Dad came into the room looking vaguely proud. Friend of yours on the phone, he said. He could drive me over if I wanted.

Drake sounded careful on the phone, like this was official be-cause parents were listening. He asked if I'd like to come over to his dad's farm tomorrow afternoon. Some friends, he didn't even say 'mates', were getting together to talk about 'Vincent'. I handed the phone to Waggoner. He'd said yes before I had time to argue.

The Drake farm was a big silver barn and buildings. Frost on the mud, making it stand up in spikes. It smelt of shit. The sun was very low, making the silver shine.

Waggoner and I got out of the car. I told Dad I'd find my way in. He said okay, he'd meet Mr. Drake when he picked us up. I had to give them his condolences about his son's friend. I was to be polite to Mr. and Mrs. Drake. They owned half of Wiltshire.

I waited until he'd driven off and turned the corner, but Waggoner had already set off across the mud. I caught up with him. He looked calm. There were sacks and boxes of stuff piled up against a barn. A label saying HORSE TRANQUILISERS. Which sounded worrying in itself, making me wonder why they needed them. 'Why are we here? We didn't have to come. Are you going to get another one of them here? It's . . . it's too soon for another, isn't it?'

'We have to wait for the times and places. This all has to be done by the book. It's got to be meaningful.' We'd got to a big white door with dog dishes in front of it. From behind it, I could hear voices: Drake, Rove . . . Angie. Other girls. Waggoner knocked.

Drake opened the door. He was wearing a tight white T-shirt, cut off at the shoulders, and jeans. 'Hi,' he said. His voice still sounded strange, but his face was stoic as always. I followed Waggoner in. Some of the football kids were in one corner of the living room, Goff and Sadiq and some others. Selway was with them. Blewly and Rove were on their own. Drake went to sit between them and the football kids.

Angie and her three friends, Jenn, Netty and Louise, were all gathered together in another corner. There were no other girls. Angie met my gaze guardedly.

Waggoner said hi and sat down with Drake. I sat beside him. I would let Waggoner do the talking.

They all had cans of lager. Drake was cutting up tobacco with his knife. I kept looking at it. He kept looking over to Angie, as if waiting for her to approve. But she gave no sign. Drake got a pizza covered in sausage and bacon out of the oven and offered it round. Angie sighed at that too. 'Vegetarian,' she said. Netty and Jenn turned it down with similar looks on their faces, but Louise took a slice.

It got dark. Drake switched on ornamental lights. His parents didn't seem to be at home. It felt odd that the death of Lang would make these kids so quiet. Every now and then someone sniggered, but nobody laughed back. They were trying very hard to be somber, forcing it on each other.

I took strength from Waggoner beside me. I was here undercover, overhearing all this. It was a world I'd never glimpsed before.

Drake lit the fag and passed it round, like it was a spliff. 'Lang always liked doing this,' said Blewly, looking at the carpet. 'He was a really good mate. He always gave us stuff.'

'And he was tough,' Selway added. 'It took three goes to

take him down.'

'My dad always said he was great,' said Rove. 'He wasn't a fucking pansy like some people fucking said he was.'

'He was ace,' said Waggoner.

The fag came round to me. I didn't know what to do. I put it in my mouth, felt the warm paper, felt the wetness of the others' mouths, handed it to Waggoner before my disgust made me spit it out. Nobody noticed.

Louise got the fag and took a great, decadent puff of it, waving it between two fingers like she had vast experience. Netty and Jenn took quick little puffs too. Angie turned the cigarette aside with a look, and Jenn quickly handed it on to Goff, having to get up and walk over to do so. Drake got up in the same second, walked to the kitchen door, looked back to Angie. She slumped and sighed theatrically. *No.* He only went out for a second, then came back.

As the night went on, we heard what had happened. The skinheads who'd painted the horse had had it in for Lang, heard he was injured, and snuck into the hospital in disguise. Melmbury, knowing Lang was so good at football ... Selway said 'Fucking hell' loudly before Netty could finish that. She looked annoyed.

Cans of lager got passed round. I took a drink. My first drink. Waggoner was throwing back cans, then stamping them flat and throwing them into the kitchen like shuriken stars.

Rove told a story about an Englishman, an Irishman and a Scotsman captured by a tribe of coons—Blewly looked to Sadiq and laughed, said 'coon' again—and imprisoned in a barrel. But after a while everyone realised he'd forgotten the punchline.

Selway went over to sit beside the girls. They talked for a bit.

Louise pushed her hair back and fixed it there, and they started carefully snogging. I tried not to stare. I looked over to Angie. She met my gaze. Just for a moment, she let me see an enormous sadness and anger on her face.

Drake leapt to his feet. Everyone looked at him. Even Selway looked up from Louise. Drake belched. Everyone laughed. 'Shut up!' he yelled. Everyone did. 'He was a sodding good guy,' he said, finally, as if deciding. 'He was too young to die. He didn't deserve it.'

I found myself curled up around something mean in my stomach again. Rove, his big hands grabbing for another can. Blewly, still sniggering at the belch. Selway, his hands on Louise's chest. But most of all Drake. Did he really believe what he'd just said? I wanted to prove the opposite, on a blackboard, with equations and diagrams. From interfering with my clothing to Kermit the Frog, it all equals Lang deserved to die. His voice meant he deserved to die. His expression meant he deserved to die. I could feel the pain all up my front and legs again. I concentrated on the pain, let myself keep feeling it. I didn't feel undercover any more. I felt like an obvious wound.

I had to go upstairs and find the bathroom. Waggoner stayed downstairs, which hadn't happened before, but I had no idea any more what was weird and what wasn't. Beside the bathroom there was a door open to what I assumed was a spare room, filled with odd stuff. I couldn't contextualise what I saw through the doorway, so I looked inside. I realised this must be Drake's parents' bedroom. There were empty beer cans strewn around, a pile of cigarette ends that obscured what might be an ashtray, dog shit on the floor. The duvet had stains on it. I didn't understand it. I backed out and found the toilet.

I locked myself in and stood there for a while. I didn't want to piss in Drake's toilet. Finally, I did.

I opened the door and found Angie waiting there. I actually tried to close the door again but she grabbed me, the first time a girl had touched me, and swung me to slam me against the wall. 'What,' she hissed, 'is going on?' I was so used to Waggoner being there that I was startled he wasn't going to answer for me. 'How can you be his *friend* all of a sudden?! Are you threatening him with what you saw?'

'What? No! D'you think I *want* to be his friend?'

She looked puzzled. 'What?'

I'd said too much. Without Waggoner there, it had come pouring out of me. But now I was looking at her face, I was angry again. 'How can *you* . . . go out with *him*?'

She looked angrily at me. But compromised as well. 'Are you just pretending to be his friend?'

'No,' I said, like I answered every playground question, but it was also sort of true, and she must have heard the true part.

'I'm with him because of when he was born,' she said. 'You wouldn't understand.' She let go of me. 'What sort of music do you like?'

I didn't feel able to buy records in the Top 40. Radio 1 was not for me. Previously, I'd learn what was Number One by overhearing what kids said on Tuesday afternoons when the new chart was announced at 12:45. But now me and Waggoner were part of Drake's lot, I heard everything they listened to, that narrow spectrum of stuff they were allowed to like: the Boomtown Rats, the Police, Stiff Little Fingers. There was Blondie too, but Blondie were complicated. They were kind of New Wave, and that was good, but they were kind of pop too, and girls liked them, but Debbie Harry was lush, and at least they weren't poofs like the New Romantics. Selway said he'd give Debbie Harry one. Or two. Differently, like.

I didn't want to answer Angie, because this was a test I'd been set, but I was undercover. 'Boomtown Rats, The Police, Stiff Little—'

'I mean, what do you *really* like?'

I stared at her. I couldn't answer. I couldn't even find the meaning of her question. She realised she wasn't going to get a reply and stepped back, shaking her head, not disappointed in me so much as missing something she needed to know.

I quickly went back down the stairs. Waggoner had opened a drinks cabinet and found a bottle of Cinzano Bianco. He was pouring out plastic cups of it, but not to everybody. He moved diagonally across the room. He went from Selway to Blewly to Rove to Drake. He left Netty blinking, her hand outstretched. He raised the bottle in a toast. 'Absent friends,' he said.

'Any time, any place, anywhere,' slurred Rove, singing like Lang would.

Waggoner shook his head. *No.*

Fifteen

The days after the end of term. Those low, dark days. Dark in the mornings, dark in the afternoon. The crisp, dry cold. Stars right across the sky that Christmas Eve. At half past eleven, Waggoner and I were sitting in my dad's car, at the bottom of the hill that led up to St. Swithin's in Compton Bassett, listening to the Grumbleweeds on Radio 2.

Why had Angie asked what music I really liked?

People were walking past in their coats, heading into church, looking over their shoulders at me and Waggoner sitting in a car with the interior light on. I'd said I wanted to go to Midnight Mass, and Mum had looked oddly at me. Dad had just shrugged and laughed. "Are you getting religion?" he said. I said no, no. So they drove us over with them and Aunt Dar, but when we got there, I took a few steps towards the church and didn't want to go in. I didn't know why I'd even wanted to come here. Waggoner stood beside me, looking annoyed. I broke away from Mum and Dad and took a step back.

Mum looked over her shoulder and called for Dad. Dad came back, looking around at the well-dressed people going into the church. 'Don't make a scene,' he said, in the voice that always made me stop doing whatever I was doing, a voice that was more fear than anger. 'Make up your mind, one way or the other.'

'It's going to be boring,' I said quickly. 'I didn't think it would be. I'll stay in the car, I'll be fine, sorry.'

Mum, afraid of the cold, tried to get Dad to drive me home. But I insisted that I had a book. It was only an hour. Because of the lack of time and the cars backed up down the hill, I won that one. Dad shook his head as he went in. Mum managed a thin smile at the people going in.

So we sat there in the car. Waggoner was reading a horror magazine he'd hidden inside his coat. The bells rang. People ran in at the last moment. The bells stopped. Then we were alone. Our breaths misted up the windows. I gave up trying to read. I curled up, my head on my knees, my duffle coat wrapped around me. I switched off the car radio. 'Why couldn't I go into the church like everyone else?'

'We could have.'

I let out a long breath. I fell back into my seat. I let my mind wander for a moment. 'Do you think there's intelligent life in space?'

He grunted.

'Mum always says they'll be just like us. But I'd hate it if they were just like us.'

———————

When we got back from Compton, Dad, who'd let all his anger fall from him and had been smiling about another Christmas from the moment he got out of church, opened up a bottle of Newcastle Brown and poured a glass for Mum and himself. He asked me if I wanted a drop, a joke as always, and I said no.

'You usually say yes!' Mum said. They hadn't noticed when I'd slept in the car on the way home from Drake's and woken looking ashen the next morning. I'd spent the rest of the party, after the benediction of Cinzano Bianco, being undercover and drinking lager, which I'd now decided I didn't like.

Dad told me to make sure I had my stocking out. I told him there was no need this year. It was a waste of money.

'A waste of money! Father Christmas doesn't worry about money! Just you think on! You're not too old yet. Next year maybe you will be.'

I tied my stocking to the bedpost. Waggoner hadn't bothered with one. It *was* a waste of money. I was an adult now. I closed my eyes, pulled the curtains closed, got into my pyjamas and got into bed beside Waggoner. I thought of Drake's lot and was angry still, and was pleased by that.

Something woke me up.

There was a light. A white light at the window. White on black.

The moon.

The curtains were open.

I was awake. I was afraid. I had grabbed the sheets in my fingers, hanging on.

There was someone moving about in the room.

Waggoner was still beside me. No. No. This is Father Christmas, right? My dad. He'd have pulled back the curtain so he could see what he was doing. I mustn't look. He mustn't see me looking. He mustn't know I know he's Father Christmas.

I looked sideways. Waggoner was sitting up, grinning. The bastard. The bastard!

I leapt up myself. To apologise to Dad. To say I hadn't seen anything, to make up some story–

It was Father Christmas. He'd come in through the window, in his red coat with white fur trim, his sack over his shoulder. He looked comically surprised to see me for a moment, then smiled and put a finger to his lips. He upended his sack, and started carefully packing my stocking with presents. There were candy canes and balls that had segments of different colours and teddy bears that climbed up on their own and whizzed down into the stocking like they were on a slide. It all looked very expensive. I was very frightened. I started to protest. He looked suddenly furious at me. He opened his mouth and roared.

That doesn't sound likely, does it? How about this?

I looked sideways. Waggoner was sitting up, grinning. The bastard. The bastard!

I leapt up myself. To apologise to Dad. To say I hadn't seen anything, to make up some story–

I shouldn't have done that. I'd caught him as he was leaving. He was closing the curtains. He looked back at me, and for a moment he looked so lost, helpless, angry, disappointed.

'Dad. What are you doing in here?' I said.

He stopped whatever it was he was going to say. 'The curtains had come open,' he said. He came back over. 'I was checking up on you. I see Father Christmas has been. But you get back to sleep.'

That sounds more likely. But how about this?

I looked sideways. Waggoner was sitting up, grinning. The bastard. The bastard!

I leapt up myself. To apologise to Dad. To say I hadn't seen anything, to make up some story–

It stood by the open window. It was naked. It had a wound on its throat and a wound on its forehead, and it was white from suffocation. It was Lang, the victim, back. No. It was what had become of him. Its eyes were pits.

It ran at me.

I yelled, wrenched up the covers to hide. It ripped the covers out of my hands.

'It's not my fault!' I shouted.

It grabbed for me. Waggoner seized it by the throat. He had the sharpened 50p piece in his hand. He shoved the coin into the thing's mouth, then pushed and twisted until, with a great cry of pain, it swallowed the coin. 'Back to the barrow from which you were born,' he said. I thought of the roundness he'd seen on the downs, when before there'd been a depression. 'Take the blood back; complete the connection.' He hauled the being over to the window with the billowing curtains, and shoved it out, sent it scampering and sobbing back into the dark.

I pulled the covers over my head and curled up into a ball and was instantly asleep.

Sixteen

By the time the Christmas holidays ended, Phil Collins was at Number One with 'You Can't Hurry Love'. *Doctor Who* had started a week earlier. That was a big thing for me, something I loved which wasn't okay to love. Mum and Dad would stay silent as I watched it, knowing I had to hear everything. Waggoner had sat through it, empty again, incapable of having an opinion.

When we got back to school, the building looked different. Just slightly. When you went down a corridor that was meant to end in a junction, it felt like it was on a vague curve. The angle of the school against the ground was different. The lines of the playing fields seemed complicated. It tired my eyes to look at them.

I heard a crash that first day. Angie, her friends running to her, was lying at the bottom of the stairs, looking round in surprise. She did it twice more in the next week. Waggoner saw that and laughed. 'She thinks she knows more than the rest of them,' he said. 'But she's got everything the wrong way round.'

Games now had become warm-up exercises followed by athletics, probably because Mr. Rove felt that was the least dangerous option. Mrs. Parkin was in charge of boys and girls together. In the changing rooms that Tuesday, Surtees must have said something about Drake, or Drake thought he had. Showing no anger, Drake hit him hard in the stomach, kicked him across the back and spat onto the top of his head, then used his bare foot to rub it into Surtees's hair, knocking his head against the ground with it. Surtees kept screaming in alarm until Drake marched off.

The next morning, in the corridor outside the form room, I heard Surtees behind me, talking to Fiesta and Cath. I turned round and punched him on the arm, then grabbed it, got his fingers in a lock, with him trying to wrestle back at me. I enjoyed hauling at him, feeling him push against me. I thumped him hard in the stomach. He went down.

Applause. Glorious.

Waggoner looked tiredly at me.

———————

On the minibus, there was Elaine, who was two years down from me and also stood on the town hall steps in Calne. She had short black hair. On the way home that night, she pointed at all the boys in the bus, and told us where we'd all be on her list of who to send Valentine's cards to. All the others were in the top two hundred. Though none of them placed higher than one hundred and fifty, and that was Grayson, who was in her year. I wasn't on the list. She said I was the last person, below girls, below her mum, below the bus driver, below the bus itself, that she would ever send a Valentine's card to.

I said she was only saying that because she really wanted to send me one. That surprised everybody. I'd talked back.

She said she really didn't.

———————

On the town hall steps the next day, I mentioned it again. I asked if she'd chosen what card she was going to send me. She said she wasn't, and if I wasn't careful, she'd send me a snake.

I asked Mum if I was a Catholic. She said no, we were Church of England; why was I asking? I said it was because I knew a Catholic. She said, Oh.

That day, I'd joined in with a group of kids clustered around Cath, shouting 'Cath, Cath, Cath!' at him. He'd looked around, going, 'No, I'm not,' over and over again.

Surtees and me, the next week, in an alcove off a corridor. He was slapping and putting his knees up. I was thumping him in his stomach, and then on his back, on his head, throwing him down.

'He's much tougher than you are, Surtees,' said Selway, watching.

I swooned at the pleasure of the boy who'd helped rip open my cock.

Other boys on the bus joined in, a couple of days later, when I asked Elaine again about the Valentine. 'What are you going to send me, then, a snake? A chocolate snake? Is that because you love me?'

There'd been a snake in *Doctor Who* the previous night, and just for a second I thought I'd left myself open to admitting I'd seen it, that she was going to say something about that. But she didn't! Even if she had, I'd have said something back. I was sure I would.

She just looked angry at me, then turned away.

———————

That day at school, Surtees was showing people his five special offer cards which he was going to send off for his Top Trumps Sports Cars pack. I grabbed his hands, prised open his fingers one by one, pulled the cards off him.

'They're mine!' he screamed. 'I'll tell!'

I tore them into pieces and threw them onto his shoes.

He bent to scrabble and pick up the pieces. I laughed, the most free I'd ever felt, the laughter bursting from me like piss.

———————

I started to ask Elaine about the valentine every day. She sat there, ignoring me now, ignoring everyone on the bus, because we were all looking expectantly at her.

One night, when she got off, I blew her a kiss, then all the boys were doing it. I looked around. I had done something that was copied in a good way!

She walked quickly off into the dark.

———————

'You're happier these days,' said Dad the next Monday on the way back home. That night, there was going to be a big meeting of the parents and teachers about what had happened to Lang, and the horse on the football pitch. 'You were singing under your breath. Are you having a good time with your mates? Helps you to work hard. It all goes towards that bursary.'

I listened that night after they came home from the meeting. Lang's assailant hadn't been seen. Many motives had been guessed at, but none of them had anything to do with the school. No connection with the vandalism on the soccer pitch, which was done by local hooligans. No parents had taken their children out of the school.

I kept grinning. I was trying the expression, seeing how it felt.

I kept on at Elaine every day, and now the whole bus did too. Men at Work went to Number One with 'Down Under', the lyrics of which were meant to be different, ruder, to what was on the radio. I sang it at her on the bus, and all the other kids, including the ones who'd been her friends, sang along. 'When the women blow and then chunder.' We did it over and over, until the bus driver bellowed at us to stop.

On Valentine's Day itself, which was a Monday, Elaine wasn't waiting on the town hall steps. But she was at school that day. I saw her across the playground. I went over, I walked through her friends. Waggoner came with me, irrelevant, looking awkward. I asked Elaine what had happened about my card. Was it waiting for me at home? She didn't reply. She looked at her feet. Her friends started saying things loudly at me. But I didn't care. I kept on asking her.

Then suddenly Angie was there. She stepped between me and Elaine. Waggoner looked alarmed. 'What are you doing?' she said.

'Dunno,' I said, pretend punk stupid. But I walked off. They called things after me. But they were just girls now. Elaine wasn't on the bus that night, either.

———

Dad picked something up from the table when we got in through the door that evening, a red envelope, held between finger and thumb like a dead mouse. He'd said in the car that there was a surprise. 'And what would this be?' he comedy murmured, raising an eyebrow.

'I don't know,' I said. I took it.

'All right, all right,' he said. 'We shall want to know.'

I took it into my bedroom. I hadn't wanted to open it in front of him, because I thought it might be from Elaine, that it might say something bad inside. I decided that if it did, I'd wait until tonight, set fire to it on one of the cooker rings, flush the ashes and tell them I'd lost it. Then Elaine was really going to pay.

On the other hand, could it be a real valentine? It must be. Because I was tough now. That was what girls liked. I was being tough without Waggoner's help.

Waggoner stood there, empty, caring nothing about all this. He caught my glance, finally, and sighed. 'All this stuff, how you are right now, is nothing to do with getting your revenge.'

'Yes, it is,' I said. 'It's everything. It's victory.'

He just shrugged.

I opened the envelope. The card had a strange design on the front. Two stick figures, drawn quite well, like someone might draw stick figures for an advert. But it was homemade. One figure was a man, and the other was a woman, because she was wearing a skirt. They were looking at each other, quite far apart. That was weird. There was no writing on the front.

I opened it. I don't know if I expected a name. But there wasn't even a rhyme inside. The card was blank apart from, tucked in the lower right corner, in tiny letters that could have been written by a boy or a girl:

YOU'RE TOO SHY. Capitalised like that.

I read it a dozen times, looked at the back of the card, held the envelope open to see if there was anything else inside it.

I was too shy? That was fucking stupid! Nobody could say that about me now! This must be from someone who really didn't know me! I was thinking that I might make myself come that evening, thinking about who this was from. But I wasn't going to be able to do that, with it being like this.

Finally, I showed the card to Mum and Dad. Because at least that would be all right. Mum seemed scared by it. Dad slapped me on the back. Then he did it again.

Seventeen

The next day, Kajagoogoo went to Number One with their song 'Too Shy'. I'd heard it before I got the valentine. Now I listened closely to it, wondering if I could work anything out from the lyrics. I thought the sender was probably Laurie Coxwell, though Elaine wasn't out of the question. Nobody at school the next day had taken the piss. I couldn't ask anyone about the card, apart from Elaine. I kept asking her. She kept her head down.

I saw the video for 'Too Shy' on *Top of the Pops* that Thursday night. My worst fears were confirmed. Kajagoogoo were like Culture Club; they weren't a band one of Drake's lot could like. They might turn out to be gay, or sort of gay, like Duran Duran. So the card had been an insult. Probably. In the video, Kajagoogoo's singer, Limahl, was wandering through a modern disco, and everything kept changing back to the 1940s. I didn't like that. *Too* shy. Too unable to say anything. Too trapped to speak up.

When that wasn't true any more!

I leapt up and switched the set off.

———————

The next Tuesday, Michael Jackson went to Number One with 'Billie Jean', which everyone said was shit. Selway told us all that he was going out with Louise.

I didn't know what going out meant to kids at my school. There was a club in Chippenham that Selway sometimes claimed to sneak into, Gold-Diggers, but I couldn't imagine a girl from our school going to it. It was a place I could only imagine glamorous adults at, drinking Babycham.

I knew, sort of, that nobody was having sex. 'Virgin' was a common term of abuse, but we all were. Just as we were all 'tossers' and 'wankers', and maybe 'benders', depending on what Madness meant by that line in 'Baggy Trousers'. If Selway and Louise were even just 'going out', that would make Louise, as far as I knew, the only girl from school who had anything to do with a boy from school, apart from whatever Angie and Drake were doing. When any girl on the bus mentioned her boyfriend, it was like she was talking about a different sort of being to us. Possibly an imaginary being. Even the football kids didn't seem to be what boyfriends were.

'Which means,' said Selway, 'I make her gobble my knob.'

I saw Selway talking to Louise that first week of March. He talked to her with her friends nearby. He couldn't have held her hand or kissed her or anything like that. That would have meant he was a poof. What did they have to talk about? Louise would be saying stuff about music Selway couldn't like, or about baking things, which he couldn't have any opinions about. Selway would be saying stuff about Marvin Hagler and Brighton and Hove Albion. He probably wasn't talking to her about his cock, like he did when he was with Drake's lot. Angie, Jenn and Netty held off laughing, and then laughed when he went, not at him. They looked like they had been told wonderful and mysterious things about Selway. I did and didn't want to know what.

Louise started giving Selway things to eat. Things she'd made in Cookery. She'd open a Tupperware box for him to take something sweet out of. Drake's lot would crowd round whenever Selway brought something back from her, asking him urgent questions. Had he shagged her yet?

My dad owned a whole homemade bookcase full of Nick Carter and Tobin books. They were meant to be spy thrillers and comedies, but they were mostly about sex. In the case of Nick Carter, that was lots of violent death, and then sex with gowns and suspender belts and girl guerillas of the Amazon. They would fight him, and then give in. In the case of Tobin, it was about insurance salesmen and frustrated housewives who wore enormous pants on the covers.

Were Selway and Louise doing anything like in the books? Where had their parents been? Had they done this in the lounge or in the dining room?

Such things weren't for me now. Not until I was healed. My sex scene would be:

Why, Mr. Waggoner, it's so cold in my room, why don't you come in and share with me? Oh dear, your slacks have caught on a nail! Let me sew them for you. My, that bulge does look big! Shall we shall what's lurking under—?

AHH! AHH! IT'S INFECTED! IT'S DISEASED! IT'S ROTTEN! IT'S CUT OPEN! IT HURTS! IT HURTS! TAKE IT OUT OF ME! IT HURTS!

One Monday, Waggoner stood with me as I was watching Selway and Louise eating together. I'd been trying to come all week, but my cock had stopped responding to my awkward touch. I hadn't even been erect. This was very weird, and so I was getting slowly, deeply, scared. I wondered if something was growing inwards from the wound. From the moment I'd read that Valentine's card, I'd felt like I was the card, cracked open, that something wasn't right with me. If I hadn't been 'Too Shy' before, part of me now certainly was.

Waggoner saw my expression. 'Selway next,' he said.

Eighteen

'Turn around.' I kept hearing that lyric. Bonnie Tyler's 'Total Eclipse of the Heart' was at Number One. Waggoner and I ran into Selway as he was heading back from where he'd met with Louise, a piece of shortbread in his hand. We fell in beside him. 'What're you up to with her?' said Waggoner. 'Really?'

'She's *really* gobbling my knob,' said Selway.

I didn't want to hear that, but Waggoner asked for all the details.

———

Over the next few days, Selway, like he was teaching us, started to talk about his great experience in the field of sex. He told us about rubber johnnies, how there was a pinprick in one in a hundred of them so the population wouldn't die out. He told us about how no girl at school could be on the pill, because doctors would tell, and so a blow job was best.

I remembered Selway hitting me. My head bouncing off that tree. I remembered him helping in slicing my cock open. I wondered what would happen if I'd said, 'You know, I can't come now, and I think it's because of you.'

Selway said you could say what you liked to a girl. He told Louise to show him her fanny, and she'd do it, because she fancied him. I couldn't imagine Louise's face hearing things like that. Then I could but didn't want to. Then I did want to. Then that feeling didn't reach my cock. The awfulness stayed warm and hard in my stomach and my throat and made the back of my neck lock in tension. I thought again of Elaine. And felt immediately terrible to have thought about her then, though I didn't quite get why.

Louise and Selway, we were told, did it in a shed at the bottom of the Selway family's garden, that had been done up as a den for Selway. Their parents didn't know they were boyfriend and girlfriend. The Selway property backed onto the landscape garden of Mr. and Mrs. Callidge, Louise's parents, built beside their farm and stables. The shed had a couple of loose timbers. So Louise and Selway would both take a walk down their gardens, and get together in that shed, like *Huckleberry Finn* with sex.

'You want to come over and see?' asked Selway, like he had a point to prove.

———————

One Sunday in early spring, Waggoner and I took our bikes over to Selway's house, which was only a couple of miles away from Calstone, just outside the village of Heddington. Waggoner had a Raleigh Chopper. I had Aunt Dar's girl's bike with a basket on the front.

Selway's mum made us toast and jam. The kitchen was warmed by an enormous cooker, with a copper kettle on top of it. Everything smelt like it was warm all the time, even at night. Selway grabbed a bottle of Dandelion and Burdock, which I'd never even heard of, from a crate. We went down to the shed together, and Selway reached round the back of some boxes and found a couple of porn magazines: *Penthouse* and *Fiesta*. Selway pointed at that title and laughed. I managed not to. Waggoner calmly took one of the magazines. I peered over his shoulder. There was an article about stock car racing. All the rest was incredibly naked women. Waggoner's hands did not shake. I hoped Selway's mum wasn't about to come in. I worried about the women in the magazines.

There were a lot of bright colours in those pages. Pink underwear. Orange stockings. Silver hair. Bright fluffy white rugs. These women were doing it in the lounge, sprawled on the sofa, their arses in the air in front of the wallpaper. There was one feeding her goldfish, in a carefully round bowl, rather than a tank, in her lingerie. Whenever any of the women had a dress on, in the first photo of the set, it looked like a cartoon of a dress, something you'd never actually see a woman wearing.

Selway took the magazine out of Waggoner's hands, like he didn't want to leave it too long, or there'd be the question of what they might do next to share this experience. He showed us he had a key to Louise's house. 'Nobody home,' he said. He pushed open the planks. Waggoner and I followed. We were in somebody else's garden. We were trespassing. We walked up the ornamental garden of the Callidge house together, Selway still carrying his bottle of Dandelion and Burdock. I could hear tractors moving in the farm beyond, low moans from the cattle. Selway opened the patio doors and led Waggoner and me inside. We waited a moment, listening, then Selway made a cartoon 'hee, hee' and rubbed his hands together theatrically. If I'd ever done that, in the sight of anyone at school, I'd have spent years with everyone doing that gesture. Waggoner copied Selway, mirroring him perfectly. He followed Selway upstairs like they were two Disney characters, stepping with their knees high, avoiding nonexistent creaking timbers.

I followed.

Selway led us along a corridor with a fluffy white carpet. We came to a door with a white horse on it, purple stars and a swirl of glitter falling from its mane. Selway opened the door. The smell of a girl's room: lavender soap and clean white towels, and underneath that, her. She had her own sink. Was that something girls always had? Why? Selway opened a drawer. He held up what I initially took to be a pair of swimming trunks. 'Her special pair,' he said. 'Just for me.' He showed us several more items of Louise's underwear. At the time they seemed spectacular, luxurious, part and parcel of the porn magazine. But thinking back now, Louise probably didn't own anything glamorous that her mother would have boggled at.

We went back downstairs to the Callidge kitchen, and Selway went to the fridge, which was fed by three huge chest freezers. 'They get cuts of meat straight off the farm,' he said. He took a pie and cut himself a slice. Beside the pie, there was a glass bowl with cling film over the top, a kitchen label on it: *Louise's steak and kidney for school.* Selway held the pie over his mouth for a moment, then gobbled it down in one like a cartoon snake.

'They got any beer?' asked Waggoner. Selway said he'd go and look, and left his Dandelion and Burdock on a shelf.

Waggoner went straight to the bottle and took a handful of crushed leaves and flowers from his pocket. He ground them again between his palms and let them fall into the bottle, grabbed a pencil and used it to mix them in. Then he went to the glass bowl and used the pencil to pull up the edge of the cling film. "No," I said. "Why—?"

"Necessary," he said. "I can't do this all on my own." He took from his other pocket a handful of white powder and dropped it into the steak and kidney. Again he mixed it in.

"What is it?"

"Just chalk." Waggoner finished mixing, then used the pencil to reattach the cling film as best he could. He put the pencil back in his pocket.

I was about to ask why that was necessary, when Selway came back in and said—and this was probably a lie because he was getting worried about staying this long—that there was no beer to be found.

We went back up the garden to the shed, and got there just as Selway's parents pulled into the driveway. Waggoner and I said hello to them, then rode off home.

———————

Louise came to school the next day and brought her ingredients for Cookery. She made her steak and kidney pie. That lunchtime she came over to Drake's lot to offer Selway some. He took a piece, but didn't eat it, and later, when he thought nobody was watching, I saw him throw it away. He looked too ill to eat anything. That grey colour in his cheeks made me feel sick too. If what happened to him was going to go as far as what had happened with Lang, I didn't want to watch it over days. I was afraid I'd say something.

'She'll give some to her mates,' I said to Waggoner as, alone, we watched across the playground as Louise ate the pie she'd made.

'No,' he said, a satisfied look on his face, 'because they're vegetarians.'

At the end of the day, Selway looked even worse.

That night I couldn't sleep. I walked through the hallway in the dark, and passed myself in the mirror. I didn't look at myself. I went into the lounge and put the television on with the sound down. On HTV, in a gap when there were no adverts, was the video for 'Total Eclipse of the Heart'. Bonnie Tyler was wandering around a school like ours, in a tight dress that billowed, and she seemed to be saying that she wanted the schoolboys, and there they were dashing around her, monsters now.

I put my hand on my wounded cock. Was it going to be okay? No.

The next video was Kajagoogoo with 'Too Shy'. I switched off the set and went back to bed and still couldn't sleep.

The next morning, to my half relief and half agony, Selway was at his desk as usual. When we moved rooms for History, though, he wasn't there for the start of the lesson, and Mr. Land asked where he'd gone. Nobody knew. Mr. Land said he assumed there had been a call of nature, which drew laughter, but when Selway hadn't returned after half an hour, he set us some work about enclosure and went out to search. He returned towards the end of the lesson, looking shaken. I heard footsteps running past the door. Something had happened, he said, and lessons were to be suspended for the day. We were all to report to the hall for activities.

Gradually, in one excited report after another, we heard the details of what had happened. Selway's body had been found in one of the disused rooms on the upper floors. His mouth was open, and a pool of blood had flooded out from it.

I looked over to where Angie and her friends were sitting with Louise. She was looking slowly around her, her shock so deep it seemed to have dragged her down to a place where her surroundings were entirely strange.

The inquest found a number of poisons in Selway's system, all of which could have been found in cleaning supplies present at the Selway house. The police found a suicide note in the shed. It was written in what was taken to be Stewart Selway's handwriting, but we'd all been taught to write in the same style. The note said Selway couldn't stand the pressure to succeed at school, and missed his friend, the murdered boy Vincent Lang. The newsreader on *Points West* said it had been found inside a pile of magazines.

Nineteen

The day before Louise came back to school, Duran Duran went to Number One with 'Is There Something I Should Know?' Angie, Netty and Jenn tried to rally around their friend. I saw them from a distance, holding her hand as she cried. Louise suddenly disentangled herself. She didn't look comfortable. There was a special assembly for Selway where hymns were sung and the nature of his death wasn't mentioned. I was relieved that Waggoner could stand there singing the hymns. I couldn't join in.

Drake's lot were now us and Blewly and Rove and Drake. The others said tough and impassioned things about their mate for a couple of days. They said they were angry at him for being a coward and taking his own life. That was the only emotion about suicide they'd ever heard on television.

The curves of the school were obvious now. If you dropped a marble, it ran down to one side of the corridor and set off along the skirting board, roaring along the plaster. Everyone started playing marbles.

On both mornings I'd kept it up at Elaine on the bus as always, making her silent, making the bus driver talk along with my usual question, in a sing-song voice, and say I was lucky I'd gotten any Valentine's cards, because I was bloody obsessed.

On Tuesday at second break, Waggoner went to take a piss,

and I didn't need to. That was odd. I turned a corner and ran right into Angie.

'We *should* be friends,' she said. 'We could be. I'm your best friend's girlfriend, and you've loyally kept our secret.' I turned around to look for Waggoner. She stepped in front of me. 'What's your favourite Number One single of this year?'

'There's only been . . . six.'

'From this *school* year. Your favourite Number One in the singles chart. What is it?'

I did a quick mental calculation. That was easy. There was only one that one of Drake's lot could like. 'The Jam. "Beat Surrender."'

She rolled her eyes and gave a little hiss of frustration. 'Wrong,' she said. She walked off past Waggoner just as he arrived. He looked at me, alarmed, but quickly calmed down. 'She'll learn soon,' he said, 'Louise will be more than she can deal with.'

———————

Since I'd started sexually harassing Elaine, I'd been doing better at my schoolwork. I'd recovered completely from the dip that had come after half-term, when pain had made me stare at the pages of my workbooks and wonder why I was bothering at all. I was going to get the bursary and not let down my mum and dad. I would let Waggoner do what he had to do. I would in the end be healed.

I thought about what Angie had said. I couldn't understand it.

———————

That Saturday, I was invited over to Rove's. Rove's, of course, was actually the school. Dad came in when he dropped us off this time, shook Mr. Rove by the hand, talked about the bursary. Mr. Rove carefully called me and Waggoner by our first name. It sounded like he had planned to do so from the moment he woke up that morning.

Mr. Rove's bit of the house was just like the rest was: dusty and awkward. There were cracks and broken things. It was all at a curving angle, leaning towards the school. It felt like school with bits of a home sitting in it. Like a display.

Rove, Drake, Blewly, Waggoner and me sat in Rove's room, which smelt weird. We were going to play a computer game, which Rove was finishing typing out from a magazine. Blewly started talking about Selway again, but Drake made a noise, and he shut up. I looked at Drake. I wondered if it was getting to him. Two friends suddenly gone. He was just the same. Drake got his fags out, but Rove said no, his dad would smell them. Drake considered for a moment, then put them away. He looked under the bed, and after a bit of fumbling, found a video cassette. 'What's this?' he said.

Rove looked furious. 'I've nearly finished the game,' he said. 'Fifty more lines.'

The game took ages to debug. We played it. Two blocks that were knights, and on the cover of the magazine had been drawn with flaming swords, bright shields and moustaches, moved back and forth, intercepting a green block that was a dragon.

Mr. Rove knocked, and came in with hot chocolate. The tray shook in his hands. He stopped, and it stopped doing that. He said the school was going to get computers next year, that just by chance were called Dragons. We would all prepare ourselves for whatever future there was, no matter how worrying. He wondered what we thought about Mr. Reagan's 'star wars' plan to protect us all from nuclear missiles. We didn't say anything. Rove finally asked if he could get on with the programming. Mr. Rove nodded and left. We drank our hot chocolate. It had got dark.

Drake put the video cassette in the VCR and hit play. Rove said it was a horror movie, with a monster.

I looked down at my cup. The lights weren't on, so nobody could see my face. The movie started. A topless woman in the smallest pants I had ever seen was being raped. She was strangled, then stabbed. The hands of the man doing the stabbing were green and calloused. He was a monster. The soundtrack was very modern, a synthesiser. She made huge gulping, screaming sounds as we saw the blade going in, in, in.

Blewly laughed. 'She's thinking did *she* pick up the wrong guy in the bar!' He sounded as if he wasn't used to saying anything, ever. Rove laughed nervously. He kept looking at his watch, wondering when he could tell us it was time for us to go and we should stop watching.

The woman's body lay now on a mortuary table, still topless, her stomach open. A pathologist peered into the hole, looking closer . . . closer . . .

The synthesiser blared as a green mass leapt at his face. 'He wasn't expecting that!' said Blewly.

Three more women had their clothes slit off and then blades or claws in cheap green gloves slit through them. The expressions on their faces were agony and ecstasy at the same time. Kill me, oh please kill me. This movie was too old for me. Were they allowed to put this in a film? Were we meant to laugh?

A full-sized monster, who was a mass of tubes, was shot by

a cop, but not before it had raped the cop's female partner, who'd gone undercover as a topless dancer. As the cop helped her away from the warehouse, covering her with his jacket, the camera zoomed in on her eyes, which glowed green.

I was shaking. I could feel my wound hurting, and I didn't want it to and did. I was so angry. I was so desperately angry with someone. I wasn't 'Too Shy'. I'd seen this movie, hadn't I? I'd taken part. Waggoner kept looking over to me, desperately trying to make eye contact. I wouldn't look at him.

Drake spat tobacco into his handkerchief. 'Fucking stupid shit,' he said, but it sounded like the highest possible praise.

Blewly was laughing. 'I'd give her one.' He rewound the tape to the last rape and froze it, white bands shuddering across the girl's gaping mouth.

I let out a noise.

They all looked at me.

I held my face until my jaw ached. My teeth were bare. My eyes were full. I let out another noise. There was a huge sound inside my head, of something starting to crash down in slow motion.

Waggoner leapt up. 'Don't tell!' he shouted. 'Don't tell!'

Then I was sobbing, actually crying, in front of them, and I couldn't stop. I couldn't see. My nose was full. I got up to run out. I dropped my mug. I blundered into a wall. My sobs were loud now, my body curling around it.

The others had got to their feet, were grabbing me, pretend kindly and actual kindly and roughly all mixed up. There was sudden horror on the faces of Rove and Blewly, maybe something dredging up inside them about what I might be traumatised about. Drake's face stayed cold, but it was coldness like a brittle sheet of ice. For the first time then I saw that everything he was could shatter. The video in the player reached the end and started to rewind. The light came on, and I was sobbing incoherently amongst them, and Mr. Rove was in the room, asking what had happened. He dived at the TV and hit PLAY and saw something on the screen.

———————

Dad didn't say anything as he drove me home, though several times it seemed like he was going to. Mr. Rove had taken him aside. Waggoner sat silently beside me, looking angry. Just before we turned off the A4 towards my house, I said to him, 'Dad . . . when you got that samurai sword . . . was he trying to kill you?'

'Of course he was!' he said. It had been a shout.

———————

When I got into bed that night, Waggoner only reluctantly climbed in beside me. 'Why the fuck did you do that? I got you into Drake's lot to protect you.'

'You mean so you could get close enough to Selway.'

'So? We're on the same side.'

Mum and Dad hadn't said a word to me about what had happened. I couldn't imagine them finding the words. 'What did you mean about Louise?' I said. Did you poison her too?'

'Of course not. She's taken something in, but it's not poison. This has to be done right. There are rules. This is important.'

'How long is it all going to take?'

'It has to finish on the day it started. On Halloween.'

Twenty

As we got off the buses and headed into school the next Monday, Drake walked right into me. His chest pushed me against the wall. He spat into my face, grabbed me by the collar and threw me down. 'Fucking twat,' he said. 'Rove's dad thought that video was mine! You thought we were your mates. Fucking fooled you. Fucking poof! Fucking *girl*!'

I had left Elaine alone that morning. The rest of the bus had been amazed at the silence. I'd looked at the ground. They'd started talking about other things. Elaine remained silent and still wouldn't look at me.

As I lay there, spat on, I felt a little better. I had no idea why.

———————

Drake's lot were split up onto different desks in the form room, with Waggoner on his own beside me, again. I hadn't heard anything else about what had happened that night at Mr. Rove's. My mum and dad never said anything more.

We had English that day with Mrs. Frenchmore. She had once locked herself in a cupboard during class, by accident, I think. Mrs. Frenchmore never shouted at anyone; she never sent anyone to see Mr. Coxwell. We'd once read *1984* in her class. She said we should like it because it was like *Star Wars*. Which made Drake's lot start using it as a weapon. 'You love

Big Brother, don't you?' Blewly had said to me. Mrs. French-more's weakness terrified me. It made her classroom into a space where anything could happen.

Mrs. Frenchmore set us an essay as homework. The title was 'The Contents of a Suitcase'. 'You find a suitcase that contains (there followed a list of objects). Write a story about the exciting and interesting things that happen concerning your use of one of these objects.' English wasn't one of my best subjects. My essays were minimal, functional.

At first break, I went back over to my lot, to Surtees and Cath and Fiesta. They let me and Waggoner walk straight back into their circle without a word, and we started talking about stuff without any mention of where I'd been in the meantime.

I watched Angie's lot go past. Louise these days always had a strange look on her face, like she was trying to remember something. She looked ill. I kept wondering about that chalk. I don't think any adult ever realised she and Selway had been going out. She managed to keep that secret. Angie stopped and actually nodded to me. She reached up to her collar and rubbed at something under there. She held up her hand and I saw ink on her fingers. She'd erased something she'd written there, and wanted me to know. Then she was gone again before I could work out what that was about.

———————

That night, I opened my English essays book and squatted against my bed, my head curled over my body, the book on the ground. I always tried to do my homework immediately. I couldn't start.

I stood and walked around a bit. Waggoner looked puzzled

at me. I dropped back onto the floor and made myself start to write. 'It looks like suicide, Inspector, but actually it was murder by poison.' I let go of the pen. I had to put my hand over my mouth to stop myself from shouting. I grabbed the pen again and crossed it all out and looked at the page from the other side to make sure it couldn't be read that way, either.

Waggoner was staring at me in shock. I shook my head. 'Sorry, sorry.'

I paced the room that night. I didn't want to think about what Selway had looked like when he died. Or Lang. Not seeing them made it worse. This was what I'd wanted, though, and I hadn't done it. I had just let it be done. I shook my head, trying to shake away whatever this feeling was. What had Angie been doing? She'd asked a real question of me before, the sort I was hardly ever asked, about what my favourite Number One had been, and I had given the wrong answer, but there must be a right answer. I felt like I should write a list of Number Ones and try to work it out. But I couldn't do that now. This story I had to write was in the way of everything. I curled up around my exercise book again. I didn't want to write anything that wasn't true. I didn't want to write anything that was. The contents of a suitcase. I could have picked my own list: a foreskin, a knife, a 50p piece, a Valentine's card, a frog, some chalk.

I thought again about what had been cut from me, wherever it was, decaying. What if Drake had found it? What if he showed it to me on April Fools' Day? 'Remember this, mate?' The knife would still have bits of me on it that would have been crushed up with the tobacco he cut. He had smoked part of me.

I made myself concentrate. What did I really have to work with? The list of objects the essay question stipulated included a bicycle pump, a hairdryer, a chef's hat and a tin of boot polish. I kept starting the essay, kept stopping and crossing out. Waggoner sat beside me, placidly. 'Why don't you just–'

'Fuck it,' I said. I could say it quite loudly; Mum would never hear. Then again: 'Fuck it.' And again: *'Fuck it!'* I started writing about finding this fucking suitcase, and about the exciting and interesting things that happened concerning every single fucking thing in it. I made those happenings *genuinely* things I found exciting and interesting, and it would serve them right.

The story happened at Fasley Grange School. There was an alien in it, and she was called Louise. She was from the tree people. Angie committed murder using a bicycle pump to inflate Selway, in, in, in, until he exploded all over the Portakabin. Surtees burnt Lang to death with the hairdryer, cooking his face. Drake put boot polish on his cheeks and led a commando raid to take back the school from Louise's reign of terror, because she was making everyone do these things against their will, and there I was, at the end, in a chef's hat, stirring soup in a huge pot, made of everyone who'd taken part in the story. I didn't display any prejudice: everyone went in the pot. In the end, it was all a dream, caused by a piece of pie before bedtime.

At the end of it, I looked through the essay, and I was horrified. What had I done? This essay was obviously going to get me expelled. It was huge, for one thing, twenty pages long. Someone would punish me for this. Someone should. I was asking for it. No more bursary. No more Drake. No more Waggoner? Blewly and Rove and Drake just carrying on. Why had I done this? I grabbed the pen again, but I couldn't cross it all out. Page after page. What would that say? I put my hands to the pages of my exercise book, and started to pull them out so I could burn them.

But no, I couldn't deliberately damage an exercise book.

I paced and paced and finally shoved the book into my schoolbag. It would have to do. I had made something, and I would have to suffer the consequences. I felt weirdly worked up. In bed, I thought of Angie holding up her hand to me to show me she'd rubbed something out. I reached down, and, though I could feel Waggoner stir sulkily beside me, I put my fingers into the gap of the wound, and felt what was inside my cock. I experimented, I allowed myself to feel something, and suddenly I was desperate again. I found a place which felt good, though there was also a lot of pain, and aimed into a sock which would immediately go into the laundry-

I came.

I lay there panting. I didn't think it had injured me. I waited for the pain to die down. It took a long time.

I sat through the next English class. At the end, Mrs. Frenchmore asked me to stay behind. That got a howl of laughter as the class filed out. Waggoner's in trouble! I took a deep breath. I was ready to be expelled.

'What a lovely story,' said Mrs. Frenchmore.

I think I made a little noise.

'This was a complete flight of fantasy! The way you used the terrible recent events and made them into something . . . golden! Do keep your innocence. I've given you an A-plus.'

I had to lean on a desk. Mrs. Frenchmore's classes continued to be where anything could happen, and it was terrifying.

Waggoner threw his head back and laughed, and slapped me on the back. He wanted me to join in laughing with him. But I wouldn't.

———————

When I got home that night, I wrote seven twenty-page stories. One was a rip-off of *Star Wars*, with Drake, Blewly, Rove and me pretending to be space fighter pilots. I emphasised the pretending, saying that was what we did at break time. One was a rip-off of *Alien*, with an alien laying eggs around the school over the Easter weekend and infesting Lang and Selway. Then there was one about football, where Drake led us all in a team. I didn't understand the offside rule when I started writing that, so in that one we all talked about it a lot, and I think I got it sorted out. There was a vampire story, where Louise was chasing Angie around the school, and they were both in old dresses, and there was a lot of yearning. Louise ended up putting a stake through Angie's heart. There was a thriller, where I played an innocent man who chose to defend himself in court, and was let out of the dock immediately to universal applause. There was a *Doctor Who* story, with Peter Davison and Nyssa landing at our school, and battling a snake that was made up of what everyone secretly wanted to do. The whole school was destroyed at the end of that, and Fiesta was the only survivor. Peter Davison took him away to be his and Nyssa's new companion. Lastly there was a fantasy story about hill people. They came to raid the villages below. They seized our women. They killed everyone from Heddington to Calstone and set Compton Bassett ablaze.

I stopped, not knowing what time it was. I found Dad

watching snooker. I said sorry, but I'd needed the paper. I'd only just noticed the name of his insurance business at the top of every page.

'What are you using the paper for?'

'Nothing.'

He took the pile of stories out of my hands. I panicked, couldn't grab them back. He took a look at the top sheet, then picked up his glasses from the table and said he'd have a read of these.

When he drove me to the school bus the next morning, he asked me how much of the stories was true.

'We don't think we can really go into space. And the people from the hills—'

'I mean, all these children at school, Mr. Rove's son and all the rest. Are they all still such close friends of yours?'

I considered what had happened last time I was at Rove's, trying to figure out the right answer. I finally said they were.

Dad said he'd like to read more of my stories.

That Thursday, during assembly, Louise shrugged off Angie's consoling hand, and called her 'bloody immature', so loudly that Mr. Land heard and pretended he hadn't.

I heard them talking outside at first break. Louise's voice had become strange, high and low, a roller coaster ride. 'You don't care about anything important! Don't let me stop you distracting yourselves!'

She marched off. Netty and Jenn tried to run after her, but Angie stopped them. She was muttering something under her breath.

I ran into Louise standing alone beside the big tree in the freezing mist. She had one hand on the wood, like it was the only thing that could reassure her. She was looking slowly around her, like she was new here.

Twenty-one

That Friday was April Fools' Day. Now we weren't in Drake's lot, that was as scary as it used to be. At the end of the Thursday when Louise had broken away from Angie's lot, Mrs. Mills had announced that Louise had asked to be, and had been made, school chalk monitor. Angie's lot looked surprised as Louise inclined her head, looking serious. Mrs. Mills went on with her announcements, deliberately casually saying that tomorrow Mrs. Pepper was going to begin her Biology classes in human reproduction. We were to tell our parents that tonight, in case they wanted to deny us permission to attend. Mrs. Mills had deliberately not used the word 'sex', but still she had to call out to stop the laughter before it settled down into whispers. I didn't like the sound of those lessons, but being denied permission would be the worst thing.

That night, I sat down beside Dad in the lounge and pretended to be interested in snooker. 'Are you going to ask about that sword again?' he said.

'No.'

'Well. No point in raking up the past, is there?' He asked me if I was looking forward to my Easter egg. I said I was. I decided that he'd agreed to the lessons, that I would save him that uncomfortable conversation.

———

The job of the chalk monitor was to check how much chalk was left in the groove that ran along the base of every blackboard. Before the start of lessons on Friday, Louise was given dozens of new packets of chalk. Every lesson she went into, the first thing she did was to go to the board, run her finger along the groove, and, if there wasn't enough chalk there, take a stick from her bag and add it. At first break she was meant to do all the rooms she hadn't had access to. Just before she went to do it, Waggoner went over and gave her something from his pocket. I didn't see what.

The first human reproduction class was going to be at 11:00 a.m. on April Fools' Day. Various April Fools had been tried that morning. Fiesta had kept telling everyone that Shakin' Stevens was dead, but nobody cared.

'Right!' said Mrs. Pepper. 'Oh yes, everyone's giggling, and nobody knows where to look. You needn't worry, you're exactly the same as every year. What you have to deal with is exactly the same as what boys and girls always have to deal with.' She picked up a new piece of chalk and started to draw on the board, with deliberately quick strokes. 'Now, can anyone tell me what I'm drawing? Fifty pence to the first one who gets it right. I know, I've never offered that to you lot before; it's just for this picture, every year. I always get to keep my fifty pence, because once they see what it is, nobody wants to say . . .' I realised at the same time everyone else did that she was drawing the outside and the inside of a normal penis. Maybe I got there first, because I was more familiar with the inside. It looked like Mrs. Pepper was going to keep her fifty pence. 'And that's a mercy, if you think about it. It's one long line of people having sex . . . yes, there's the S word, and not a snigger . . . and being just the same as you.' The cock depicted was erect, and judging by the size of the balls, carefully not enormous. It did, however, stretch from one side of the blackboard to the other. Inside it were many double lines, and there were gates going back into the body, and a gap that led up at a curve into the wider world.

I looked over to where the girls were sitting. Louise was looking furious. I thought for a moment that she was going to say something. That maybe she had asked for a note to be excused from this. Because she looked like she profoundly disagreed. With exactly what, I had no idea.

Mrs. Pepper finished her diagram with a flourish that took her chalk down to a stub. She took her fifty-pence piece out and showed it to the audience, then dropped it back in her pocket. The trick was done, the power invoked; we were silent. 'Right!' She thwacked the tip of a new piece of chalk onto the board and drew one hard line up to the diagram. 'This is a—'

There was a screeching noise. The chalk broke in her fingers. The board divided. Then the topmost part broke under the weight, and the two halves fell off the wall. Mrs. Pepper leapt back with a shriek as the blackboard crashed onto the ground and shattered into pieces. A cloud of chalk dust burst up into the room. Kids jumped up from their chairs and shouted.

From outside came the sound of the village clock striking twelve. The time for April Fools' jokes was over.

Louise raised her hand. 'Please, Mrs. Pepper: is it a penis?'

Mrs. Pepper shooed us all out of the Portakabin, saying it wasn't safe. On my way out, I saw something glittering amongst the dust under the board, and picked it up. It was a narrow point of flint. It was covered in chalk from where it had been inside the stick. It wouldn't have been enough to cut the board. That must have been done beforehand. But it had served to draw a line.

———————

Louise stayed on as chalk monitor. How could a child have put that much effort into an April Fool? Perhaps the board had just somehow broken? I'm sure she denied everything, if they even asked her. In Art, she started painting in a different style, one that excited Mr. Kent. The people and grassy surroundings she smudged onto the paper were peat bog old, greens and browns, rubbed in and in. The girls started to copy her, and even though Mr. Kent was pleased by it, it looked kind of against what we should be doing anyway, so some of the boys copied her too.

———————

On Easter Sunday, Mum made me an egg out of cooking chocolate. Dad reminded me, as I broke open the egg and ate one small piece of the chocolate, that this wasn't all that 'my Easter egg' was. Last night, we'd seen local news pictures of the crowds on the first day of '*Doctor Who*, A Celebration: Twenty Years of a Time Lord' at Longleat. There were meant to be monsters going, and actors and props from the series. It was on all weekend. There were thirty thousand people there, the reporter said. The roads were blocked with cars for miles around. I felt excited as I watched, but tried not to show it. Mum and Dad had looked uneasily at each other when the reporter had said how much the tickets cost, and how many peo-ple were complaining that their children hadn't got to see any-thing. 'Well, that doesn't look very good,' Dad said.

I kept my face still.

"There's Doctor Who," said Mum, as Peter Davison could be seen in the distance, surrounded by children, trying to get out of a car.

"And they're not even showing any of the new episodes there, only the very old ones." Dad looked over to me. "Are you bothered about going to that, or shall we go to Longleat after it's all over, next weekend?"

"We'll go next weekend." I nodded, not taking my eyes off the screen, trying to soak it all up. "It's a waste of money." If I'd said, "Please, can we go right now?" he'd have leapt out of his seat and gone to put his sheepskin coat on, and ushered us all out to the car. I have a recurring dream about my father: there's a war, and boys are being conscripted, and the authori-ties come to the door, asking for me. Dad tells me I don't have to go. He'll go instead. Again.

On Tuesday, David Bowie went to Number One with 'Let's Dance'. I saw the video on *Top of the Pops* two days later. 'If you say run, I'll run with you.' I wasn't sure if it was something Drake's lot could like. The video looked more real than real was, the newest thing possible. I felt that I liked it, and wondered if I could. The playground offered varying verdicts, and I didn't want to ask. I saw Louise pass by a group of girls talking about the video and suddenly start swearing at them, to the point where they all walked off together, calling things back at her.

Term ended next Friday. We'd resumed the human reproduction lessons in a classroom without a blackboard, and Mrs.
Pepper had sketched a huge, very colourful penis on a white-
board with squeaky felt tips. She didn't offer the fifty pence
again. We'd been left dangling over the holidays to learn the
rest of it when we came back.

The Saturday morning, after the end of term, waking up. I
knew from experience that it would take a couple of days before I'd feel school wasn't suddenly going to happen again. I
opened my eyes and saw that Waggoner was standing by my
bedroom window, looking out. I had no idea what he would
do now we weren't in school until May. The mock exams were
next term, so I'd have to revise during this holiday. I even had
to go back to school for revision classes. But there would still
be a long while of blissful . . . *nothing*. Or so I thought.

On Sunday, as promised, Dad drove us to Longleat House and
Safari Park. There were signs that led to an ornamental gateway,
then a long, winding drive that led through gardens and forested
hills, and then over a rise, and we were looking down onto the val-
ley where the stately home was. The air through the window of
the car was still cold but full of approaching summer. There below
us were the house and gardens, and the flags and the lake already
with boats chugging away on it amongst the sea lions and hippos.
That sight made you want to get down there quickly, quickly, before they closed it or something!

Dad glanced back at me, hoping every minute for a smile, so I smiled for him. There were a line of other cars in front of us, and a line behind us, but there weren't thirty thousand of them, so we were all sailing along at ten miles per hour. I lay back and closed my eyes, and breathed.

Waggoner sat beside me in the back seat. He said nothing. He was purposeless.

I still love Longleat. It's a country estate that's been planned so that the lord of the manor owned everything he could see. There's nothing he doesn't want to have there, all the way to his horizon. In the 1960s, it became the first place to open a safari park: the Lions of Longleat. I associate the house entirely with the summer months, because it was closed all winter. It was the opposite of my school. We parked in one of the fields, excitingly flagged into our own space by a girl in an orange jacket. I could already see, even from this distance, that the ground to one side of the great square house was churned up into one huge sheet of mud. That had been where the *Doctor Who* event had been. We walked over the little bridge to the huge gravel expanse at the front of the house. There were just a couple of steps up to a front door here. I could imagine walking out of that door and looking up the long, straight drive that led from it right to a big gate about a mile away, and thinking that this was all mine, that there were big hedges and strong gates and wild animals between me and everybody I didn't want to get in. Nobody would ever make you run up *that* driveway. This was *my* house.

We'd do the safari park at the end, Dad said. We had to hurry, to do everything the ticket let us do. We did the house first. You went from room to room, keeping behind the red rope, looking into lounges and dining rooms, all of which smelled of some extraordinary polish which I never smelt any-where else. Mum said that if she had a chair like that one, which looked like it was ancient and yet had never been sat in, she'd sit on the floor, except that the carpet was quite nice too. Nothing was cracked. Nothing looked like it was about to fall down. Things were right.

We went on the sea lion and hippo boat ride, to see the go-rillas on their island, and Dad even bought some fish for the sea lions to eat, and he had them pursuing our little corner of the boat. He was chucking pieces in expertly, dangling them only for a second and then giving it to them as they leapt, his face alight, like he'd learnt this on the rail of some boat that had guns and camouflage and a big, muddy river behind him. 'Frank!' said Mum, as if he were setting a bad example, but he just laughed.

Out around the back, by the stables, was the whole point of Longleat for me, but we had to do everything. We even went into Pet's Corner.

I saw her first, a figure squatting by the low fence around the rabbit enclosure. She was wearing a long pastel orange skirt that looked very crumpled, with purple tights and flat black shoes, and a big white blouse with the tops of the sleeves all puffed out. She'd pushed her hair up somehow; it was nearly a quiff. Now she didn't know anyone was watching her, she looked very sad.

'Isn't that Mr. Boden?' said Dad.

Angie looked round, looked suddenly careful, stood up. Her parents were with her. They looked rich. But I thought everyone else's parents did. Dad had already stepped for-wards and was shaking Mr. Boden by the hand. 'Frank Wag-goner. We met at the parents' evening.' Angie and I looked awkwardly at each other. Waggoner sighed.

It turned out Dad and Mr. Boden had a shared interest in horse racing, Dad through betting, Mr. Boden through having shares in two horses. They fell into talking almost instantly, and so did Mum and Mrs. Boden, the wind blowing at their hats. Dad glanced covertly at his watch. 'Do you think these two would fancy the maze?'

'It's Angie's favourite,' said her mum.

———————

Angie and Waggoner and I were walked to the gate of the maze, and tickets were shown, and we had the gate closed behind us. I wanted to ask Angie about her smudging her collar with ink, about all sorts of things, but as soon as the gate clicked shut she was off, sprinting away into the maze without a glance behind her.

I made to follow, but I realised Waggoner hadn't moved. He was standing at the entrance, looking angry. 'Why would you want to get lost deliberately?' he asked. 'It's stupid.'

So I went on without him. The Longleat Hedge Maze is a square box made of 16,000 English yews. The path runs for 1.69 miles. The aim is to get to the wooden tower in the middle, and then out of an exit at the other side. I'd never completed it. I'd always had the feeling I was working against the clock, that I wouldn't get to see the attraction I'd come to Longleat to see unless I got out of there. I'd always flipped open the covered metal plaque that showed you the way out.

This time, with my thoughts on trying to find Angie, I was lost almost immediately. I found myself at the crossroads of three pathways.

'Hi.'

I stopped at the sound of her voice. She must be behind one of the hedges. 'Hello?'

'So you've stopped pretending to be friends with Anthony?'

I hated the way she called Drake by his first name. I wondered again how they could be together without her having heard all about what he'd done to me. But if that was the case, why would she ask all these questions? I didn't like 'pretending', but it was the closest approximation to what had happened that might still sound possible. 'Yeah.'

'And you've stopped bothering Elaine?'

I had to close my eyes. Just hearing her say Elaine's name now felt bad. 'Yeah,' I said. 'Sorry.'

Silence. Then she spoke again. 'Okay, then. So. *What's* your favourite Number One single of this year?'

This time she had said it like the answer should now be obvious, like she had proven something to me. I suddenly realised, with perhaps the most intelligent thought of my childhood, that I had been sent a message. Could Angie have been the person who'd sent me that valentine? If so, I had no idea why. 'Kajagoogoo?'

'Bless you,' she said, like I'd just sneezed. Then I heard the sound of her running off again, and her laughter along with it.

I stood there, puzzled. Had that joke been the whole point of the card? Had she April Fooled me on Valentine's Day? What had that to do with how I'd been treating Elaine? 'Hey!' I shouted. I chose a path, ran down it, and found I was at the plaque that told you how to get out of the maze. I flipped it open.

When I got out, there was Angie, standing with our mums and dads. They were all laughing about something. 'Bless you!'

said Mrs. Boden to me. My relief turned to anger, but there was Dad, his eyes meeting mine with quick fear. Don't let us down. I looked to Angie again, not knowing what to make of her smiling at me.

Waggoner arrived sullenly beside me. Did I require his services?

Dad nudged me. 'Do you think Angie would like to go and see the Dalek?'

Twenty-two

The best thing about Longleat was what stood on the corner of a cobbled square: a police box with an open door, through which could be seen a ticket window, the *Doctor Who* Exhibition. It had been here for as long as I'd been coming to Longleat. Its presence was the reason, presumably, why last weekend there'd been the huge *Doctor Who* event here. Reluctantly, my ticket in hand, I led Angie into the stable block area, heading for the exhibition. Waggoner came with us. Every now and then I thought I saw Angie's gaze turn to him, but there was an irritated look on her face when it did. We stopped at the threshold of the police box. From inside, I could hear the cries of the Dalek. I desperately wanted to ask Angie about the Valentine's card now as well as everything else, but how could I? Not only did it open me up to the possibility of her laughing at me again, but the words I was putting together in my head, the form that question would take, sounded to me just like what I'd been tormenting Elaine with. That question had now become too horrible for me to ask.

'Aren't we going in, then?' she said.

———————

The Dalek had retreated into the shadows at the back of its glass case. As soon as we tripped whatever the mechanism was, it surged forward, lights blazing, shouting that we would be exterminated. Some small children beside us screamed.

'Are you scared?' asked Angie.

'No,' I said.

I expected her to ask more questions I'd have to say no to, but she didn't. We walked around cabinets with costumes and monsters from the series hung on dummies. For the first time in all the years I'd come here, I felt kind of disappointed. There were displays of guns and spaceships, which were just dusty things that had been hung up. In the face of Angie, they seemed slight. I didn't want her telling me this was just a dusty room. That would mean it suddenly would become that.

We entered the central area, where the control room was, all sorts of mechanisms on the TARDIS console flashing on and off, and buttons you could press, and the column lit up, rising and falling. Angie pushed some buttons, found they didn't do anything, and looked around like she didn't think much of it. 'This is all very futuristic,' she said. 'Do you like the future?'

I nodded enthusiastically, which made her smile. Waggoner looked furious at me.

'Is your favourite Number One single *really* "Too Shy"?'

I felt, weirdly, like I could tell the truth. The TARDIS, after all, was outside of time and space. 'No,' I said.

'Why did you say it was?' She didn't seem upset, like I'd expected her to be. She sounded pleased, like she already knew the answer.

'I . . . just . . . needed to say that then.' Because of the Valentine's card. *Could* I ask about that? The words still felt like they'd be horrible.

'Great.' She nodded as if I'd just confirmed something. 'So. What's really your favourite?'

I took a risk, hoping against hope. 'It's "Let's Dance".'

Angie beamed all over her face. 'The Number One of right now!' she said. 'Interesting!' She stuffed her hands in the pockets of her skirt and headed for the door.

I stood there for a moment, impressed beyond measure. She had looked and sounded, in that moment, exactly like Doctor Who.

———————

We all walked back to the cars together. Just before she got into her family's expensive car, Angie looked to me again. 'I could lend you some records if you want.'

Waggoner stepped between us, suddenly furious.

'Yeah,' I said, wanting to get him into our car. 'Fine.' And then, 'Thank you very much.'

———————

The very next day, in the afternoon, Mum found a package outside the door. Nobody had rung the doorbell. The package was bound up in three colours of tape: red, gold and green. I took it into my room and closed the door. There was a note attached: *Here are some records you should listen to.* There was Angie's signature, which was so big it went right off the page. There was another sheet of paper in the envelope, a Photostatted document. It read:

NUMBER ONES OF 1982–1983

'Do You Really Want to Hurt Me' by Culture Club. I asked the mirror if the boy and I would always be together, and if he'd grow up a bit to let that happen, and it turns out the answer to that is another question, one I don't understand, by a band he wouldn't like. I avoided him completely on Sunday night because I didn't know what all that meant, and because of the usual family stuff. I danced to the track as usual, to thank the mirror, but when I got home that night, I found the mirror was buckled and cracked! Something huge is happening.

'I Don't Want To Dance' by Eddy Grant. This is terrible! I asked the cracked mirror if we were going to be found out after Waggoner saw us, and now it tells me it doesn't want to dance, it doesn't want to have anything to do with me! I won't be able to ask it any more questions! I'll only be able to imagine what I might have asked, and then hear the Number One and hope that would have been the answer to my question. There was an accident on the football pitch, and someone's painted a horse there and I feel weird even to think about it, it feels impossible. I tried to talk to Waggoner, but he didn't answer. For some reason, I don't think he'll give us away. When he saw us in the clearing, I said a few good lyrics and got rid of him, but before that it looked like he spazzed out. There's something weird about him now. Something new.

'Beat Surrender' by The Jam. The lyrics go, 'As it was in the beginning, so shall it be in the end'. What would I have asked the mirror to get this track as an answer? I got the feeling something big was about to happen, so I took care to be everywhere and do everything, so I'd see it. Sure enough, there was an accident in the swimming pool. One of the boy's friends has been badly hurt. He must be feeling so bad about it. I felt sick after. The whole school's feeling weird now.

'Save Your Love' by Renée and Renato. Well, that's pretty obvious. There's clearly a threat to the boy, and I have to do something about it. Damn Terry Wogan of Radio 2! He got this to Number One! The only good thing is it kept The Shakin' Stevens EP off the top, because how hard would that be to decipher? This so-called song is ancient, but maybe that's saying the threat is from something ancient. I wish I could discount it, but I'm too scared to. So I will dance to it. In thanks, even though that bloody mirror doesn't deserve it. Sorry. Waggoner has suddenly become one of the boy's friends. That doesn't feel right, that's so weird, but everyone else seems to think it's fine.

'You Can't Hurry Love' by Phil Collins. It's been two weeks since Vince Lang died, or was killed, rather. The boy's been very brave. I think I would have asked the mirror if this was going to have an effect on our relationship. And this single is an answer which would have made me feel better. I asked Waggoner what music he liked, but he just said the usual, nothing interesting. Something big has definitely happened to him, something weird, like with the school. If I knew what he really thought about pop music, I might be able to work out what's going on.

'Down Under' by Men at Work. Either I've started to be very clumsy, or what happened to my mirror has started to happen to the school. It's very worrying. I can guess what the next Number One will be. I'll make use of that to help Elaine with that fucking Waggoner, who is being the biggest arsehole. What question would I have asked the mirror to get this answer? I dread to think! No, it feels like a big, empty desert. Those lines about dying and temptation.

'Too Shy' by Kajagoogoo. Ha, ha! Got it right about the next Number One! I've used it to help poor Elaine. I wonder if Waggoner will realise what I've done to him?

'Billie Jean' by Michael Jackson. Louise is going out with one of the boy's friends, so that's good. 'Not my lover' worries me. The whole song, the performance, people vanishing in the video, Michael Jackson looking out from under his hat, it all worries me.

'Total Eclipse of the Heart' by Bonnie Tyler. What?! This one is Noel Edmonds' fault! Am I supposed to be paying attention to what the top of the charts would be like if these DJs didn't keep making records Number Ones that aren't supposed to be? How do I do that? The video is horrifying. I think this says something huge is going to happen to the school. The changes are going to get worse. Who's the eclipse going to happen to? I might have asked, 'Will Louise and Stewart work out?'

'Is There Something I Should Know?' by Duran Duran. About a week ago, Stewart Selway killed himself. Another one of the boy's friends. He must be really going through it, though he won't say anything. But Louise is changed, bent out of shape by what's happened. If I'd asked the mirror a question, it could have been, 'What question should I be asking?' I'm missing something huge.

'Let's Dance' by David Bowie. Oh! Thank you! Finally! Phew! I can ask questions again. Although with the mirror broken, I don't know how good the answers will be. I danced to this so much, straight away, up and down my room. Louise is being so weird. The school is getting weirder all the time. Something happened in human reproduction. Waggoner has stopped being the boy's friend, so that's some-thing that's jerked back to being normal, at least. Elaine says she think he might have finally shut up, so I've, errrrr, let him off. This Number One tells me there's hope in the middle of this horror movie. I know exactly what question I'm going to ask before the next Number One comes along.

I stared at the piece of paper. The note felt dangerous, for all sorts of reasons. The boy she talked about must be Drake. This could actually be evidence, in that it said Louise and Selway had been going out.

But in the middle there was the most incredible thing of all. What did Angie think she'd done to me? How had she let me off? Why had she sent me this note and told me that without telling me what all that was about?

Waggoner tried to look at the piece of paper. I crumpled it and put it in my pocket. 'Does she say anything about me?' he asked. I said she hadn't. I had to use a kitchen knife to open the package. Out onto my bed fell what turned out to be ten singles. They were:

- 'Goody Two Shoes' by Adam Ant.
- 'Cat People' by David Bowie, this one a 12".
- 'Hungry Like the Wolf' by Duran Duran.
- 'Mirror Man' by the Human League.
- 'Human Nature' by Michael Jackson.
- 'Party Fears Two' by the Associates.
- 'Suspended in Gaffa' by Kate Bush.
- 'Don't Talk to Me About Love' by Altered Images.
- 'Senses Working Overtime' by XTC.
- 'Back on the Chain Gang' by the Pretenders.

Waggoner looked at them with increasing incredulity, shaking his head and laughing. I laid them out on my bed, trying to read a message from them. This was urgent now. Angie had said in the note she knew what question she was going to ask next. Was it going to be about me? What might be the next Number One, and how might it apply to me? I went into the kitchen, grabbed the paper and took a look at the Top Forty. 'Beat It' by Michael Jackson? 'Sweet Dreams (Are Made of This)' by Eurythmics? 'Church of the Poisoned Mind' by Culture Club?

I went back to look at the singles again. Some of these were by acts Drake's lot hated, like Modern Romance, Michael Jackson and Duran Duran. Some of them they'd like, like XTC and Adam Ant. Was this a test? Was Angie asking if I was gay? Playing the records, I found no clues. I hid them under my bed, the note under my pillow.

In the middle of the night, I woke, suddenly thinking the window was open again. I leapt out of bed, about to close my eyes and lunge for the curtains.

Something sharp went into my foot.

I fell to the ground. The curtains were closed. I held my bellow of pain inside. I grabbed for my foot. I pulled the sharp object out. I looked. I was getting good at looking. There wasn't much blood. I was holding a jagged bit of the XTC record. The sharp point had been part of the label at the centre. Now it had a small lump of my blood and gristle on it, across the name of the band.

I looked around the room. The floor was covered with bits

of broken record and scraps of their sleeves, a carpet of spikes and confetti. I tried to stand up, fell, crushing more record shards under me. They spiked my hip and leg, and my hand where I put it down to steady myself.

In the corner stood Waggoner. He had in his hands the Bowie record, whole. Now he was sure I was watching, he broke it over his knee and let the pieces drop. He went over to my bed, lifted up the pillow, found the list of Number Ones, and, while I lay there, he read it.

Twenty-three

In the early hours, I crawled about, picking pieces of record and sleeve out of the carpet, and then out of my pajamas and skin, and putting them in a carrier bag. It took a long time, with no thought, just something that had to be done. The dust from the carpet made my eyes stream, but I finished it, running my hands along the surface as dawn came up, finding the last particles.

Waggoner watched me do it. When I'd finished, he screwed up the list of Number Ones and ate it.

———————

When it was light, I went on one of my long walks. I left the carrier bag in the dustbin. I waited until we had turned the corner around the road.

'Why?'

'She has a system of her own. It's about stupid shit. She's trying to draw you into it.'

'How am I going to replace those records? They cost–'

'It was all right when there wasn't a girl about, wasn't it? You were into it then. Listen. There's her version of stuff and ours. Our version says that everything means something. That's what's real and right and just, what's important. Her version is just about what things look and sound like, just distractions from the big stuff. You were *maimed* by them, don't you remember? She's *going out with* the man who *cut* you! Don't you want them to answer for it? Don't you want to punish her too?'

I shook my head violently. 'We could have just given the records back!'

'Then she wouldn't hate you. She can't seduce you if she hates you.'

'Seduce–?' I really doubted that was what she was trying to do.

'What's the point of getting to know what she thinks about anything? You can't have her. You can't have any woman now.'

'Why are you saying that?'

'Oh, you're thinking I'm part of you, a figment of your imagination, the naughty angel out of *Jimmy Jinks and What He Thinks*–'

"Are you even a real person?" I reached out and tried to touch his face, but he backed away.

"Listen, you like justice and law and cause and effect, reasons. That's why we're here. You called out to us. You're not like her. You're like us."

"Stop . . ." I wanted to say he was bullying me, but I couldn't say the word. "You're . . . like Drake!" I stumbled away from him across the rough grass.

He followed. I put a hand to my temple. "I'm not in there!" he shouted, so loud it made me duck and look around like lightning was about to strike me. He was there again at my shoulder. "Don't get distracted. You have the bursary to aim for. You have the mock exams coming up. Don't go looking for other things. Or you'll lose it. I will do what I have to for your revenge. Now, because she's clearly dangerous, I've added Angie to my list."

Shit. Shit. What was I going to do?

I had to return her records to her, get her out of my life, show Waggoner she wasn't a threat. I couldn't think of any excuse that would work for having destroyed all of the records. I got fifty pence pocket money a week. I hadn't any savings that I could get at, only some premium bonds and a Post Office savings stamps account that I could access when I was twenty-one. Odd jobs were something I'd read about kids doing.

I didn't revise at all that day. In the end I wrote a story. This one.

                    The Chalice of the Queen
                      By Andrew Waggoner

Starring:

    Anthony Drake as Blake.

    Angie Boden as Northstar.

    Mark Ford as the Teacher of the Arthuria.

    And Andrew Waggoner as Himself.

It was a hot day. My boss called me into his office and told me gruffly I had to keep the Chalice of the Queen, that was part of the Crown Jewels safe. He had information that someone in particular wanted to steal it. A very special someone. But he could not tell me who, for security reasons.

'You don't trust me!' I bellowed.

'I don't trust you, but I do trust you to get the job done!' He bellowed back. But he offered to pay me for the job. All the money I needed.

I grinned grimly. The only way I could keep the Chalice of the Queen safe was by stealing it. So steal it I would. And I would do it that very evening.

The Chalice was kept in a safe at Fasley Grange School. This was run by a teacher who was part of the secret Royal Bodyguard, the Arthuria, who were charged with keeping safe that which could only be kept safe. Or the realm itself would be in peril.

I arranged on some pretext to go and see him, during a school day. The safe was kept, intriguingly, in the office of the bursar in that old building. It had only one guard. But she was very dangerous. She was an expert in the ancient French martial art of panache. She wore a big skirt to allow her lithe limbs freedom of movement. And a cruel smile marked her features. Her name was Northstar, at least, that was the only name I heard. The teacher called her that when he introduced us. I bowed deeply in the traditional Oriental way. She bobbed a bob.

I took dinner with the teacher that lunchtime, because he said he had to be at an important meeting in the evening. He was very thin, and smiled a sinister smile. Which was strange because he was good. I tried every trick I had to send Northstar away from the safe. I told her there was a fire that needed her attention. But nothing worked. On some pretext, I excused myself. I went to the staff room. There I found a teacher who was more exciting. He was heading a football against the wall. This was Mr. Blake. He had an eye patch. But he was very muscular. On a pretext, I talked with him about Northstar. He sighed and said he loved her. He didn't like to talk about it. I told him to phone her up. So he did.

They talked for a while, and I knew this must mean

she was on the phone. So I went back to the bursar's office. The teacher had left on his important meeting, so I went to the safe. I only had seconds to open it. My training came in handy. I put my ear against the tumbler and rolled it in my fingers. When three clicks came up in a row, jackpot! I flung open the door.

And there was . . . nothing!

'Were you looking for this?' A quiet voice said from behind me.

I spun round like a cat spins.

It was Northstar. She was holding the Chalice. Which she had filled with deep red wine. 'You are too late,' she purred in a Soviet accent. 'You should have known who I really was from my code name. I am here to steal the Chalice. That is what your boss could not tell you.'

I kept calm. 'Why have you filled it with wine?' I asked.

'Because only wine will activate its special properties. Like with men.'

I frowned. I didn't want to demonstrate that I knew exactly what she meant in every detail. 'What special properties are those?'

She drank the wine in one long, deep gulp and flicked the last dregs away from her lips with a well practiced claw with red nail polish on it subtly. 'This!' she bellowed. She turned the Chalice around so I could see the bottom of it. It glowed like the heat of the sun.

I moved without thinking. I dived aside. And as I

did that someone dived in front of me. It was Blake. He was clutching his chest. 'My heart!' he bellowed. And then he died. He had a hole right through the centre of his body, from the beam from the Chalice. Blood flowed everywhere, apart from where it had been too hot, and the wound was cauterised.

Northstar dropped the Chalice and ran to him. 'Blake!' she bellowed.

That took me by surprise. I didn't know she could really love him. I ran and got the Chalice, and ran for the door. Gunfire blazed around me just before I got out. But then I was away.

The Chalice was mine. And now I would find out why 'they' had wanted to have it! And that would give me all the cash I needed!

To Be Continued!

That night, I waited until my parents were asleep, then went out to the kitchen. I had to find at least twelve pounds. I took one five pound note from Dad's wallet, which was sitting with his keys on the kitchen table. I took another and two pound notes from Mum's purse.

Or perhaps my window opened that night, and in flew the money.

Twenty-four

The next morning, I heard a row start, and it continued through the week. Mum said Dad had put it on the horses. Dad said she'd lost it. Dad stayed in every night, and the rows continued, and I stayed in my room, writing my stories. Mum finally made Dad go out. When he got back, everything was quiet.

———————

On the Tuesday afternoon, after having experienced the new dread and pleasure of listening to the Top 40 being revealed live on Radio 1 (Bowie was still at Number One, so I had no relief), I cycled into Calne on Aunt Dar's bike, and went to the shop that sold sofas and carpet, fridges and records. I found nine of the singles, but they didn't have 'Back on the Chain Gang'. I'd been planning on putting the remaining money into a charity tin. Now I'd have to keep it until I could find that last record.

Tomorrow was the first of Mrs. Coxwell's revision classes. I could give Angie back the other records, but say I wanted to keep that one a bit longer. If I had to admit that I'd broken it, well, it was just one, that could be explained. I would stop Waggoner from hurting her, and stay away from her after that, and try not to think about all the amazing possibilities raised by her note, and not ask her any questions about it that might make Waggoner act against her there and then.

How could I make sure Waggoner wouldn't break the new records overnight? I pretended to go to bed, waited until I was certain Mum and Dad were asleep, and then got up again. I tried to revise, but I couldn't. So I wrote stories through the night. I fell asleep around 5:00 a.m., and he moved straight for the package, but his movement jerked me awake, and I put my hands on it and stopped him.

'I can give her back the records,' I said, my voice as quiet as it could be. 'Then she'll have no more power over us.'

I sealed up the nine records in almost as tight a package as they'd arrived in, and clutched it to my chest, wary that Waggoner might try to grab them or trip me.

Being driven all the way to school was weird. I told Dad to drop me off, and walked up the long driveway. The buildings were silent. There was just that wind in the trees, the noise that had been under all the misery on the run. I looked back down the drive and considered being here and not feeling horror, not feeling the ache that still stretched down my abdomen and into my legs.

It was weirder still in our form room, to see everyone dressed not in uniform, but in what they would normally be dressed in. This was bad. I was in my brown cord slacks and green jumper. Everyone else wore jeans. Mum had asked if I wanted jeans, and I'd said no, because they were what kids like Drake wore.

You didn't have to go to Mrs. Coxwell's Maths revision class, so Blewly and Drake weren't there, and neither was Fiesta. Incredibly, now I think about it, neither was Rove. Angie smiled at me quickly and looked away again.

Waggoner took a step forward, but I held him back. He went to sit with Louise. She looked up at him with a smile. She seemed otherwise to be deliberately keeping herself apart. They started whispering to each other, sometimes looking at one kid or another, planning, judging.

Angie was wearing very clean jeans, and a huge black jumper that fell off one shoulder, revealing her T-shirt underneath. Her makeup looked like she was ready to go out dancing, great swirls of red and black around her eyes.

I sat down, and put the package under the desk. The lesson was a run- through, with examples, of everything we'd need to remember about Maths for the mocks next term. Mrs. Coxwell treated the class differently, maybe because we weren't in uniform, or because we were there voluntarily. 'Do you want five minutes' rest?' she asked. The class awkwardly said they did. Everyone stood up and walked about a bit. It was weird to have nothing definite to do. Mrs. Coxwell had sat down and got a flask out of her bag. She hadn't called for silence.

Louise left the room as fast as possible. Waggoner stayed, drawing endless patterns of circles in a rough book, so hard as to almost carve the pages. Angie was suddenly beside me. 'Did you like the records?' she said. Waggoner looked over at us, expectant.

I picked up the package and handed it to her. 'I . . . liked . . . some of them.'

'Which ones?'

'XTC.'

'I thought you'd say that.' She looked disappointed.

'I liked Kate Bush as well.'

'Did you?' Her whole face lit up.

I found that I was smiling too. Waggoner had gotten up and came over to stand behind me. I made myself stop. 'But the best one was–'

'Yeah?'

I thought about the consequences of what I was about to do, but I also knew how I was going to get out of them. The white line I had in my head at times like this was just for once crossed out. '"Back on the Chain Gang". That's why it's not in the package, I'd like to keep it for a bit–'

She'd grabbed me, got halfway to hugging me in a moment, and then stopped. She'd let her hands quickly slap my shoulders and then let go. That incredible feeling of a girl having touched me, not violently, as she had before, but so tenderly she couldn't actually complete the action. She'd leapt off the ground in delight. Now she took a couple of steps back, sweeping her hair away from her eyes.

I cringed. I nearly curled up with the weight of it. But as I looked around again, still nobody was watching. It was like the world had changed to allow us this.

'You read the Number Ones list?'

'Yeah.'

She looked suddenly vulnerable. 'So . . . what did you think?'

'Interesting,' I said.

She nearly grabbed me again, perhaps saw my startled reaction, and settled for touching my shirt. 'I knew!' she said. 'I'd knew you'd understand.'

Waggoner stepped between us, tried to shove me away. I pushed him back against the desk. He went sprawling between us. He glared up from where he landed.

On Tuesday, Spandau Ballet went to Number One. Whatever question Angie had asked this mirror of hers, the answer was—

'True.'

Twenty-five

May 1st was a Sunday. I pushed my bike along the A4, the long trudge up Cherhill Hill. It was raining. The wind buffeted my ears. I had to go somewhere, to get away from attempts to start revision that continuously failed.

I was thinking a lot about all that I'd said to Elaine on the school bus. A meaning had been slowly condensing out of a cloud of things that had happened, and I was just starting to grasp the idea that I had done, that I *could* do, something terribly wrong.

But Angie liked me anyway. She could like me despite knowing what I'd done. She could like Drake despite all he was. Maybe she knew about what he'd done to me too? I hated the idea that Drake and I could be held in the same mind, in the same breath.

She'd done something to make me stop behaving that way to Elaine. She'd sent me the Valentine's card for no other reason I could see, so that must have been it. It had worked, but I couldn't see how. Was there another set of impossibilities in the world, going off in another direction from Waggoner's, against them, even?

Waggoner rode effortlessly beside me on his Raleigh Chopper, the wind at his back, looking determined. Cars passed us at high speed. My foot still hurt from where the shard of record had pierced it, and that connected with the continuing ache from my groin. I pointed to my foot. 'You hurt me.'

'For your own good. To stop her hurting you. By next Halloween, it'll all be over, and you'll be healed.'

'Why by then?' He didn't reply. 'Do you still have to do all this other stuff, with the horse, and whatever's happened to Louise? Why did that happen with the blackboard?'

'Because the teachers keep saying nothing's ever changed, that people are people, and that's a lie. Things have changed and changed, and people have changed too, and we hate it when people forget that, forget what's underneath. We want to get back to before all the changes.'

'We?'

No answer. We were passing the entrance to the 'easy way' up to the downs, the track that led steeply, but more quickly, up the backs of the hills, right to Oldbury Castle. It looked wet and wild up there. 'Answer me! Or I'll . . . get rid of you!'

'How?'

'If I think hard enough–'

'No. It's bigger than you. It's very old, not like her music.'

We walked and cycled all the way to the Beckhampton roundabout, which people always said was made out of an old barrow, but no archaeology has been done on the bump in the middle. If you go one way from the roundabout, you end up at the prehistoric artificial mound of Silbury Hill, with West Kennet Long Barrow down that same road. If you go the other, you get to Avebury. We stood on the curb across from the Beckhampton roundabout, and I listened to the wind whipping the trees about with rain, and I wanted to be with people

I didn't know. I'd never had that feeling before.

Waggoner was making to go towards Silbury. I cycled off in the direction of Avebury. After a while, I looked back through the rain, and saw that he was following.

———————

Avebury is a village built inside an enormous prehistoric stone circle. Inside that circle, there are several smaller features made of standing stones, like the various interior chapels of a cathedral. There are earthen banks, still huge now, that, before thousands of years of erosion, must have been like the seating of a gigantic stadium.

There's a pub right in the middle of Avebury called The Red Lion. I cycled around the big turn that led into the village, let the bike run fast into its car park and stopped. I felt awkward at what I saw through the rain. This being May Day, there were travelers sitting on the steps of a bus decked out in anarchy symbols. They'd started a tiny campfire on the tarmac.

Back then, Stonehenge was surrounded by barbed wire with claxons and security lights. So on festival days, the travelers tried to get in there, had a clash with the police, and then ended up at Avebury instead. Today and on the winter solstice, it was just the committed ones, but on the summer solstice, there'd be a lot of tension and large numbers of people hanging about the town. In the 1980s, there were riots about paganism on my doorstep.

Waggoner wheeled his bike past the bus. 'May Day,' he said to me. 'If you were at school, this would be a fine day for a blood sacrifice.'

I'd never heard him talk quite like that before. It was like he was putting it on deliberately. 'Don't talk about sacrifices. That doesn't feel . . . real.'

'She's luring you into saying things like that, judging what's real and what's not. As if pop music is *real*!'

'What you just said, it's . . . an excuse! For you to do . . . what you do.'

'Look who's talking. For you, it's the excuse. For me, it's real.'

I started shouting. Suddenly. Out of nothing. 'What you saw up on the downs, what made you, I think it's all made up! You can't use it as a *reason!*'

He threw his bike down and walked right into me. 'You want your revenge and nothing else? You want it simple?'

'Yes! No! Yes!'

'See? Revenge is complicated. It's mixed up with everything, and something else got mixed up with it for you. Something else got mixed up with *you!* Don't you want to be healed?'

'I don't want it. I don't want it anymore.' I was crying now, hot tears bursting out of me in this car park. I didn't care who saw.

He put his mouth right to my ear. 'You want her. That's all this is about. I understand you're weak. That's okay. You get a whiff of a girl, and you throw away law and justice and logic and history. You do what they all do. Something nice comes along, something like her, something like one of her "hit singles", and you grab it, and you use it as a shield and you forget.'

I let my bike fall to the ground. I grabbed my head. I was sure the people in front of the bus had been looking at us and laughing for a long time now but I didn't care. 'I'm going to do it!' I shouted. 'I'm going to get rid of you! I started to push my fingers into my eyes, into my nose and ears, grabbing my head like a melon that I wanted to burst. I was denying this reality.

He came at me. He tried to punch me in the stomach, but I saw it coming, and his fist rebounded off my hip as I twisted out of the way. I grabbed his head, and we went round and round in a headlock. He lashed out at me with his foot and made me jump out of his way.

The travelers were clapping and laughing. One girl in a long frock looked shocked, and was getting to her feet. I could hear shouts from the tables outside the pub. He shoved me, sent me reeling back. I fell into the fire. I felt the urgent heat through my coat. I yelled, tried to roll, heaved myself up. He threw himself on top of me, his fists driving into me. He was shouting like an animal. We rolled off the other side of the fire, kept rolling, slammed into the tyre of the bus. The traveler girl was staring at us, so hurt and astonished, not knowing what to do. I wonder if she hadn't been included in the alteration to the world, or was wise enough to see past it. Did she see me fighting Waggoner, or was it just me there, a child slamming himself against the bus, having a punk fit?

I know now that on Beltane, or Walpurgis Night as the Scandinavians call it, May 1st, kids leap through bonfires. That it's part of what's said to be an ancient ritual of sacrifice. It's possible that even trying to break away like this, I was still locked into what was planned for me.

I rolled away from the bus and ran, and he was after me. We ran past buildings, through tourists, through locals, out onto the grass, with the sheep and the stones. 'Listen to me,' he was bellowing. 'I'm the one who's free! You get rid of me, and what's left? You get rid of me, and you'll be spat on all your life!'

I flew down into the trough between the earthen banks, tried to climb up the other side. He caught up with me, grabbed me off my feet, punched me hard in the face. I fell into the trough. It was wet down there, rain and mud. I was already soaked, and now there was blood coming from my mouth. I had a sheet of mud up the front of my clothes, and the back of my coat was burnt. He jumped on top of me, his knees on my chest. I punched him as hard as I could. He fell back, and I shoved my feet hard into the mud and was away. I ran the whole circle of the ditches around the village, with him just a few paces behind me. Then there was a path, hacked out of the grass, leading up to a gate, so I scrambled up on it, chalk and flint beneath my shoes again. I got through the gate, onto the road.

A car shot by my hip, the driver blaring his horn.

I ran on, my arms everywhere, mucky all over now, twigs and shit in my hair, yelling, blood from my mouth, the boy screaming out the bounds. There was a bring-and-buy sale set up outside the old barn. I ran to put the tables between me and Waggoner. He caught me; we hit the tables. What was on them went everywhere, and the lady behind them leapt up, crying out. He put his fingers into my throat, and held me there against the table that had collapsed onto the ground, my muddy hair slammed against the white cloth so hard it smeared. He held, but he could not choke. His fingers would not close. He started hitting my head against the table. Pounding and pounding. My hand found something. A hard corner of card in my palm. I swung it, intending to hit him with it, to get his hands away. I stopped because it felt too thin to hurt him. The square blocked the low sun.

I realised what I was looking at: 'Back on the Chain Gang' by the Pretenders, on sale for 50p.

Waggoner saw it at the same moment I did. He seemed surprised. He let go of me. He stumbled back. I got up. I held the record in front of me. 'Not her,' I said. 'The others . . . but not her.'

He finally nodded.

My shaking hand found a 50p piece in my pocket. I handed it to the woman, who was starting to yell that it would cost a lot more than fifty pence, what I'd just done. 'I'll take this,' I said, and ran.

Twenty-six

Monday was the start of the summer term, the term of the mock 'O' Levels and the bursary. Ripples of heat across the playing fields. The grass getting less wet and muddy. The shedding of coats, then pullovers, then not bringing them in at all.

The mocks and the bursary. Nobody talked about them. They were written under everything. They were geography and history. Kids had still been talking about Selway at the end of last term. By the start of this term, he was a different sort of history.

Groups of boys in the distance, on the grass, and then suddenly there'd be a flurry, and two of them would be out of the edge of the group, grabbing at each other. It'd go on for a few seconds and then stumble into nothing, or get worse.

The girls were silent, sitting together with books, forming sudden groups of solidarity with looks and comments and then breaking them again, every now and then one of them suddenly in tears, sometimes with a few to comfort her, sometimes left wandering into nothing on her own. Louise was in her element, joining a group for a few moments, talking determinedly, gesturing angrily, pointing at others in the distance, saying how so and so was a slut, how wrong they all were, how it was all getting worse and worse, how they needed old-fashioned values, which made one group of girls burst out laughing. The girls had given her a bit of leeway, but no more. They were all starting to shake their heads, to say she was mental now, to walk away when she approached. She seemed to secretly like that. I saw her smiling at it.

Building, building towards something.

It was hard to see where the changes to the school ended and where the feeling of pressure began. The completion of Waggoner's plans felt obvious and likely.

Drake and Blewly and Rove came after me all the time, telling me every chance they got what I was, who I loved, what I wanted to do. They got worse, by a tiny increment, every day. Waggoner stood beside me, not protecting me. It felt like they were cycling back towards once again cutting my cock off.

In the evenings, I would walk around the lounge, telling Mum about *The New Horse-Hoeing Husbandry*, Jethro Tull and the Seed Drill as she was doing the ironing, all the things in the stories in my history revision. She'd stop me when I sounded like I was making stuff up. There was revision with me all the time, a book beside me at the dinner table, a book beside me as I was curled up around one of my stories. I heard Mum and Dad talking about taking my stories away from me until the mock exams, but they never tried.

On that first day back, I had 'Back on the Chain Gang' in my bag, ready to give to Angie. I'd carefully made a little tear in one corner, like I remembered from her copy. She looked over to me at first break, across the grounds. It felt again like everyone was watching. Even more so, with the gravity bearing down.

She came over to me anyway. 'Hi,' she said.

I could feel Drake looking. Waggoner beside me turned aside. I put the record into her hands. 'Thanks.'

She frowned at it, then at me. 'This is a different one. Like all the others were. What did you do?'

I couldn't answer.

'Did you break them or summat?'

I nodded.

'Never mind. Same singles. So. Do you want to talk about my note? Do you want to know what was "true"?'

I managed another nod.

'Great. Mum says you have to come over and visit, so that's on the first weekend of half-term, okay?'

I think I must have nodded once again.

———————

Kids had started playing British Bulldog. Someone had said it had been banned once. You formed two teams, facing each other across a stretch of playing field. You wrapped your arms round yourself, or put your hands in your pockets, and then each team ran at the other, and tried to knock them over. Anyone who got to the other side stayed in for the next round. Sometimes you ended up with loads of kids from one side all running at one kid on the other.

So many fights in those weeks. Not just Surtees and Fiesta and Cath and me getting wrestled and punched. Even the football kids, with each other. Surtees and I grabbed each other, we slammed each other, we tumbled with each other awkwardly, and me and Cath, punches that bounced off each other's fists, stances and expressions that made the other kids laugh, and sometimes leap in. Fiesta just ran away, shouting carefully that no, he wasn't going to fight us. The teachers had stopped coming outside at break times.

On the Tuesday, I listened very closely to what kids in the playground were saying about the charts. I had no idea what would be Number One. Whatever it was would affect Angie's life again, like 'True' must have, and I was going over to her house that weekend, and would get some answers. The Number One turned out to be 'Candy Girl' by New Edition. I thought for a moment that DJ Gary Davies had made a mistake.

That evening, the phone rang, and Mum answered it. 'It's Angie Boden, for you,' she said. She sounded as scared as I was.

'You see what it's like?' Angie said as soon as I picked up the phone. 'Where did that come from?' That's what you'll be thinking to yourself. It's like a bloody roller coaster ride!'

'What?'

'The charts!' She wouldn't say anything more about that. She wanted to sort out the details of me coming over.

Angie's parents lived on the married quarters at RAF Lyneham. On the way over there, that Saturday, the first day of the half-term break, Dad proudly told me that Mr. Boden was a squadron leader with Transport Command, and he'd now done some business with him. So what did I think of Angie?

It took me such a long time to find the right words. 'Good,' I said.

Dad told Mrs. Boden he'd be back to pick me up at six. Angie's bedroom door had a wipeboard on it, with COME IN written on it in big red letters. I knocked.

The curtains of Angie's room were half drawn. There was a bed that I looked at, and then didn't. She also had a sink. It took me a moment to realise Waggoner wasn't beside me. I looked back to the doorway. He was standing in the hall, trying not to look angry. Around the doorway were Blu-tacked sheets of paper. I went to look. I recognised song lyrics. Waggoner glowered for a moment more, then walked away.

'Close the door,' said Angie. She was sitting at her dressing table, wearing jeans and a baggy black jumper. 'You can sit on the bed.'

I did. It gave slightly beneath me. I put my feet firmly on the floor. On the ceiling was a piece of bright blue glossy paper, like a window to a blue sky. On it were *Smash Hits!* stickers. There was Bananarama in the middle, a ring of twelve others around them: Spandau Ballet, Wham!, Eurythmics, Duran Duran, Heaven 17, Tracey Ullman, JoBoxers, Yazoo, The Belle Stars, Paul Young, New Order, UB40. The paper looked ragged, like the stickers had been replaced many times.

'Bananarama?' I asked. I couldn't help it. This list was so utterly divorced from anything Drake's lot could like. If Drake ever lay on this bed, he'd spend the next hour taking the piss out of Angie. Probably. Hopefully.

'Bananarama.' She stood up, and for one horrifying moment I thought she was going to sit beside me, but instead she went to the window. 'Somehow, they seem to *know*. When they were on *Swap Shop*, I wanted to call them up and ask. Keren, the young one. Sarah, a bit serious. Siobhan, it's her group; she's in charge. They're missing someone. There should really be a secret fourth member, or one we only hear about later. If I called up, Siobhan would understand what I was saying. She'd want to keep me on the phone, take down my number so we could talk more later. But she couldn't do that, because they wouldn't have let me give out my phone number on live TV. So in the end I didn't call.' She was different here, still serious, but calm. 'Mum and Dad think I'm a bit mental. They keep sending me to see doctors and keeping me off stuff at school. But I'm all right; I have my stuff. It's that school that's wrong.'

'Yeah,' I said. Then I found I was nodding violently. 'Yeah.'

'We're meant to think the school building is historic and epic and everything, but it just looks shoddy to me. The future's better than the past. Or what's the point?' She went and sat on the stool in front of the mirror on her dressing table, and beckoned me over. 'Here's where I ask the questions.' So this was the mirror from the list. It was indeed warped and cracked. A jagged line ran right across its centre. The mirror had spaces for pictures in the frame all around the glass, and in those gaps, Angie had slotted images of loads of pop stars, more than one in each gap, crowding in. 'That's everyone I could find a sticker of who's ever had a Number One. I think me putting them in there from years back was why it started answering me the way it does. I started doing it because it worked in fairy tales, and then I realised that, three times in a row, the questions were answered by the title of the next number one single. The question I asked this week, if you're wondering, was about who most hated me. Turns out it's who I thought it was, the "Candy Girl". Louise. You know, she gives out all that stuff from cooking? She says she hates everything about me now. I don't talk about serious things, apparently. I'm being "distracted". I think she's gone weird like a lot of things have gone weird. But you want to know about the Number One before that. You want to know what's "True"?'

I nodded again.

'I asked the mirror what you were.' I must have looked astonished, because she burst out laughing. 'So I've decided you're weird like I'm weird, and not weird like school and Louise have got weird.' I wanted to say that she'd made a very dangerous assumption. I could think of another way I might be 'true', that my story was true, not my friendship, that she should listen if I told her about Waggoner and what had made him, what Drake had done to me. The mirror had a limited vocabulary. To really answer her question would have required such a prog rock title that it could never be a Number One single. 'Pop music,' she said, 'can change everything, take you away, tell you what people are really like, let you see the future. It can take you from being one thing and make you into another.' I had only ever danced the once in public. It had felt like that. 'You can draw on it when you need to, using the words. I say them under my breath or write them down hidden on me to try and make things happen, only the most current stuff, what I think'll be in the charts next week. I think it lets me see a bit ahead, because I'm trying to live in the future. That's how I got you out of the clearing. I used "Should I Stay or Should I Go?" I was so afraid of you then.'

I remembered when I'd seen her wiping off the Biro on her collar, ink on her fingers. I found my voice. 'Did you . . . did you send me a . . . card?'

She sighed. 'I had to do something to make you stop hurting Elaine.'

I closed my eyes. I couldn't describe the ache I was feeling. I don't think I registered feeling guilt, as such, until I was somewhere in my thirties, but I hope what I felt then was that.

'I told you you were "too shy" to make you calm down. But I was angry and the lyric ended up having the power of a Number One single behind it, so I think it might have done a lot more.'

I found that my mouth was open. Could that really be the reason I hadn't come until she'd rubbed the lyric out on her collar? I was sure I believed in science, but there was also Waggoner, so why couldn't there also be this?

'I'm sorry about it being a Valentine's card. I don't want to get your hopes up, okay? I wanted Mum to see that I'd sent one to someone who wasn't Anthony, and you're quite safe.'

I heard Waggoner, outside the door, make a muffled noise. Angie reacted to it with a frown. I didn't want to hear anything more about the valentine now. 'You said there was something weird about me–'

'Sometimes I can half see it. Do you know what it is?' I felt able to shake my head. 'You weren't Anthony's friend, and then you were, and now you're not again, but it wasn't like how that normally works. It was all too fast, which is why I had a go at you about it, sorry. Do you know why that happened?'

Again, I shook my head.

'You seemed to change just before the school started changing.' She ran a hand back through her hair. 'God, if you're going to think I'm mad, now's the time!'

'What do you think's happening to the school?'

'It's changing into what someone else wants it to be. It was squares, and now it's becoming circles. It was old already, but with us in it, it could be young, but now it's getting older, and it wants us to be old. I think Lang being . . . killed – it feels so weird to say that – and Selway killing himself, *two* of Anthony's friends, that's got to have something to do with it too.'

A terrible suspicion had formed in me. I pointed to the crack in the mirror. 'Your note said that crack happened on Halloween night, after the school disco?'

'Well, I came back here to find it cracked, so yeah, I guess.'

I heard another noise from Waggoner, a growl. I closed my eyes, and Drake was inside the darkness. She couldn't have been told what had happened to me. Not if the crack in the mirror was what she thought was important about that night. Could I tell her? I opened my eyes again. 'Why are you going out with . . . him?'

Angie paused, surprised by the sudden change of tack, a little disappointed in her safe boy. 'I told you,' she said. 'Because of when he was born. The singles I sent you were a random casting of stuff from my records box. When I want to know what someone is like, I think hard about them, close my eyes, and pick their Top Ten at random.'

I thought for a moment about 'Goody Two Shoes' and 'Hungry Like the Wolf' and the lyrics of 'Cat People' and the words I couldn't hear in 'Suspended in Gaffa' I had felt that all the records were about me, but I sort of thought that was what pop music was about for everyone, that that was why I'd always denied myself it, because I didn't deserve it.

'But,' she said, 'if I want to go deeper, I check out the birth chart.' She went to her bed, reached under it and produced a copy of a book called *Top Twenty*, compiled by Tony Jasper. She flicked to a page of tables for the year 1968. 'His birthday is April 27th.' I didn't want to know, but she put the book in my hands. 'Look.'

I did. 'Wonderful World' by Louis Armstrong was at Number One.

'So?'

'So it took me a while to work this out, but the highest placing of a record is how much it influences you. The whole chart contributes, though. Sometimes it's not about the title, but the lyrics, or the feeling of the music. When I started to think I should have a boyfriend, I found out the birthdays of everyone in our class, and I listened to all the records in the birth chart for each one.' I wondered what the chart for August 17th, my birthday, was like. But then my gaze caught something else on the page, at number nineteen in the week Drake was born, a song by Jacky, 'White Horses'. Was Drake destined to be part of what Waggoner was doing as much as I was? How much of this was already written? I hated the thought of it being already written.

I closed the book. 'So that's why you're with him? Because of Louis Armstrong?'

'And "Lady Madonna", and "If I Were A Carpenter" and "Can't Keep My Eyes Off You". And I thought *maybe* you'd understand.'

I took a deep breath. I was on the edge of telling her. 'Do you . . . know what he's like?'

'I know he's too rough. Because he's been terribly hurt. Have you seen what's on his back?'

'Where the horse kicked him?'

'It's a burn in the shape of an iron. I think his dad did it to him.'

'But he says his dad–'

'I've seen his dad hit him. Anthony tried to say it was a joke, but his dad meant it. Being hurt makes people bad. They can get past it, though.'

Outside, Waggoner slammed his body into the wall, and the

impact made my wound hurt and my teeth grind.

'You were his mate for a bit; you must see there's lots more to him. He's also been hurt by what happened to his friends, but he'd never show it.'

A great roar forced its way up out of my throat. 'He hurt *me*!'

'I know he's done some awful things to you–'

'He cut me.' I gestured towards it.

'What?' She didn't understand what I meant. 'Show me.'

I stared at her. I could hear Waggoner thumping on the door, like he was beating his head against it.

She realised I wasn't going to do anything. 'Then we need to heal you too. Someone needs to. Someone needs to heal everybody. Before it's too late. I know I can heal him–'

I went quickly to the door. I didn't want her to see I was on the verge of tears. I pushed my way past Waggoner. I was out of the house and walking towards home before he caught up. I found a phone box and called for Dad to pick me up. I said Angie was ill. Angie didn't follow.

———————

The next time I went to the library, I checked out my birth chart: 'I Pretend' by Des O'Connor, 'Here Comes The Judge' by Pigmeat Markham, and at Number One, The Crazy World of Arthur Brown, with 'Fire'.

Twenty-seven

The next Number One was The Police with 'Every Breath You Take'. I had started scanning the charts furiously. I was angry at Angie and comforted by the thought of her. I wrote a lot of stories about her.

On the night before we were due to go back after the half-term break, Dad came into my room and said that he and my mother wanted to have a word with me. His tone was half serious and half mocking, as always. I sat down at the kitchen table with them, Waggoner beside me. 'Now,' Dad said, 'we know you've kept saying that you want a skateboard–'

I really hadn't. They looked insanely dangerous.

'You creased that page in the catalogue,' said Mum. 'I had to flatten it out again.'

The Great Universal Catalogue. The skateboard page was opposite . . . Oh. The women coming out of the ocean, pulling off their snorkels. I quickly nodded.

'So call it an incentive scheme,' said Dad. 'The mock exams start on July 11th. It's your birthday in August. If you win the bursary, we'll get you that skateboard and a helmet and set of pads to go with it.'

It was an awkward smile, but at least I managed one.

———

On the Monday, I got through Woodwork, quietly planing away at something while Waggoner expertly chiseled the lines and swirls of the long, decorated pole he'd been working on. From the first day back, the weight had immediately dropped back onto everyone's shoulders. The grass was dry, and the mud was dirt, and the tarmac sang with heat and the stone of the building shone. I kept my gaze away from Angie and kept walking, faster and faster, to try to stop Drake and Blewly and Rove from catching up with me. It didn't work. They caught me every time.

On the Wednesday, in Physics, Mr. Brandswick was going over all the important formulae, for the pressure of a gas, for energy and time. He said there were only a dozen things to remember, and if we went over and over them before we went into the mocks, we'd be fine.

On the Thursday, Mr. Kent in Art slapped a newspaper in front of everyone and told them to rip it up and make papier-mâché. This was meaningless now, because this was nothing to do with the mocks. Mr. Kent said he was trying to keep his mind off the general election. That had closed John Bentley and a lot of other schools that day, because they had to be polling stations, but not ours. There was ripping. Then throwing of lumps of paper. Then spitting, then bowls of water getting knocked over. Mr. Kent went from place to place, faster and faster, trying to stop it.

On the Friday, it happened. That morning, Dad had looked at his newspaper and nodded, happy. 'A landslide,' he said to Mum. 'That'll show them.'

I was walking with Waggoner in a straight line across the playing field at afternoon break. It was hot. We were walking towards a particular point at the corner of the tennis courts, out in the heat haze. Also walking for that point at that second were Blewly and Rove and Drake.

They broke around us, and circled us, and we all ended up on the one spot. The other three started knocking into each other, hands in their pockets, shouldering each other like they were playing British Bulldog, not letting us out.

Waggoner stuck his hands obstinately into his pockets and played back. He followed the rules. He ran at them. He shouldered into Blewly, sent him stumbling, ran after him, did so again. Blewly fell, rolled, got up. He tried to shoulder Waggoner back, but Waggoner was skipping sideways, dodging. Suddenly, he leapt forwards again, and Blewly fell again, winded. He made a high noise and crawled to his feet. He leapt at Waggoner, teeth bared, fists flying. He kicked up at Waggoner's stomach, but Waggoner dodged again and pushed Blewly, his fists still randomly swinging, into Drake. A fist caught Drake in the mouth. Drake yelled, 'Fuck,' and went apeshit, pummeling. Blewly fell into Rove, blood spurting from his mouth. Rove yelled as it went all over his shirt. He lashed out, and Blewly fell.

Kids were running in from everywhere now. I saw Louise walking purposefully towards us. Drake and Rove started to kick Blewly, seriously kick him. The first kid to arrive was Grayson from my bus. He started kicking at Blewly too. Kids rushed past me, faster and faster now, like I was in an avalanche. Surtees ran right into the middle of the knot that was getting bigger and bigger, and used his momentum to send his shoe right into the side of Blewly's face. 'See?' he was screaming. 'See?'

I'd never seen a fight get so big. It was drawing in everyone, kids coming out of the forest, from behind the school buildings, running and yelling. Girls as well as boys. A girl fought her way to the front and leapt for Blewly's face, trying to stamp down on his nose. I looked up to see Louise standing back, nodding, laughing. She seemed to be anticipating something. Now there were scuffles breaking out on the edges of the group. Surtees was lashing out at two kids beside him as they tried to pull him away. Some kids were treating this as British Bulldog, their hands in their pockets, arriving at a run, throwing themselves at the pile of bodies.

Hands were starting to grab at me. I ducked under and wrestled away. Girls in the middle now, rolling about too, and then more boys, rolling on top of them. Blewly was somewhere under there. Kids reached down to grab or punch or scratch. They all wanted something of his. Everyone suddenly grabbing everyone else, round where Blewly was, the whole thing starting to swing, to totter, to spin on its axis.

Blewly was rising up out of it. The anger. The anger. He was bloody about the face, and the red went right down into his skin. His mouth was open and bellowing, and on each arm he was heaving a mass of kids who were trying to hold him down and wrestle him back onto the ground. The kicks and spittle flew at him harder and harder, and the nails of girls ripped into his cheeks. But still he rose up and up. He wanted to take them all with him.

Now there were screams coming from the mass, and the sun was being blotted out by dark clouds overhead, that were rushing in, in impossible time. Somewhere I could hear the voice of Angie, shouting, shouting, trying to put some words into the way of this. I heard another female voice, a mocking one, questioning her, saying she was mad, getting her own words in the way.

A gap bloomed in the middle of the crowd. Blewly looked up. He was suddenly free, but terribly afraid. He'd never looked so alone.

There was the loudest noise I ever heard. Overhead and round me. The light flashed all around at once. Our shadows lay in every direction in that moment, including all the impossible ones.

But my eyes were open.

Waggoner had kicked up into Blewly's throat.

Blewly's head had flown back. Frozen in time. In the light that made everything white. It had flown back at too great an angle. He could not live with his head there.

The flash let go for a moment. Then came again. A gap of darkness in between.

Now Blewly's head had left his shoulders completely. Blood jetting. The look on his face, of something so unfairly taken from him.

I fell with it in front of me as the sound shot past and then back. I looked into his face. He blinked. What he was never quite left his face. It just went further and further and further away as the echoes died, and so it stayed there, just the last bit of it, trapped in that spot.

His body exploded into ashes, and the head with it. Concussion and light. White. Too loud to hear.

Everyone was falling with me. The rain started to blaze down around us. Now there was a patch of shining water, no, black glass, and in a moment the glass would be lost under the water that was pooling around us, cooling our bodies, the steam rising off us, that made us stand and stumble and slide and slip and start to yell and cry out and justify. Louise was sitting, her palms on the ground, her eyes closed, heaving in deep breaths through her nose. Angie was sobbing, a hand over her mouth, staring.

Teachers were amongst us now. Mrs. Parkin. The lightning! The lightning!

There was Blewly's head, one lump amongst all the other lumps of him, fried and lying beside the fused black glass of the grass, his body distributed and his self never given back, locked to that spot forever.

Twenty-eight

The school was shut down. So many hospitalisations. So few actual injuries from the lightning. Cuts and bruises and compression injuries. I was unscathed, of course. Nobody else had seen his head go flying. Everyone blamed the lightning.

Mr. Clare the bursar had called the parents and asked them to pick up their children. We hadn't seen Mr. Rove. I had lain there shaking, staring up at the school buildings. It was all seriously different now. There was a green shine across everything, like an echo of the lightning. The car park had police cars and fire engines in it.

Dad was silent in the car going home. He hadn't approached Mr. Clare, just waved from by the gate, and I'd finally seen him and scuttled over without telling anyone I'd gone. 'Not your fault, then?' he said finally, ironically. He pulled the car off the road at the Quemerford post office. 'I think you could do with an ice cream,' he said.

So I had a Lolly Gobble Choc Bomb. That had a core of a chocolate bar, which wasn't like any other chocolate, under a layer of ice cream, under a layer of chocolate with hundreds and thousands on the top.

The way Blewly's head had bounced. I'd seen what was inside the bottom of someone's neck. It hadn't looked real. The smell of burnt meat. What I wanted had summoned that. It was too big. It was too big.

I let Mum dry me off. She thundered the towel over my hair.

———————

I tried in that week to start revising again, but the information bounced off me. I felt my thoughts go to what was too big and then fall away again, and that feeling of falling away ended up as an ache in my stomach, and I thought of other things. Would I get my stuff back from Blewly's family now? Could I ask? How could I ask? I shouldn't be thinking that. What would Angie be thinking? Her boy had lost another close friend. She must be planning something, trying to work out something. Dad would come in more often than he had before, and look at where I was curled up, reading or writing.

I listened to Radio One. I hoped David Bowie's new hit, 'China Girl', would get to Number One, because while its meanings would be complicated for Angie, its tone was comforting. She hadn't tried to talk to me since I'd run from her. She must have been wondering if I would tell other kids about how weird she was. She must have kept waiting for some sign of that. I liked having power over her, but ever since Elaine, that had bad feelings mixed up with it. I didn't like to think of Angie feeling as desperate as I was. I wanted not to hate her for her wanting to heal Drake. I felt a complicated sort of anger and care about her at the same time. Both feelings made me hard. I kept saying to myself that she wanted to heal me too. What kept getting in the way was that it didn't feel like there was room for her to do both. I ground my teeth at the thought of her and Drake, at the thought of Drake.

Waggoner just kept looking at me and sighing. He shook his

head whenever I thought about her. 'You have to keep going,' he said.

For the first time, I tried to write just the truth, but I couldn't get to it. I finished the story, and realised that some of it wasn't true. For the first time, I threw away that version, burnt it on the stove late at night, washed the scraps away down the sink. The second time I wrote it, I knew, even as I wrote, that some of the stuff that was true sounded like I'd made it up, that it wouldn't be accepted. So I did the same with that. The third time I stuck to what was true, except that I didn't include anything impossible. I wrote about what it was like on the playing field. How there were no teachers. How anything could happen. How anything had been happening for a long time now. I mentioned the lightning because there would be the patch of black glass on the ground, there would be evidence. Even if there wasn't, that sounded like it could happen. I wrote about how things really were between me and Drake and Rove and Blewly, though I didn't say why, but I gave them, and Louise, false names. I didn't mention Angie.

On Monday, June 20th, we went back to school. There was no special assembly about Blewly. There was no connection made between the murder, the suicide and the act of God. I hated that term. An act of God working for what I'd wanted, what I still wanted, despite everything, every time I thought of Drake. Getting off the bus felt like walking uphill. The green shine persisted, blaring against the green of summer. There was no corridor now that remained straight; they all curved so you couldn't see what was at the end. The sound dropped off between classrooms. Winds moved through the building in ways that shouldn't have worked. I saw Louise standing at the junctions of corridors, her dress flapping, enjoying the new breeze. In the days to follow, I saw her, every other break time, walking far out on the boundaries of the playing fields. I went to look sometimes, and found pieces of glass or coins. She was changing the school in many small ways: swirls of mud she'd made that had been baked hard; quick little three-stroke carvings on fence posts; paintings too high to reach that now hung at awkward angles.

There had been a meeting of parents and teachers. Dad came home from it saying, 'Well, that was a waste of time.' We thought the mock exams might have been called off. But they weren't. Nobody said anything about that. The bursary depended on the results of the mocks.

How was Drake feeling? He and Rove walked together, and it was just the two of them now, but they were still attacking randomly, still the same.

At first break on that first day back, everyone went over to see if the patch of black glass was there, if there was still any blood. The area around the patch was surrounded by four sticks, and police tape and some blue plastic sheeting covered the ground. It stayed that way until the end of the school year. I looked at that plastic sheet and I saw a patch of a different sky, waiting to be born.

———————

On June 28th, Rod Stewart went to Number One with 'Baby Jane'. Optimism, he asserts, is his best defence. The mock exams would start on Monday, July 11th.

- July 11th: History.
- July 12th: R.E.
- July 13th: Physics.
- July 14th: Maths.
- July 15th: Biology.
- July 18th: English Lit and Chemistry.
- July 19th: Geography.
- July 20th: English Language.
- July 21st: French.

I woke up on that first morning, and I hadn't revised. Not recently. Not enough. We went into the dining hall, which was filled with evenly spaced desks, and echoed like we'd never heard it echo. Waggoner hadn't come with me. What could he do in an exam? I was astonished to be here. I wanted to wake up now and find that I'd revised after all.

On the way in, Angie smiled at me. She was on her way to try for her bursary. I thought about it for a moment and smiled back. There was also that line in the Number One saying the narrator 'knew secrets about' the subject of the song, but the tone was conciliatory. She would know by now that I hadn't told anyone about her. It was like she was half of something that could save me. She was facing the same thing I was now. I wanted to talk to her again, to be in her room again, to hear secrets again, but I didn't know how to start getting there. She would have to ask me.

This History paper was mostly concerned with the Corn Laws. I started to write at high speed. I wrote what I thought had really happened. I had to ask for more paper. I did it a bit too loudly. I brought my last page to a screeching halt when Mr. Coxwell said to stop now, and I stabbed the ballpoint into the inkwell that still sat meaninglessly in the top corner of the desk and I looked at the rest of the kids in the room with a tension grimace at having to stop.

In the RE exam, the questions were historical ones, like Saul's conversion on the road to Damascus. I wrote about taking an eye for an eye.

In Physics, I wrote about how two big things rubbing against each other could produce lightning between them.

I did the paper in Maths, but got lost, my equations all over the page.

For Biology, I wrote about smoking will kill you.

In English Lit, I wrote what, judging by the mark I was given, was regarded as a reasonable piece about Hamlet's reluctance to act, but which at the time I thought was me taking the piss.

Chemistry was about turning grass into glass and nothing more.

Just before I went in to the Geography exam, I heard that Paul Young had got to Number One with 'Wherever I Lay my Hat, That's my Home'. I'd been distantly hoping for that: all those lines about the narrator's worthlessness as a boyfriend.

Geography was about how everything around us is just what glaciers did to what was underneath them.

For English Language, I was invited to write an essay. I continued the series of stories I'd been writing about Angie's adventures with the power of pop music. I called her Rosamund.

For French, I just made up all sorts of words.

On the way home from school after the last of the mock exams, Dad asked me if I wanted another ice cream. I told him I didn't.

That night, I put my headphones on and spun the dial on the radiogram to AM, to hear strange, distant channels in French, and something that sounded like Russian and then the surging, pounding beat that was meant to be something to do with radar tracking submarines, and nuclear missiles waiting to be fired. I was calm, listening to its regular electronic pounding. Although it was what lay under everything, it sounded like science fiction. I knew now that the end of the world was coming not from the future, but the past.

Twenty-nine

The next day was the last day of term. It was going to be one of those days when there were no real lessons. Mum and Dad hadn't asked how I'd done in the mocks. They'd looked at me questioningly, frightened, every evening when I'd got home. At first, I'd made myself look hopeful. Then I realised I was getting their hopes up, and so I started to look sullen. Mr. Land, in what was supposed to be History, handed out a list to each desk instead. 'A treasure hunt,' he said. 'A bag of sweets for the winner.' The list said:

- An item of sporting equipment.
- Something Irish.
- Something of great value.
- A book with a bird in the title.
- Something good to eat.
- As many individual things as possible that can be held in one hand.
- Something with a Latin motto on it, and its translation.
- Something of scientific interest.
- A picture of a famous person whom your teacher will recognise.
- An apple for the teacher.

Mr. Land told the class that we had one hour to find all

these things. He stopped me as the others ran out. 'How are things working out,' he asked, 'since we had that chat? I haven't noticed you giving anyone a jolly good thump.'

'No, sir,' I said.

Waggoner and I walked the curving corridors of the school, and went in all the rooms, and nowhere was locked. We heard distant music from a record player in the staff room. It wasn't like Angie's music. It felt like everyone was hiding, on this day that was halfway between two things. Waggoner and I walked through all the old and important things that had been left here and made into a school: the paintings of people we didn't know; the architecture that was for the use of someone else. I didn't feel the need to do anything about the list of objects. I didn't want to do anything. Something was coming, and I wanted it to, to make things end. I was empty, released from worry, because that ending was coming. I felt I deserved it, in a good way and in a bad way.

We encountered Louise, standing on a balcony, looking down into the hall. She had in her hand a painting she'd made in Art. I looked over Waggoner's shoulder as he inspected it. It was an intricate map of the school and its surroundings: two lines where every one should be, swirls with suns and ripples. The school buildings were rounded. There were tiny stars in a lot of the rooms. One of them, up in the roof, had a big red circle in it that radiated out, swirls from it flowing into all the other rooms. The doors looked like breathing, sucking orifices, or the layers of geological diagrams. The big tree outside was a spike which generated, like a map of currents, circles and spirals of its own, all around. The lines of the horse were still visible on the football pitch, its eye marked with bright red. There was a black spot closer to the school, and that, like the eye, had swirls that swept right off the edge of the map, including the bright yellow of lightning. Among the green of the forest, there was a circle with a lot of influence too, a ring that I had a terrible feeling was meant to be my clearing, Drake's clearing, the clearing where I had had something cut from me. Furthest away of all, on the edge of the paper, there was a green circle, surrounded by three upon three lines of current, which stretched all the way back to the school. 'What's that?' I said, putting my finger on it and feeling that the paper had been pushed up in a little dome where I touched it.

Louise ignored me. She spoke only to Waggoner, saw only Waggoner. He looked at me and relented. 'The barrow,' he said. 'Chippenham hospital.' Before I could ask anything else, Louise said there was chalk in every room now, that the territory nearly matched the map. The two of them talked like old friends, like people in a TV show who knew a lot more than they were telling. She took a packet of coloured chalks from her pocket. She was going to do some more drawing, ready for next year.

In the next hour as we walked the halls, we saw blooms of colour on some walls, lines leading along others, swoops of it across the black and white tiles in the hall. It would all be washed away by the cleaners, or perhaps some of it would remain, in corners, neglected rooms, but it would have been there, Waggoner noted to me, and that was what was important. You couldn't get rid of this stuff.

Ahead of us now were Drake and Rove. They were making hushed, hurried plans. Drake was saying to Rove that he should be somewhere and do something, okay? Rove was nodding. I walked up to them, looking at them like I was looking at everything else.

'What are you looking at?' said Rove.

'You,' I said.

He tried to grab me, but Drake smacked him on the shoulder. 'Fucking don't waste time. What are you fucking doing here, fucknor Waggoner?'

'Doing the treasure hunt.' I'd decided in that moment that I was. It was something to do. I took the list of items from my pocket and held it up to him. I wondered about the wounds on his back. I was glad he had them. They were nothing compared to my wound, I decided.

'"Doing the treasure hunt!" You fucker. You know what the future's gonna be like for you? You're gonna be so beaten up. People will just see you and say, "Who's that cunt?" and look at your face and want to fucking fuck you over.'

How did Angie see anything inside that that was like a person? 'It's all going to change.' I didn't know how he couldn't see it. Waggoner nodded solemnly beside me.

'You wish. It's always gonna be the same for you. Out in the real world, it's just like it is here. It doesn't get any better.' He shouldered past me on his way somewhere, with Rove after him.

We wandered until we got to the bursar's office. I didn't see anything much that would do for the treasure hunt. I found the door of the office was unlocked, and went inside. The room was empty. It smelt of Mr. Clare, like citrus that had gone off. There was a corkboard with keys hanging on it. I looked around. The list asked me to find something of great value. I opened a little cabinet. There it was. The Trilateral Cup. I put my hands on it.

'Don't do that,' said Waggoner.

'Why not?'

He was silent for a moment. 'All right,' he said. 'You take it for the treasure hunt, then you bring it right back.'

I lifted the Cup out of its cabinet. It looked cheap. The surface was flecked, like the gold was falling off. It smelt musty. I took it out of the office and closed the doors behind me. Now I had this, I didn't know if I wanted to fulfill the rest of the list after all. Either this would be enough or it wouldn't.

We wandered up the small stairs, into the roof. I found the room where Selway had died. There was nothing to be seen now, but like Waggoner had said, it felt like something had remained. There was sunlight across a clean wooden floor instead of a dusty one.

I saw Netty and Rove standing in one of the corridors off the art room, near the old chimney. It was an old fireplace, to be exact, in the middle of a corridor, perhaps from some room for servants, now demolished. There was a wind that came through that chimney, only in winter, sucking the warmth out of the heights of the building. The grate was always full of dead cigarettes, ancient and modern, never cleaned up. That's what kids came here for, if they were inside the building and so couldn't get to the woods. They also left messages for each other, stuff that needed to be hidden, placed on a ledge up inside the chimney, because the fag ends said that no cleaner or teacher ever stopped here. Of course, I kept myself away from it. Those with particular messages would always write in code, and those mysterious phrases would be repeated, whispered amongst kids who had no idea what they meant. Everyone would reach up the chimney from time to time to see what they could find, except me.

Rove was looking at his feet; Netty had her arms folded. It looked like they were on guard together, but didn't want to talk to each other.

They were so busy looking away from each other they didn't see us. We tiptoed past them. We were now in the servants' quarters: dust and dust sheets and paint pots and ladders that were themselves dusty and jobs never completed. There was new chalk here, lines and swirls that might never be seen.

I heard her voice crying out. It was coming from one of the rooms ahead. I tiptoed forwards and looked inside.

There were Drake and Angie. She had the buttons down the front of her dress undone, and her underwear was carefully hung over a chair. Her eyes were closed. He had his trousers and pants around his ankles. His pants were blue. His hand was up her dress. Hers was holding his cock. His cock was perfect, smooth, large.

Behind them on the blackboard was drawn a huge golden knot of chalk.

'It's good they're doing it with that there,' said Waggoner, pointing to the chalk. 'Louise put that there for us. Next she'll add it to her map. We're now in charge of everything that happens in this building. Angie's not playing by our rules, so we're going to use this to get her out of the way.' He must have noticed my reaction. 'Not like that. You stopped us from hurting her. So we're not going to. What happens here is really your fault. It's good you're seeing this, anyway. Let it make you angry. It'll make it easier for you to keep going.'

'Go on,' Drake was saying. 'Let me. Just a poke.'

'No,' said Angie. She was taking quick breaths. 'Sorry. Sorry.'

'No,' he said, 'come on. Go on.'

'No,' said Angie. She kept saying no.

'Yes,' he was saying, gently, insistently, a voice I'd never heard from him before. There was a note of pleading in it.

Waggoner put a hand on my shoulder. 'She wants you as a

friend. A pet. Not a man. You can hate her. It'd be okay.'

I looked at the Cup, still gripped hard in my hands.

Angie took a deep breath, made a decision. 'Okay. Just for a second. Just, gently–'

There was a bit more awkward fumbling, him prying her open. She kept saying, 'Not yet, not yet.' He kept saying it was okay. Then he was inside her. She cried out. I saw the movement. I saw him start to move faster. She opened her eyes. She saw me. She started to shout.

I wrenched Waggoner's hand from my shoulder. I ran into the room. I grabbed her hand. Drake fell with a yell of rage and surprise, his trousers tripping him. I heaved Angie out of the door.

She resisted for a moment, but then she ran with me. We ran down corridors. We ran for the door of the school. We burst through that door. We sprinted across the gravel. The tremendous shining green was dragging at us, unwilling to let us go, but we were off into the forest, soil flinging from our heels. We crashed through bushes and low shrubs and banks of ferns and dead nettles. I had the Cup in one hand, Angie's hand in the other. We ran past the path that led to my clearing. We fought the current with our feet. We ran further into the woods than any kid had ever been. Ahead was a row of trees. We ran at them. We burst through. The forest expanded around us. There was a burst of birds from a thicket. The trees shot up and towered. The light slammed into being ordinary, glorious, summer treelight. The air got thick and still. There was silence from behind us.

Angie was in a summer dress, and she was dignified again and standing calmly with me. We were in a different forest, the New Forest, maybe three weeks later. Our families were on holiday together. It was so quiet.

Thirty

The summer holidays lasted from July 23rd to September 4th, but I can't pin down what happened during that time to specific dates. There was nothing beyond the forest that summer, no distant road with the noise of traffic. The trees were tall and deciduous. There was a warm carpet of soil. Life moved in every thicket. Natural sounds came from the distance. The light spread through the branches. There was no horizon.

In that forest I walked with Angie Boden. She was sad, to start with, and I was awkward. Mr. Boden got his insurance from Dad's business now. My mum would say how outrageous Mrs. Boden was, but in a good way. I'd never heard Mum talk that way about anyone before. The caravans and awnings and deckchairs of the two families were parked in the Caravan Club's official New Forest site. We were allowed to wander off together. They seemed to like us doing that. Mr. and Mrs. Boden didn't know what had happened to Angie on the last day of school. I heard them talking with my parents, and they all seemed, though the exam results hadn't come out yet, doubtful about the bursary, relieved to say that to each other.

'You should have him arrested,' I said. She shook her head and scowled at me. We walked in silence for a lot of the time, especially in the first few days. Waggoner stayed away from us. We saw him sometimes through the trees. I'd kept the Cup in my bag. I hadn't told anyone about it.

There was a fireplace, on its own, standing in the middle of nowhere. We saw it in the distance and walked to it. A sign said this was the Portuguese Fireplace, the last remaining bit of a barracks built by Portuguese soldiers staying here during the First World War. I decided the First World War was more complicated than I thought it had been. The fireplace was very well built. It hadn't crumbled when everything else had. Angie put a hand on it and started to cry. In the past few days, KC and the Sunshine Band had gone to Number One with 'Give It Up'. 'I thought it was going to be that song,' she said, 'when I asked the question.'

'What question?'

She looked at me like I was stupid and like she hated feeling that about me and wished I was someone better. I reached into my bag, took out the Cup, and held it out to her. She took it. Her tears fell into it. She whispered all her lyrics over it, and let herself cry into it. It took into itself all we felt and couldn't say. From then on, she never suggested taking it back to school, even though she knew that was where it belonged. When we headed back to the campsite, I let her take it with her.

Angie and I started to talk more, about stupid stuff. I was allowed to talk about stupid stuff with her. I made many mistakes and said many alarming things, but it was all okay. Lying in a field, we watched families of deer. With a few days left, we went to visit the Rufus Stone. It's a metal pillar marking the spot where William Rufus, the son of William the Conqueror, is said to have been killed in a hunting accident. I've heard some people say that both his name and the day he died are auspicious, a sign that he was a sacrifice. Amazingly, he made sure his killer, Sir Walter Tyrell, was pardoned. I tried hard to understand that. I thought I could see the point of it, out of the corner of my eye. It hurt to think about. The sun had started to go down a little earlier, and the shadows of the trees were longer.

Angie put her hand on the Rufus Stone. 'What *did* he do to you?' she asked.

I walked around and around. It was too big to deal with. Finally, I had to come back to her. 'I can't show you.'

'You can.'

I had in my mind an image of her pouring water from the Cup onto me. Of me becoming healed and hard in her hands. But the hardness ruined the purity of the healing, stopped me from putting her on a pedestal, where I needed her to be. I pushed my top teeth into my bottom lip. My whole face went rigid.

'There's nobody around. We'd hear them from miles off.'

I couldn't stop myself now. I tried not to look like I was trying to be sexy. I turned away and unbuttoned the top of my cords, unzipped them. I took them off, and folded them. I took my grey Y-Fronts off and put them on the ground beside the trousers. Then I turned to her.

She was standing with her hands by her sides. I thought in that moment that she was being so brave. She looked at me. She wasn't horrified. She was so sorry for me. I didn't want her to be sorry for me. But I did. 'Okay,' she said. I put my clothes back on.

It was dark by the time we headed home. I tried to backtrack, to talk about the Number One single. Instead, she asked me a lot of questions about what had been done to me. I told her. She was very mature. She accepted all I said. She grabbed my hand quickly before we parted and then let go, marching off towards her caravan.

Back in the caravan, I reached under my bed and found my bag. All that holiday I'd been writing, many stories. A lot of them featured Angie and her music. They contained much that was true, much that was impossible. They included, for the first time, a lot about the people on the downs, events based on Waggoner's experiences up there, and about how much of that had come down to the school. By the light of the moon, I made the stories into a bundle, and tied them with a red ribbon from Mum's sewing bag. I felt different. I felt freed and forgiven. I had to thank Angie and celebrate the purity of us.

———————

The next day, we were due to leave. I went straight over to Angie, and if she was going to be embarrassed about what I'd shown her, she didn't have time to show it, because I started talking straight away about my stories, and how many I'd written, and that she was in these ones. She took the bundle from me and said she'd read them and tell me what she thought. She had the Cup, and now she had my stories too. I had given her all I could.

———————

I feel like I should buy her flowers and fine wine and dresses. Not

*that I could. I want to write poetry and songs for her. We're the
Queen and the Knight, who loves her romantically and purely. I lay
my sword at her feet. The two of us have always been together, the
ones in all the songs. Like in 'Wrapped Around Your Finger', that
Police song about magicians.*

*All the tracks we hear on the radio sound the same: they're
about us being together in the summer, right now. Level 42's 'The
Sun Goes Down', The Lotus Eaters' 'The First Picture of You', The
Style Council's 'Long Hot Summer'. Roman Holiday and Tom
Robinson. Freez and Club House. There's only right now. This one
wonderful summer. I hope I always stay here. We could come and
live here. I'm still here.*

———————

Angie went into her mum's and dad's caravan, and came out
carrying a tiny pink lozenge-shaped box. She gave it to me.
'The *box* is the present,' she said. 'Don't open it.'

'Okay,' I said.

We went for a last walk; we touched hands again. I walked
off into the forest, and couldn't see Waggoner between the
trees. I decided I was now keeping him inside the box Angie
had given me. I came to my own edge of the forest. There was
the corner where my house was. I walked down the hill to it.
My own impossible forest moved back into the tapestry of the
world behind me and time started again.

Thirty-one

August 17th was my birthday. Which, it had said on TV, was in the middle of the week when the BBC was going to start showing some old *Doctor Who*. Mum and Dad kept on looking worried about the bursary, wondering whether or not they should phone the school. The letter seemed to be taking a long time to arrive. I still hadn't seen Waggoner.

The letter arrived on Friday, August 12th. I saw the school crest on the envelope. Mum dropped it onto the telephone table like it was hot. She called Dad at work, and he said to wait to open it until he got home. That night, he sat down at the table, managed an ironic flourish with the knife with which he was going to eat his cod in butter sauce and opened the letter.

I made myself be there. It was only justice that I was. I kept my face still. Dad read the letter. Then he looked at Mum. He smiled. 'Oh, well, not this year.'

I asked to see my marks, but Dad said the letter didn't include them, and folded it into his jacket pocket. So I had to wait until that night to take it out and see them.

———————

So I wasn't expecting anything for my birthday on Wednesday. I spent the weekend being relieved about that. I was talking to Angie on the phone, and writing stories. Dad said I should see if she would call me, rather than calling her all the time and running up our phone bill, but halfway through saying it, his voice changed from angry to quieter, and he went into the kitchen.

I was waiting to hear what she thought of the stories I'd given her. She hadn't mentioned them on the phone. Did her voice sound different now? Had something crept over my horizon without me noticing it?

———————

On Wednesday, Mum and Dad said happy birthday and gave me a card. Another arrived in the post from Angie. It had The Creatures drawn on the front of it; that was Siouxsie from Siouxsie and the Banshees and someone else from her band, with 'Right Now', which was the name of their single, in big, spidery letters above them. *Is the time for your birthday,* followed inside. Followed by Angie's huge signature and a kiss.

That was all right. Wasn't it? There was nothing extra to it. Did she understand what my stories had meant?

When Dad arrived home that teatime, he called me into the kitchen, and Mum and Dad were standing there, and on the table was a pile of presents. 'Well,' said Dad, 'aren't you going to open them?' I did. It was the skateboard, helmet and pads. They felt up-to-date in my hands. They smelt of now. They looked like they worked. They were the most expensive things I'd ever touched. I told Mum and Dad this was the best present ever.

I decided not to call Angie. I'd let her call me. She didn't call. I couldn't call her. Now I'd stopped, I couldn't start again.

Had seeing my wound got worse for her the more she thought about it?

That Tuesday I made myself listen to the last chart before we went back to school. I wanted to feel the connection of what a new Number One single would mean to her. 'Red Red Wine' by UB40 was the new Number One. It sounded very sad.

Thirty-two

A Story Andrew Waggoner Never Heard

By Waggoner

Starring:

Louise Callidge as the Imposter.

And Angie Boden as Herself.

Angie sat on the edge of her bed, reading the stories Andrew had given her. Andrew had been wounded by her boyfriend. She was so sorry for him, but now it had gotten complicated. She had followed what she'd thought the mirror was trying to tell her, but it was like she had walked into a trap. The stories told her terrible things about what had happened to the boy's friends, but how could any of it be true? Who was this other Andrew that was in the stories? Was that just fantasy? She was starting to feel that she, of all people, didn't have time for fantasy now. Something horribly real was calling to her, something she was trying not to think about. It wasn't definite yet, but it was probably real. She wondered desperately how fantasy could deal with it.

She hadn't won the bursary— she had come second to Netty—but that seemed to have pleased her mum and dad enough. It had convinced them she was reasonably normal. Except now there would be this.

Her mum called that there was someone here to see her. It was one of Angie's friends. Angie put the stories carefully away in her hiding place and went down to see. 'Louise,' she said.

'Hi,' said Louise, as if nothing had happened.

They had coffee in Angie's room. Louise didn't make much effort to resurrect a dead friendship, as Angie thought she might be here to do. She talked in her usual brittle way about what she'd been up to that summer, but at least she didn't dig in with sharp questions. Angie hadn't talked to Netty or Jenn about Andrew, or about Anthony. Nobody else knew what had happened. Now she felt a terrible urge to talk to Louise about both of them, but she stopped herself.

Louise knew that Angie kept all that she didn't want her mum to see under her bed. When Angie went out of the room to get some more coffee, Louise reached under and found the stories, still bound in a ribbon that had been tied and untied many times. It wasn't what she had been looking for, but after a moment Louise realised that it would do. She put the stories in her bag, and when Angie came back in, she talked to her emptily for another hour and then said it was time she was going. She paused at the door. 'Don't think we're going to be friends again,' she said. 'You're getting everything so wrong, you could send everybody in the wrong direction. So you're about to find out what distraction really means.'

Angie cried out and damn near threw Louise down the stairs, until her mum, screaming in social horror, stopped her.

―――――――

On Monday, everyone went back to school. Sometime during that day, Louise made her way to the old chimney near the art room. She took the bundle of stories from her bag, shoved her arm up the chimney, and found a place for the papers to lodge. She slammed them home and fixed them to the lining.

―――――――

At that exact moment, Angie, sitting in a toilet cubicle, cried out and put a hand to her mouth and looked at what she'd bought that morning. All the hope she'd had of this place and time not being her life forever, of escaping into the future, had gone.

Thirty-three

When we went back to school in September, there were visibly fewer kids there. A couple of the more well-off families had had enough. The buildings were full of circles, of green, of the coloured chalk spirals, so much so they hurt to look at. The light and the smell were different. Kids kept falling on those stairs, like there was slippery moss under their feet. The weirdness wasn't growing. It was waiting. There was still no sign of Waggoner. I had expected him to be here. This was where his mission was; the buildings were shaped and ready for him. I didn't know how I felt about that any more. If I didn't see Waggoner again, if he never completed his task . . . No, I still couldn't bring myself to think that would be okay.

It was announced at the first assembly that Fiesta and Netty had won the bursaries. Mr. Coxwell, making the announcement, called Fiesta by his real name. Fiesta shrugged as everyone looked at him. That shrug had got him through a lot.

I kept looking across at Angie. I wanted her to know that I was looking to her, to see if she was okay when Drake was about, to support her. I also desperately wanted to know if she and Drake were still together. I didn't see them together, but that was how things had always been. She didn't look back at me. I went home sitting in the back of the minibus, staring out at the trees again, wondering if the horrors of my cock could really have taken that long to sink in.

That Wednesday, Elaine walked right up to me and said, 'You loved her, romantically and purely!' She ran away before I could ask what she was talking about.

'By the power of Bananarama!' yelled Franklin's sister later that day, flinging her hands into the air like a magician.

As I went round the playground with my lot, everybody was laughing. The boys had heard from the girls. 'Are you a king?' Surtees said. 'Have you snogged her? Have you shagged her in your corpse?' He meant my copse, but I couldn't reply to correct him.

By the Thursday, everywhere I walked, kids pointed and laughed.

I couldn't look at Angie without anger warping the shape of my vision. She'd *told*! She marched proudly along, her expression calm.

The bus every day became joke after joke. Elaine led it. She deserved to. I was silent. I looked at the telephone at home. I didn't want to look at the telephone. I couldn't write stories. I would never write stories again. It felt like I'd betrayed myself, that something vital had fallen out of me into those pages and would never be mine again. I found it hard to pick up a pen, then had to pick up a pen in school, many times a day, so I did. No music. Except Dad would put Radio 1 on in the car now, and so I heard 'Red Red Wine' all the time.

I lost the desire to come, because that had got wrapped up with her too. It must be diseased. It would fall off me now. I would be nothing. That would be better.

At one point, the phone rang, and I picked it up. It was her voice, but she sounded so angry. She started accusing *me* of all the things *she* was doing to *me*. I put the phone down and left it off the hook until Mum saw it like that and put it back. Angie didn't call again.

One day at first break, I saw Angie talking with Drake. She was being serious with him. He had a faltering look on his face. He actually had an expression.

That same break, he suddenly came for me. He hit my nose so hard that I fell back onto the gravel. I lurched, groggy, blood going everywhere. I could hear cheering and clapping, kids talking about kings and queens and copses. 'You thought you could get your hands on her. Show her your cock, did you? Could she even see what's left? Fucking cunt.' He kicked me hard in the ribs. I curled up around it.

Rove spat on my blazer, and they walked away.

Late that night, after Mum and Dad had gone to sleep, I found the box Angie had given me. I had considered throwing it away, but that would have meant seeing it again. I took the box into the lounge, where the television was on, me waiting for *The Outer Limits*. In one of the drafts of one of my later stories I say I opened the box.

Inside was something small, brown, curled up in cotton wool. It looked like an ancient leaf. There was no dirt on it. It seemed perfect. Washed. Dried off. Tended to. It was the part of me that had been cut off.

'I knew something had been hurt,' she said. 'Because of "Do You Really Want to Hurt Me". "Let me love and steal." That was my first clue. So I knew I had to look after it. I found it in the clearing just before Anthony arrived.'

———————

I did open the box. There was nothing inside.

Waggoner wandered back into the room. 'Shall I just get on with it, then?' he said.

There was nothing left to decide now. 'It's just going to take until Halloween, isn't yet?'

'Yes. Not long to wait.'

'And all the stuff you want to happen as well–?'

'That's when *everything* goes back to how it should be.'

———————

All I heard from other kids at school now was about Angie and me that summer, especially the impossible stuff: the magic on the downs and in pop music. It felt as if, like Fiesta's nickname, soon the teachers would start to refer to it too. 'Now,' Mr. Brandswick would say, puffing on his cigarette, 'we're going to do wave motion, just like Waggoner says Angie held back the waves by singing "The Tide is High" so she and Waggoner here could talk a bit longer on the dock.'

Our form teacher Mrs. Mills once told us, when she'd got really angry at Lang for sniggering, about how history was a natural progression towards collective ownership and the abolition of capital. That when two big ideas hit each other head on, the result was called a synthesis, a new idea, and that this process of things hitting each other was how the momentum of the universe towards those ends came about. Lang sniggering stood in the way of that process.

One Wednesday morning in winter, when all the other buses had been late because of the frost, and for the first five minutes it had been just me and her in the form room, I had put my hand up, and she had said to put it down and asked what I wanted.

'What did you mean? About the two forces?'

She came over and sat down beside me, which was scary. 'It's a bit old for you. I was talking about natural economic forces.'

'Natural economic forces that make history?'

'You could say that.'

'Would people be able to see them?'

'You see it all the time. Like when the Harris' factory closed down.'

'I mean, would they see the actual forces?'

'No. Okay, it's like–'

'So it's not seeing one thing over another? Like a montage?' I'd seen a documentary about *Top of the Pops* a few years ago. Cameramen had explained how what one camera saw could be mixed in with another. 'Like there's a competition for what's the most true. When one thesis, one picture, is stronger than the other, that's what ends up being true.'

She had laughed. 'I think that's something you saw on *Doctor Who*. That's not the way the real world works.'

I was reminded of that conversation a lot as kids kept asserting to me that these two different and opposed sets of impossible things I'd talked about in my stories–the magic of the downs and the magic of pop music–were impossible and yet also had happened to me. 'Is that what happened with the horse on the football pitch?' said Rove. 'Did Bananarama want Mr. Rushden's eyeball? Or was it the things on the downs?'

The questions got stranger. They began to ask about Lang's accidents and death in hospital, about Selway killing himself, about the lightning and the glass in the ground, always in that tone of voice, like it was all a joke, but the answers were important to them too. Waggoner walked beside me again now. So I wasn't saying no to everything they said. I started to say yes.

———————

Mr. Rove had decided to sit at the side of the stage as Mr. Coxwell led every assembly now. He nodded along, but kept nodding after Mr. Coxwell had finished talking.

That dry cold of early autumn. The fogs in the morning. The blankness. The trees changing colour, just starting to shed leaves. Everything was going to come around again, but there would come a point where things would stop. I desperately wanted that. Wanting that was all I had left. The school had become permanently rounded and green and hard and old. There was going to be an end, and in that end, I would be healed.

One Tuesday in late September, I saw Angie and her friends listening to the radio at lunchtime. I saw the look of horror on Angie's face. I was glad she was horrified. Culture Club were at Number One again, for the first time since last Halloween. I was sure they would stay there until the next Halloween disco. The song was about how everything comes around again. It was the sound of something coming to get her, and I was glad. The title of the track was 'Karma Chameleon'.

Thirty-four

Waggoner wanted me to call Angie, to ask her for the Cup back. I hadn't thought about her still having it, but I supposed she did. I didn't know why she would keep it, if our time together had meant so little, but I wouldn't call her.

I forced myself to buy a copy of *Smash Hits!* and read the lyrics to 'Karma Chameleon'. They would have filled Angie with fear about the future. Good.

In Art that week, Mr. Kent told Louise that her wild new paintings were the best he'd seen. The kids who were copying her, and that was almost all of them now, had now forgotten they were doing that; it was just what you did in Astand up for myselfrt. Her most recent paintings were of faces that might be monsters. Some of them had similarities to kids and teachers. The chalk she'd used to draw lines and swirls along the walls had mostly vanished now, but you could feel where it had been. The rooms retained the colour of the chalk in the colour of their light. Everything contributed to the curved and lofty feeling. Out on the playing fields, I walked past the heavy grass roller, and was surprised to look through the handle and catch a line between it, the sun through a cleft in the hill, the white boundary of the football pitch, the school. There were all sorts of alignments like that. It was like we were in a huge clock, and everything was slowly swinging into place. You could see new carvings in desks, chalk lines round the boundaries of every blackboard, which reappeared within the day if I rubbed out just an inch with my finger, groupings of paint pots and erasers that swarmed precisely in store cupboards, even where nobody would see, that changed every time I looked. I kept looking. I wanted to know. I knew when it would all be complete, but I didn't know exactly what. The hardened sand in the long jump pit had been made into ripples. They spilled over the square enclosure, and made it round. They were like banks and ditches seen from the air. It all scared me, but in a good way. Rove and Drake himself remained to be punished, and I wanted that, coldly, solidly, right at the heart of who I was now. I wanted to hurt Angie for what she had done to me. But I would not. I would settle for the justice of the revenge I had originally called for.

On Friday, the last day of September, Drake made me eat soil while Rove held my nose. 'This is for Angie,' Drake kept saying, over and over. It was like he was trying to force something into himself as he forced it into me. I thought he might literally be doing it for her, that she'd asked him to do it. I had shown her my cock. This was what I'd gotten for trusting someone with that sight, for imagining the world could care about my wound.

Waggoner went behind Drake and Rove, reached into Drake's bag, took something and closed the bag again before Drake saw.

I thought of the school and grounds being swept away, with everyone inside them, replaced by the sunny hills and lovely rolling roundness and protection from the wind, protection from everything. I thought of sitting above it all and looking down at the world and judging everyone.

———————

The next day, Dad came into my bedroom, and saw that I was sitting against the bed, not doing anything, waiting for Monday. Waggoner sat beside me.

'You've been quiet,' he said. 'Aren't you writing stories?'

I said no. He led me into the lounge, saying he wanted to show me something. It was a faded cardboard folder, and in it were ten typed sheets of very thin, almost transparent paper, browned by age and cigarette smoke. I held the first one by its top corner, and I could see right through it. 'This is my book. The book I never finished,' he said.

The title at the top of that first page was *The Journal of Frank Waggoner: The War in the East.*

'*I was sent with my mates on a troop ship which spent six weeks at sea, going to Burma to fight the filthy Japs,*' it began. I read the rest of it while he sat there. It told, in almost no detail, at a huge distance, about how Dad had caught malaria the moment he landed. Then he was sent into the jungle, and spent every night awake, fearing for the lives of himself and his friends. He'd never heard the sounds of a jungle before. Things came in and out of the trees, into the camp, all the time. He tried to ignore them when he wasn't on guard, but then one of them turned out to be a Japanese soldier, naked and covered in grease, with a dagger in his teeth, and Dad stopped making a dividing line in his thoughts between when he was on guard and when he wasn't. The man got shot by Dad's bunk, and he had to spend the next morning wiping it all down. He was a private, and he was promoted four times, and demoted four times. When he didn't respond to a sergeant who wanted him to dig a ditch, the sergeant yelled about the number of stripes he had, and Dad replied that altogether, he'd had more. The funny stories were put in order, in separate paragraphs, like Dad had wanted to type them out first and quickly. Then there was a gap, and a paragraph about a Japanese charge. The angry words came thundering onto the page, without commas. How crazy and high on drugs were the Japs to do this, waving swords? Dad saw a friend of his get a sword blade through his throat. Then the officer with the sword was cut down, and they fell over together, and Dad's friend's head fell off. On leave, Dad and his friends drank a lot, and one of his friends broke a rifle out of base stores and somehow got shot. There was a tirade of abuse about the stinking coolies who followed them around, trying to sell them things. Dad played a joke on one, setting his shirt on fire. There was another gap, and then a paragraph about the joy of getting home on the ship, and the anger at the docks when nobody seemed to know if they were finished or not, if they could get onto the trains and be sent home.

'I didn't want to go home,' Dad said, when he saw where I'd got to. 'Stupid. I hung around the station. In the end, I just decided not to be so daft. I didn't write that there.'

After he'd got home, Dad signed up with the Prudential insurance company, and started selling policies door-to-door. 'Utopia, we expected. Just relief and peace. Only something else always comes along.' One day, the Lord of the Manor, a Lansdowne, a Petty-Fitzmaurice, rode past him on this turning where our house was. Dad was in his first car. His Lordship yelled for Dad to doff his cap. Dad stopped his car, ran up to him so fast the horse shied away and yelled back he'd do no such thing. His Lordship was so afraid he galloped off. 'The look on his face. The world was changing.'

'Why are you showing me this now?' I said.

'You asked me. About how I got the sword.'

'That's not in here.'

'Oh. Isn't it?' He looked fearful for a moment. He looked through the pages. 'I must never have written that bit down.' I waited for him to tell me. He didn't. 'But,' he finally continued, 'you're old enough for it now. It's not like in the war comics. Some of this stuff is a bit much. Your mum didn't want to finish it. She's had problems of her own. When I came home, she wasn't eating anything, not until her dad sat her down at the table and forced her to, and then she spent some time in . . . hospital. We weren't properly together for a long while.' He took a breath, and I could hear a wheeze. 'So, I was a soldier. What are you going to be?'

I shook my head. I didn't think I was going to be anything now.

Thirty-five

Waggoner started saying hello to Mr. Rove whenever he was seen in the corridors. Waggoner made a point of walking after him and calling him sir. Fiesta and Cath and Surtees from my lot were still delighted by what had happened in my stories, and were making up their own variations, greeting me with snickering new developments every time they saw me. I'd been crowned King of Pop in a magical land that was going to appear at the school.

———————

One Sunday in early October, Waggoner was invited over to Mr. Rove's house to earn some pocket money. Dad drove us over, and came in with us. Steven Rove had an outraged look on his face when we walked in. He looked pale, like he hadn't been getting much sleep. I expected him to whisper something nasty to me, but he kept silent as his dad made tea. Waggoner was to go into the forest with Rove, to cut logs. They were each given a small axe. Mr. Rove said distractedly that they were both nearly adults now, and would have to learn about paying their way, and it was good for Steven to have a friend over. He didn't get enough visitors, and he'd been affected by all that had happened last year. Mr. Rove said that right in front of Rove.

Rove picked up his axe like he'd never carried anything heavy before. He and Waggoner walked off into the afternoon mist with their tools slung over their shoulders. I walked beside them, anticipating and fearful.

'I don't know what you're here for, you fuckwit cunt,' said Rove, as soon as we were out of range of the house. 'I tried to say you couldn't come.'

Waggoner laughed. Rove lurched forwards to attack him. Waggoner bobbed back at him, making Rove shrink back. Waggoner chuckled and slapped Rove on the shoulder. 'You're all right,' he said. Which made Rove look at him like he was wondering who this was.

They got to a place in the woods where a few trees had been roughly cut down, and they looked at the fallen limbs, which had started to become covered with ivy. Waggoner hacked at one of the lower branches for a while, until it fell onto the floor, which gave Rove the inspiration to do that too, though much more slowly. Waggoner started talking to Rove about the revenge of Bruce Lee against the factory owner in *The Big Boss*, how he put his fingers right through the man's ribcage, how all the people Bruce Lee had beaten in fights got revenge on him by hiring an assassin to kill him using a secret ninja punch. Rove laughed, said he bet he hadn't expected that. Then he looked like he'd regretted joining in. His face went red. He came out with a string of swear words, threw the axe down near Waggoner and then picked it up again.

They sat down after having hacked a few more branches off. Waggoner used the edge of the axe to carve and plane the fallen wood, until he had made odd-looking scoops with blunt, angular ends. Then he got his fags out. 'Now I've started doing this with you, I 'spect you'll get sent out here fucking loads.'

'Fucking hope not. And you should fucking shut the fuck up.'

Waggoner handed him his cigarette. 'Why do you think your dad's making you do this now?'

'He keeps saying he won't be able to fucking "provide" for me. That I have to "stand up for myself." I do that, I tell him I fucking do. Nobody fucking messes with me. I'm going to program computers. When those Dragons get here, I'm going to put games on them.'

I watched and I waited, an enormous tension, but then we all went back to Mr. Rove's, and he made us some more tea, and Dad picked us up and we went home. I kept looking at Waggoner on the way back, and finally he took my hand: *he* hadn't changed sides on me.

———

Angie was off school a lot, and when she was there, I didn't get to see her much. I imagined her getting so much more respect than she'd had in the past by revealing all the details of my stories. I imagined her smiling as her audience laughed at me. I heard Rove complaining loudly to Drake that, on two more Sundays, his dad had made him go out and chop wood. He looked over in the direction of me and Waggoner. He looked like he was about to blame us, but then he stopped. That would have meant saying that Waggoner had been to his house.

That Tuesday, Culture Club stayed at Number One. Which meant they would indeed still be there next Monday, the night of the Halloween disco.

———

On the night of Sunday, October 30th, the tension finally caught up with me. I fell asleep in the dark of the lounge, and Mum and Dad turned the sound down low on the television and left me there.

———————

That evening, Rove was once more sent out by his dad to chop wood. He had a torch with him. He made his way through the woods, his breath billowing in front of him, his hands huge in his gloves, his breath wet on his woolen scarf. He'd raised his axe tiredly into the air over the tree when he heard a noise. He put it down again, and looked round.

There stood Waggoner. He started laughing, and called Rove a twat. 'Look at your face,' he said. Waggoner asked him if he wanted to come and have a smoke. Rove didn't question the fact that Waggoner didn't seem to have come over in the way he had before. Waggoner walked off, and Rove left the axe where it was and followed. They walked for quite a way, and Rove started to complain. They were getting way into the woods. Why were they coming all the way out here for a smoke?

'Why do you think?'

''Cos they might see the smoke from the house?'

'There you go.' They were heading towards the clearing. It didn't look that much different from the rest of the forest, in the absolute dark, with just the one torch picking out the trees. There were bright stones and coins on the path, and all around it, knots of string hanging from the branches. 'Here's where it all unwound from,' said Waggoner, stepping into the middle of the clearing. 'Do you recognise it?'

'No,' said Rove.

'You and Lang, Selway, Blewly and Drake came here three hundred and sixty-four days ago.'

'When's that? What're you going on about?'

'You've sort of forgotten, haven't you? Now here you are with me. Like nothing happened. Did you think I'd forgive you?'

Rove stopped in his tracks. He started shouting, flatly denying he'd been there.

Waggoner grabbed him and pushed him up against the tree. Rove was astonished he could do that. Waggoner pulled open the buttons on Rove's coat and started tugging at his belt. 'No,' Rove said, like this was just irritating, trying to slap his hands away, 'get off.' Waggoner shoved his elbow up into Rove's throat, and used the moment to throw Rove's coat open, and get his belt off and pop the top button on his jeans. He pulled apart the fly. Rove grabbed his head, and really struggled. Waggoner slammed his head against the tree. He pulled down his trousers. Rove was wearing huge white underpants. Waggoner could see the lump of him. He hauled his pants down, and had to slam him back again. Once, twice. Rove was shouting at the top of his voice.

Waggoner took Drake's knife from his pocket.

Rove began to scream, huge bursts of breath, a cloud in the torchlight.

'Right,' said Waggoner. He grabbed Rove's genitals in his hand, and pulled them out in front of him. 'Let's get rid of these.' The knife flashed silver in the light. It struck at the root of Rove's genitals. Blood burst from them. Rove screamed. Waggoner had to hack again, then again, and finally they fell, and he grabbed them, and ripped off the last trailing skin and tendons and held them up in the air like a trophy so Rove could see and threw them away.

Blood flooded out of Rove onto his legs and onto the ground. He spasmed and slumped in Waggoner's arms. He was breathing in gasps. Waggoner let him fall, and applied the serrated edge of the blade to the wound. He cut expertly upwards, the look on his face that of a skilled ritual butcher. He made a crossed incision, and flicked it, and pulled. A length of purple blue black bulged out. Waggoner tugged at it, and slowly it emerged, stinking, shining like ancient treasure. He heaved Rove up, and propped him standing against the tree, his stiffening muscles helping.

I think Rove was still conscious as Waggoner started winding his intestines out of the clearing, out of the wood. He looked down at the floor of the clearing, and saw his whole cock and balls lying there at the centre of the glittering, prepared circle.

Waggoner took the innards along with him, playing them out like rope, sometimes having to haul, sometimes just easing them with his hands. He made his way out into the playing fields, under the blank, dark sky. He crossed the eye of the horse and the black glass in the ground. He genuflected towards the room in the school where Selway had perished, and towards the big tree, and in the direction of Chippenham hospital. He made for the horizon. He hitched the intestinal cord around a fence post with a mark on it. Then he turned, and walked the perimeter of the school, around the swimming pool, past the gateway at the end of the drive, around the lights of the house, round again to the forests at the back.

As he went, they were watching him. They had massed to look down. The man with the two sticks was there with them, in the gap between times that was close to opening once again.

Waggoner came back to the clearing. Rove was still standing there, shaking. The impossible length of his stomach contents was stretched out from where Waggoner had left, and now it had returned, at a sharp angle to him. He had been caught so precisely. He was like someone pinned to a clock. Waggoner wound the chord tight around the same tree he was standing against. Rove had his eyes open. He was on the edge of death. He tried to say something. Just noises.

Waggoner slashed the knife down again. The offal was cut. Blood flew into the world. It fell in the rough circles of bulges and troughs. It landed on the lines. It made the horizon. The glow remained for a moment around the perimeter, then was gone into the soil, ready. Rove fell. His blood spilled hugely into every crevice and vanished in moments into the ground, filling the circle. Waggoner produced the spades he had cut out of the wood when he was last here. He dug a deep grave and lowered Rove into it, and buried his remains until no sign of him was left. The offal and the blood were already being consumed by the animals of the forest. It would fade with the dawn, become a line of knowledge, not flesh, around the boundary, connecting it to distant points, placing it on the map. Waggoner squatted, and used sticks to build a small round house in the centre of the clearing. He stood up from his work, and felt the landscape finally ready around him. It was beautiful, full of promise like Christmas night.

Thirty-six

The next day was Monday, October 31st. Halloween. The year had turned. I'd got there. Dad dropped us off, and I stood beside Waggoner on the steps of the town hall, and I sat beside him in the minibus. The stories of fantasy those on the minibus told about me to hurt me now seemed the most glorious thing.

I hadn't thought about a costume until Mum had asked that morning. We were due to come home between the school day and the disco, and she'd asked what I'd like her to put together. Maybe something out of *Doctor Who*? I said I'd just go as myself.

After what had happened to Rove, I expected there to be phone calls saying not to come into school, or police cars waiting there, but there was nothing unusual about the day. Waggoner spent the woodwork lesson finishing off his elaborate pointed pole. Mr. Sedge's smile was faltering today. Drake was finally on his own. He was clearly not with the football kids. He stood at a separate bench during Woodwork. He grinned at other kids every now and then. He looked kind of desperate.

I waited to hear something from Mr. Rove. There was no sign of him.

I saw Angie at first break. She turned away without looking at me.

By the middle of the day, I'd started wondering why nobody

was saying anything about Rove. Mr. Rove would surely have realised he hadn't come home last night. At second break, Waggoner knocked on the door of Mr. Rove's office. There was no answer, so we went in. Mr. Rove was sitting at his desk. He was absolutely still. He could have been dead. Then he looked at Waggoner.

'I was just wondering, sir,' said Waggoner, 'why my friend Steven isn't here today.'

'Is he not here?'

'No, sir.'

'Because I thought he . . . might be.'

'No, sir, he's definitely not here.'

Mr. Rove tried to get up from his desk and then didn't. 'I was . . . working on my speech . . . for the start of term assembly . . .'

'That was weeks ago, sir.'

'I'm writing about the original intention of the school. It is a microcosm of the world. We prepare you for your place in it. History has set out a path for you. We lead you along it.'

'But that's not true, is it, sir? Did you know Harris' closed down, sir?'

'Can't be helped. Sacrifices must be made.'

'I couldn't agree more, sir.'

'I thought I saw my son at breakfast. He did have a stomach ache. There are these other people in the school now. Or are they coming today? Old pupils, they must be.'

'Shall I tell you what's going to happen, sir?'

'Please do.' He said that with irony, as if he was above whatever tiresome misbehaviour Waggoner was about to inform him of.

'Tonight this place is going to become the navel of the

world, the judgment of everything. This landscape is going to become the same as our map. You'd got it halfway there already. We'll make everything right when we're set free. Your son's blood runs through these pipes now.' Waggoner went over and tapped a radiator that wasn't switched on. 'Well, it would if you weren't so hard up.' He squatted down and, with a bit of effort, turned the tap. 'Mr. Rove?'

Mr. Rove had his teeth clenched. He made a noise like a stick had a voice. His eyes rolled up into his head. He lowered his head onto his desk. His limbs thrashed. Waggoner took a deep breath. I remember an odd smell, which I now think was the odour that a fit gives a body. Another sign of the changes that happen when one thing is put inside another. Mr. Rove was physics, biology, chemistry, history and geography in that moment, an entire syllabus. The seizure lasted a couple of minutes. Waggoner went and sat on the desk, watching it. Mr. Rove finally lay tired, taking deep breaths. 'Who are you?' he asked.

'Andrew Waggoner, sir.'

'Who am I?'

'You'll know tonight.' Waggoner stroked the headmaster's hair. 'You helped make this possible.'

I went home on the minibus. I watched through the windows in the back doors as it drew out of the school in the cold afternoon darkness. I thought that was the last time I would see the buildings like that.

The bus driver put on the radio, and 'Karma Chameleon' was playing.

Thirty-seven

Dad drove me in for the disco. I was silent. A nothing drive, but a different sort of nothing, one waiting to be filled. I got out onto the gravel in front of the school. Dad had parked the Renault Fourteen with one wheel up on the steps. I shook his hand, which surprised him. He frowned, but he couldn't find the words to express such a vague worry. 'I'll get on home,' he said.

Waggoner stood beside me and watched the car drive off. For a moment, I wished I had my two sticks.

As I walked into the school, I remembered Angie dancing in her witch costume. I'd got to know her, for a while. For the first time, I'd got to see all the contradictions and over-writings and lack of reasons and dislocations which make a person. Then I'd found out how all those flaws and features could surprise you with new horror, bursting out of nothing. I'd found out how randomly frightening people could be.

This needed fixing. I had no doubt in my mind now. No imaginings or hope for the future. I would see this fixed, and my revenge would be complete, and all would be right with the world, and I, being not all right, would be somehow, blissfully, healed or ended or both. It felt like the same thing.

I stopped at the corner of the building and looked at the kids in costume already there at the top of the steps, which led down to the cellar. It was cold, but somehow nobody wanted to go down there first. I considered seeing Lang and Selway and Blewly and Rove amongst them. But no. What had been done had been done. A few of the kids had used last year's costumes again; Fiesta was once again his nonspecific devil, maybe a bit more Michael Jackson this time. I went to join them, went to my lot, nodded. Mr. Coxwell marched up and asked loudly why we weren't getting down there and enjoying ourselves? Following the others, I ducked under the lintel of the cellar. The first record was playing, 'Karma Chameleon' again, the current Number One.

I stopped when I saw who the DJ was. Mr. Rushden. This was the first time I'd seen him since he was lying there on the football pitch in the rain. He was wearing an eyepatch. He looked up, saw who it was and gave me a big smile. He'd forgiven me. I ducked away, moved on. Louise was opening foil-wrapped packages from Cookery, putting out biscuits, making a spiral pattern on the bar surface with them, counting them, talking to herself under her breath, eager, whispering. I looked back over my shoulder. On the stairs behind me, there was Angie, with Netty and Jenn.

They had mops of hair and little troubadour hats and braces and big chequerboard trousers. Angie had half dark and half light hair, Netty had dark hair and Jenn had very blonde hair.

They'd come as Bananarama.

Oh God, oh God. I could hear the mocking laughter over the music. It started with amazement and rose to a crescendo. I backed into a corner by the speakers. I couldn't bear it. 'You'll find out!' I yelled at them, lost under the music. 'They'll fix you too!'

Grayson's sister was yelling. 'Here's the queen and her princesses. Let's all bow!'

'You love Waggoner!' a girl called out. 'You're going to marry him!'

That wasn't what I'd expected to hear. And . . . instead of laughing along and at me, Angie had turned aside. Her friends were hustling her away into a corner.

Those taunts had been at *her*.

But I thought telling people about my stories was *her* joke on me.

Oh. Oh no. She hadn't betrayed me.

I fell back against the bar. I looked round for Waggoner. He was suddenly right in front of me, looking urgently at me. 'It doesn't change anything,' he said. 'It doesn't make everything all right.'

There was a disturbance on the stairs. There was Drake, on his own. He elbowed his way down. He was in his tiny concessions to werewolf again: sideburns and a lumberjack shirt. 'What?' he was shouting at some kids near him. 'Didn't hear you! Say that again!'

The girls were silent. Just. Though they laughed again as soon as he went past. Angie was looking awkwardly at him and then away from him. Drake looked horribly on his own. Like an animal about to be brought down. Angie looked like she needed a lot more from him.

I tried to get over to Angie, but her friends blocked my path with looks and muttered words and then with their bodies, until the crowd, intent on being close to them to catcall at them, shoved me away with comments that now meant nothing except I was, after all, the same as her.

I stood in a corner, panting. She must have felt like I'd abandoned her, all those weeks when we could have been strong.

Louise was calling kids over, putting cookies into their hands, saying there were always more, replacing them every time one was taken, keeping her spiral pattern intact. Waggoner went over and got two. He ate one himself, and, before I could do anything, grabbed the back of my head and shoved the other into my mouth. It was choke or swallow. I swallowed.

While I was still staggering, Waggoner took a dirty handkerchief from his pocket. He opened it up. Inside was a congealed mass, but what was at the centre of it was unmistakable. An unbroken eye. It moved. It was swiveling. The pupil was huge, panicking. Waggoner closed his hand round it. Mr. Rushden took a giddy step back from the decks and had to steady himself. Then he stepped forward, suddenly certain again, and put another record on the turntable. It was 'Red Red Wine'. He carefully took the microphone. 'Now we are going back,' he said., 'All the Number One hit singles, from this Halloween to the last!'

I stumbled away from Waggoner. It felt like the dance floor had tilted. Or I felt drunk. But that couldn't be. I fell into the bar, and saw, as I turned around, that others had fallen with me. I saw where Angie was trying to get up, and made my way back across the dance floor, foot after foot, in long steps, and landed at her feet. There was a great roar of laughter and applause. Wolf whistles. Suddenly every reaction had got bigger. There had been teacher laughter too. Netty and Jenn looked daggers at me, but Angie indicated something to them, and Jenn got up, and I landed in her seat and Drake stopped where he had started to come over from, swearing and pushing at someone.

'I'm sorry,' I said.

'It's too late for that,' said Angie.

'I didn't tell them about the stories.'

She looked at me hard, not believing me. Then she did. 'Oh. I thought you did.'

'I thought *you* did.'

'Why would I do something moronic like that?'

Waggoner was watching me, like he was afraid of what *I* might do. 'Why would *I*?'

She had to pull herself together before she could continue. 'It's childish anyway. I've got bigger things to worry about.'

'What?'

Angie suddenly laughed. Then she looked like she might cry. She pushed her hair back. 'Fuck. Anything else you want to ask? I've brought the Cup back.' She indicated her enormous Virgin Records bag. 'I'm going to try and sneak the stupid thing back to Mr. Clare's office.'

'The Cup isn't stupid. The Cup is really important.' Or it was to Waggoner. I wanted to say that she shouldn't have brought it back.

'Oh, go on, tell me a story.' I'd never heard anyone say anything the way she said that. It started out ironic, but then in the space of one breath, I was sure she meant it. I looked round. Everything in the cellar was starting to shift. I could feel the boundary Waggoner had set up around the school. It was tipping. My body was shaking. I was having trouble pushing my thoughts out. They were tied up around what was turning. I yelled, and so did some of the others.

The shaking stopped. We had nearly gone right over then, but something had stopped us. An imperfection had got in the way.

Louise was glaring at Angie. I looked to her bag. Louise started forward.

Drake stumbled over and hauled me out of my seat. The kids around us burst into more laughter and applause. I could see he hated it, because some of it was for him. Ignoring Angie's screamed protests, he hauled me away.

He ran straight into Waggoner.

Drake reacted, startled. He could see Waggoner! He spun and looked at me. He could see both of us now. He staggered back, showing so many new expressions.

The teachers had all been eating Louise's biscuits too. Mr. Coxwell was gesturing in the air now. Nobody was listening to him. He looked afraid. Mrs. Coxwell arrived beside him, swaying, trying to pacify him. Mrs. Pepper was laughing and laughing, a high, neighing laugh. Mrs. Frenchmore had sat down in a corner, looking seriously at the kids who were dancing now, trying to understand. Mrs. Parkin was dancing to KC and the Sunshine Band, her girls all around her. Mr. Sedge was walking, nodding, across the dance floor, back and forth, sizing things up. Mr. Kent was just staring, such sadness on his face. Mr. Clare was looking for something behind the bar, on his hands and knees, his arse stuck out in his purple suit. Mr. Brandswick was grabbing at individual pupils, trying to shepherd them together into one corner, but as soon as he went for another, the ones he had slipped away. Mr. Land, at the decks, was lecturing Mrs. Mills, trying to make the bloody woman understand, but she wasn't listening; she'd got her hands to the walls and was feeling it, feeling it, feeling it changing. She thought it was toppling back onto her, and she fell backwards, and hit the far wall and rolled up it.

The kids from the dance floor took that in their stride as

Paul Young came on. Every Number One would be played. The teachers and pupils walked down the dance floor and walked up that wall. The laws of physics going apeshit was the only way anyone could dance to that.

Drake looked slowly back and forth between me and Waggoner.

Rod Stewart came on. The kids were all dancing now. Elaine had her arms above her head, pleading for nobody to look at her. Surtees was dancing spastically, punching invisible assailants, nearly falling, was overwhelmed by them, hissing through his big teeth. Laurie Coxwell had come as a cat girl again. She was swaying, her eyes closed.

Mr. Rushden, a look of panic on his face like he alone could see there was something wrong, was pulling out disc after disc, putting on each one in turn, faster and faster: The Police, New Edition, Spandau Ballet with 'True' . . .

And there was that enormous start to David Bowie singing 'Let's Dance'. I looked over to Angie and saw a determined look on her face. She had to do something. She stepped out onto the dance floor.

Thirty-eight

The bottles of spirits in the Halloween disco were falling and breaking as the room rotated about an axis that nobody understood. The bottles broke near secret lit cigarettes. The room spun to the sound of Duran Duran and Bonnie Tyler and Michael Jackson, which made Fiesta dance onto the ceiling. The room resounded like a drum with people inside. Forever's going to start tonight. Forever's going to start tonight. There was snogging and fighting. Surtees was lashing out at anyone he could connect his fists to, in a strange sort of pogo divorced from the music. There were bodies all around him, flying in and piling on. Mrs. Parkin was grabbing for her girls, to be with all of them, to be one of them. The first small fires broke out.

I felt Angie's dance trying to push against what was happening. She was thanking her broken mirror for this chance, asking it for more assistance, her two friends helping her, dancing beside her, in a ridiculous, passionate way, as if nobody was watching. She was leading up to something. I had no idea what. I had no idea what she could do.

Drake was looking between me and Waggoner. He looked for a moment like he might start to understand. He reached for both of us, angry with us equally.

'Andrew!' yelled Angie. She was stumbling towards the edge of the dance floor like she was on the deck of a ship, clutching her bag. Netty and Jenn were dancing even more frenziedly, dancing for her. She held out her hand, it was time, she wanted me to go with her.

Drake's hands closed on me.

I shoved him and sent him stumbling back into Waggoner. I sped with big, leaping panto flying steps across the rotating dance floor. I grabbed Angie's hand.

She hauled me towards the exit.

The door at the top of the steps was rotating, like something spinning into the distance as a futuristic video effect on *Top of the Pops*. But we had the Cup in Angie's bag. Unlike all the other kids who were falling away from the door, we could escape. We ran at it. We burst through it without caring which way was up.

———————

We stumbled out into a vision of two worlds colliding. We spun on the spot, the gravel flying up under our feet. It fell in great arcs, like we were walking on the moon. Two gravities were vying for our bodies.

I looked around desperately, trying to find a horizon, a point of reference in what should be so familiar. There was the big tree, but it was also the omphalos. One thing was mapping itself onto another, like grids on a computer game intersecting. The perimeter flashed, trying to weld them together, a red heat where Waggoner had threaded the flesh. The horse was hauling itself up out of the football pitch. Its eye was blazing. Its hooves struck sparks. It had an enormous chalk cock, perfect and clean. The horse reared back and then mounted the ground, thrust into it, came into it, and the ground, pregnant, swelled up towards the sky, pushing the worlds towards each other. The rounded shape of the school buildings was becoming the rounded shape of trenches and ridges. Lightning was flaring as fast as sparks in a horror movie laboratory, connecting the black glass in the ground with the weight of the sky above, where clouds any moment were about to resolve themselves into something solid. There were earthlights floating up from the woods, lights bursting from the windows at the top of the school, lights in the far distance in the direction of Chippenham hospital.

The effort was shaking the earth and sky. The pressure was huge.

The man with two sticks stood above it all, on a promontory above the clouds. He was heaving his sticks towards each other, bringing them closer and closer. The fire blazed between them, more intense every moment. He looked to me and Angie on the ground. He was looking for the Cup. He found it in her bag. We felt the weight of his gaze. We fell off our feet, onto the gravel.

Around him now, towering over us, we saw the ones with their shields and eyes. The rain that started to fall on us then was their rust and tears and blood.

Angie and I tried to stand. I heard 'Too Shy' start to play. I hauled myself upright at the same moment she did.

Waggoner stepped out of the cellar, smoke billowing up from behind him, carrying the sharpened, decorated pole he'd been making in Woodwork. Angie looked between us. She could see both of us now too. Waggoner slowed as he approached us. 'We're about to go onto the downs,' he said. 'Get her to give you the Cup. We need to break it.'

'Why?' asked Angie.

Waggoner ignored her, addressing his answer to me. 'It's full of her ways. She's changed it. Made it into something real. Her version of real. So it won't fit any more. If it stays here, intact, as the worlds come together, there'll be a rip in the map. We won't be able to complete the sacrifice, complete your revenge. You won't get healed.'

Behind Waggoner, kids had started to leave the cellar, fleeing what was becoming one big fire. A whole bunch of teachers, led by Mr. Rushden, was holding someone who was struggling. They were forcing him to come with them. He was shouting. It was Drake. It was the first time I'd heard him afraid. Or perhaps I'd always heard him afraid. Mr. Rushden had an awful look on his face, like he was aware of what he was doing but couldn't help himself. Louise walked beside them, gesturing, cajoling them on, leading them in the right direction.

Angie looked between them and Waggoner and me. 'Complete the sacrifice?' She looked betrayed.

'Run,' I said to her. 'Please. Get away.'

'Yes,' said Waggoner, 'that would be fine. Take the Cup with you.'

She couldn't look at me. 'What'll happen then?'

'Then everything will go back to how it should have been, centuries ago. We'll be in the world. We'll be free.'

She considered for a moment. She looked over to Drake, who was being led towards the playing fields, towards the shining horizon.

To my surprise, she turned and ran.

Waggoner put a hand on my shoulder. 'Of course she did,' he said. 'What she's about is slight. What we're about is old and meaningful.'

I didn't know how I felt. I followed the procession that

was forming behind the teachers holding Drake, a line of kids amongst the billowing smoke that was obscuring the lights that were now dancing all around us. I could feel the pressure of the worlds coming together. It couldn't be long now. All it needed was the final sacrifice to seal it.

The smoke started to be buffeted by wind. The belly of the earth rose under us as we slowly marched. The horizon of many distances dropped away. We were indeed heading up onto the backs of the downs above my home, but I could still hear the distant music of Men at Work and then Phil Collins far below.

I looked at Waggoner's expression as he walked, clutching his sharpened stake. He looked purposeful, determined, on the verge of a great victory. I couldn't imagine myself looking like that. I didn't know if I ever wanted to look like that. Ahead, Drake was screaming now, a primal, urgent call for help, like a baby.

The people from long ago who were doing this, I knew how they felt. I knew how I'd summoned them. They were like me. But I realised something else now. Did they really think being born once more into the world would be enough for them? They wouldn't just be satisfied with standing again in their own hill fort, not after all they'd been through. They'd want to control the world all the way to the horizon, and the next horizon, and the next. They'd keep their plan of revenge going; they'd have to find more and more things to take revenge against. They'd extend it to the places in my world where I'd seen different possibilities, to the New Forest, even.

I still wanted Drake to suffer. I had been wondering if at some point his screams would be enough. But now I knew. Nothing would ever be enough.

In the landscape below, the school was starting to blaze. Smoke was rolling all around us. The gas main had been caught by the smaller fires working their way inwards into the old, rotten wood of the cellars.

I could feel something once again causing friction between the worlds, sparks in the sky, causing Waggoner to look around, startled. Ahead were the walls of the hill fort. A pale figure ran from it towards the procession. It was Vincent Lang, emaciated, naked and shivering, with scars at his neck and ribs. He was looking around desperately too now, hissing. I wondered what freedom he'd been promised when the worlds collided. In the sky overhead, the shape of the man with two sticks was twisting, looking all around, the fire between his sticks lighting him against the blackness.

I saw Angie standing on the first bank of the hill fort, holding the Cup. She had followed us. From the horizon below I heard that awful music, 'Save Your Love'.

The procession headed for the omphalos. Waggoner held his sharpened stake over his head, a challenge to her. Suddenly, from the bounds of the hill fort, the stern onlookers with their shields emerged and ran at her. She dashed away from them, darting this way and that across the fort, but even with the Cup, surely there were too many of them? What was she hoping to do? As we reached the omphalos, the man with two sticks started to step down the sky towards us, and his light grew brighter and brighter, and I could still just about see Angie as she was surrounded and leapt upon and the Cup ripped from her hands.

The water around the omphalos shone. Drake was hauled forwards at the same moment Angie was. They brought the Cup with their captives. The looks on the faces of those desperate ancients, their hunched backs, the nervous glee in their gasping breaths. They hid behind their shields even now, as if afraid even of the light that was going to free them. The teachers and kids stared at them, not understanding, unable to escape. Louise stood by the crowd, her fists slowly clenching and unclenching, her jaws working as she mouthed words that were like the sounds of eating.

The man with two sticks stood between all of us. He was slowly bringing his sticks together, but the process could not yet be complete. Waggoner slammed his sharpened stake into the ground beside the omphalos. 'Break the Cup,' he said. 'Bring the sacrifice.'

They hauled Drake forward. Angie started yelling all the lyrics she could think of. They seemed as meaningless now as Waggoner said they were. But among them I heard so many things that reminded me of the trust we'd shared, the trust I'd shattered all over again. She let me make eye contact with her, and she wasn't pleading with me, she was urging me. Demanding that I make a balance for all that happened, that I do it myself. I heard 'Beat Surrender' playing far below, I heard it change to 'I Don't Want to Dance' and knew that while that was in the air there was nothing she could do, that it was up to me now. It always had been.

'You said I'd be healed,' I shouted.

'After the sacrifice,' said Waggoner.

'Before,' I said. 'Now.' I leapt forwards and grabbed the Cup from the hands of the ancient warrior who had raised it in the air, about to break it. I didn't look to see if Waggoner was going to call to them to stop me, but he must have let it happen. I bent to fill the Cup with water from around the omphalos. I could hear Lang start to snigger with laughter, and then

I heard the ancients all joining in. Maybe they thought I was blaspheming against Angie's way of doing things by using her Cup to complete their plan. Or maybe they were just cruelly delighted at watching me trying to attend to my own desperate needs that had proved so incidental to theirs.

I took a look at Drake, struggling and shouting as he was shown the stake they were going to impale him on. He was to be the pin that would fasten the two maps together. 'Let her go!' he was shouting. 'Angie, you have to run, the baby, you have to run!' Such impossible words from him. I still can't hear his voice saying them, but I remember.

The man with two sticks walked up to Drake, his face obscured by the fire that blazed between them, still hauling the sticks together, waiting for the moment when the Cup would be broken, the last sacrifice made, and he could slam his sticks and the two worlds into each other.

As quick as I could I pulled off my trousers and pants and threw them on the ground. In the distance, 'Do You Really Want to Hurt Me' started to play.

I raised the Cup to pour the water over my wounded cock. I hesitated. I could do this and be healed.

Here's that line again. Here's where you *decide* to step across it.

With a yell, I ran from the pool right at the man with two sticks. I threw the water at his fire.

Water is being thrown onto my face.

I ran as fast as I could along the ditches of the hill fort. I could hear Waggoner behind me, screaming at me as he pursued me.

He held Drake's knife high above his head. All around us, the two worlds were crashing together, rebounding, out of control. I rushed out the gate and down the hillside. I leapt the wooden stile. I rolled down the hill past the Red Barn in the mud. I burst past the badger sets and sent the pheasants flying. I hauled my way through the hooks of the blackberry bushes. I sprinted as I hit the gravel of the lane that led round the curve that led to my house. Waggoner kept after me. He was catching up. His cries echoed across the fields.

I saw no lights on at my house as I ran desperately, trying to run better than I had ever run. I knew the front door would be locked and bolted many times. So I clambered over the garden wall and ran down the row of high trees and leapt at my bedroom window. I smashed through it and rolled, ready to face Waggoner as he followed. He jumped through the window straight at me, Drake's knife point downwards. I managed to grab his arm. We spun, clockwise, him trying to force the turn back the other way, to force the knife into me. As we turned, I looked up at the downs through the broken window frame. I saw the man with two sticks fighting at the last second to make the worlds come together. I could see his features, just a normal face. He was just a person. With one last effort, he heaved his sticks together. It was too late. The fire had gone out. Everything he wanted vanished in a puff of smoke.

I grabbed hold of Waggoner and thought of the riff from 'Back on the Chain Gang,' and that made me think of being connected to things I could never escape.

I saw a look on Waggoner's face, in that last second, as his features leapt in towards mine, a look of release. Then it was just me standing there, holding Drake's knife. I dropped it. I was Andrew Waggoner. I put a hand to my face.

Water was being thrown onto my face by Mr. Rushden.

He'd gotten a lot of us out onto the playing field. Kids were lying on the frosty grass in the charred remains of costumes. I realised I was fully dressed. Angie was lying beside me, Drake beside her. I coughed and heaved in a breath, sat up and looked around. There was Louise, looking to help Netty and Jenn, looking around her as if she was waking from a nightmare. In front of us, the school was burning down. There were already fire engines on the scene. The first ambulances were rolling up, kids being led towards them. Mr. Rove was staring up at the blaze. Teachers were stumbling around him.

The ambulancemen came for me and starting asking me urgent questions about how much I'd inhaled and what I'd eaten. I could still feel the awkward shape of my maimed cock under my trousers. I always would. They asked me if I was hurt.

I almost laughed.

Thirty-nine

The school closed, forever. I went to John Bentley. It was fine.

I saw Angie again a couple of years later. I'd left school, and was trying to get away from the area, from all the impossible memories. I ran into her in Chippenham. She was walking with a small child, her son. He looked like Drake. She saw me and stopped, looked shocked. I was afraid she'd run. I didn't want to scare her, I walked carefully up to her.

We couldn't find any words about anything impossible. I asked about Drake. She hadn't seen him since a couple of days after the fire. Everyone had wanted to know who the baby's father was. She had never told. Drake hadn't contacted her. She said she was sure he could change, would change, but it wasn't up to her to make it happen. She was putting the child first now. She was still in touch with Jenn and Netty and Louise. Louise now regarded herself as having had some kind of breakdown and saw herself as recovering. We didn't talk about the implications of that—that we knew better.

The only thing I could find to ask her about those times was why that ornamental box she'd given me had been empty. She seemed puzzled by the question.

'Of course it was empty,' she said. 'It was for you to put something in.'

I said sorry I hadn't called her. She said the same. We both knew we never would. She walked off, and looked once over her shoulder at me, and walked on. That was the last time I saw her.

———————

Many years later, I made a deliberate effort to find Drake. I was still wounded. I still had a flaw at the heart of me. I had done some bad things. I had made things right but not in myself. I decided, in a moment of weakness, that seeing him might heal me.

He was on Facebook. There was his face—older, which was somehow surprising. He'd never moved away. He ran what had been his parents' farm. They were deceased. I friended him. I waited a couple of days. He friended me back. I sent him a message. He agreed to meet.

I realised, as I walked into the coffee bar near Swindon bus station, that I'd come to this meeting wearing a geeky T-shirt, a joke most people wouldn't get, the sort of T-shirt that requires an explanation. I'd put it on without thinking, or maybe it was my armour today. There he was. He stood up as I entered. I thought he was going to hold out his hand to me, but he didn't. He looked nervous, anxious to start talking. We ordered. He'd already shown much more in the way of facial expression than I remembered. 'I'm sorry,' he said, speaking so fast his words collided with each other. 'I can't say sorry enough. It's not big enough. I've been an addict. I don't know what's true. I'm clean now; all that shit just gets in the way of what I did. What I did to you.'

I didn't want to hear this. I kept my own expression neutral. Everything he said was making me think of all that I myself had done.

'My wife, she's an angel. I've found the straight and narrow. I need to apologise to you. I will . . . I will do time if you want.

I've decided that. I mean . . . what that'll do to my wife and . . . but no, I can't say that. I've decided.'

I'd kept his knife; it was still in a drawer at home. I'd thought of bringing it, for some reason.

'I'm a dad now. I don't want my boy to get any of this from me. I've never laid a finger on him, I swear. He's happy. He's whole. He's not like . . . we were. What was done to me when I was his age, it stops with me.'

I wanted to be able to say the same. I stared at him, trying to find what I searched for whenever I looked in a mirror, but what was in front of me was all there was. It wasn't enough, because nothing could be. I realised I couldn't stand listening to him any longer. I got up. 'I'm glad you're a changed man,' I said. 'I'm glad that's possible.'

I left. He didn't follow. That was the last I knew of him.

———————

That evening, taking the opportunity to go and see my family, I asked Dad again about how he got his samurai sword. 'We were coming out of the jungle,' he said, leaning back in his chair, his eyes darting about as if he was still there, 'and we heard the sounds of a battle ahead. So we slowed down. By the time we poked our heads out, there was nothing. Just a few bodies. Two patrols, the sergeant said, must have met each other, fought it out, and whoever survived had moved on.' I listened, waiting for the tone of his voice to become self-mocking, but this time it didn't. 'There it was, stuck in the mud.' He blinked at me. 'I just pulled it out.'

Walking back to my car, I looked up at the downs. I didn't see anything.

Acknowledgments

Over many years, many people have helped with this book before my wonderful editor Lee Harris got his hands on it. I'd like to mention two in particular: Simon Kavanagh shepherded it from being an unreadable mess into something that worked. For that and so many other things, I owe him a great debt that I will possibly never be able to repay. Julie Crisp, working on other books with me, taught me a whole host of skills I then applied to *Chalk*. This misses so many people out, but over the years I've lost a lot of documentation, and a growing list of people I was supposed to mention here. If you think this book should be for you, believe me, it is.

About the Author

© Lou Abercrombie, 2015

PAUL CORNELL is a writer of science fiction and fantasy in prose, comics and television, one of only two people to be Hugo Award nominated for all three media. A *New York Times* #1 bestselling author, he's written *Doctor Who* for the BBC, *Wolverine* for Marvel and *Batman and Robin* for DC. He's won the BSFA Award for his short fiction, an Eagle Award for his comics and shares in a Writers Guild Award for his TV work. His recent Tor.com novella *Witches of Lychford* has been nominated for the BSFA Award and the British Fantasy Award.

TOR · COM

Science fiction. Fantasy. The universe.

And related subjects.

*

More than just a publisher's website, *Tor.com*
is a venue for **original fiction, comics,** and
discussion of the entire field of SF and fantasy,
in all media and from all sources. Visit our site
today — and join the conversation yourself.